LoveLife

Praise for Rachel Spangler

Learning Curve

"Spangler's title, *Learning Curve*, refers to the growth both of these women make, as they deal with attraction and avoidance. They share a mutual lust, but can lust alone surpass their differences? The answer to that question is told with humor, adventure, and heat." —*Just About Write*

"[Spangler's] potential shines through, particularly her ability to tap into the angst that accompanies any attempt to alter the perceptions of others…Your homework assignment, read on."—*Curve* magazine

Trails Merge

"The meeting of these two women produces sparks that could melt the snow on the mountain. They are drawn to each other, even as their pasts warn of future pain. The characters are beautifully drawn. Spangler has done her homework and she does a great job describing the day to day workings of a small ski resort. She tells her story with wonderful humor, and gives an accurate voice to each of her characters. Parker Riley's best friend Alexis is as true to the sophisticated 'City' girl as Campbell's father is to the country. *Trails Merge* is a great read that may have you driving to the nearest mountain resort."—*Just About Write*

"Sparks fly and denial runs deep in this excellent second novel by Spangler. The author's love of the subject shines through as skiing, family values and romance fill the pages of this heartwarming story. The setting is stunning, making this reviewer nostalgic for her childhood days spent skiing the bunny hills of Wisconsin." —*Curve* magazine

The Long Way Home

"Well-written and very thought out, *The Long Way Home* accurately paints the picture of a woman struggling to move beyond her past in order to look forward to her future. Spangler's characters are dynamic yet realistic, giving the reader a chance to see aspects of herself, her family, friends, colleagues, and community members within each persona. Their troubles, hopes, fears, and doubts are the same as the rest of us."—www.Cherrygrrl.com

"Rachel Spangler's third book, *The Long Way Home*, explores how we remake ourselves and the consequence of not being true to our real selves. In the case of Raine, her perceived notions of small-town life may have been tainted by being 17. The reality of what she finds when she returns as an adult surprises her and has her wondering if she'd been wrong about her home town, her parents, and her friends. Spangler's story will have you staying up very late as you near the end of the book."—*Lambda Literary Review*.

By the Author

Learning Curve

Trails Merge

The Long Way Home

LoveLife

Visit us at www.boldstrokesbooks.com

LoveLife

by

Rachel Spangler

2012

LOVELIFE

ISBN 13: 978-1-60282-655-7

This Trade Paperback Original Is Published By
Bold Strokes Books, Inc.
P.O. Box 249
Valley Falls, NY 12185

First Edition: April 2012

Credits
Editor: Shelley Thrasher
Production Design: Stacia Seaman
Cover Design by Sheri (graphicartist2020@hotmail.com)

Acknowledgments

Everything happens for a reason. Or so Diane Gaidry said when I first e-mailed her with a vague character development idea. Instead of filing a restraining order, she welcomed me into her home and then spent hours answering the most wanderingly absurd questions while my creative process took hold. This book simply wouldn't exist without her, and I can't thank her enough for sharing her time, knowledge, and faith in our shared purpose. Later in the process, my cadre of life coaches grew to include Dian Reid and Chris Hopson, both of whom reiterated that everything happens for a reason, when they agreed to chat, plan, work through plot points, and serve as beta readers. Any authenticity you see in Elaine can be traced back to these three women, and I'm gladly indebted to them.

But perhaps I've gotten ahead of myself. I would have never gone on the wild adventure of chasing life coaches if not for the constant encouragement (or depending on who you ask, bad influence) of Georgia Beers. She supported and egged me on as I broke from a previous project and refused to let me cave in to either embarrassment or insecurity at any point in the process. Thank you, GB.

There were many points in the process when I wasn't sure I knew what I was doing, and a few times I knew for sure I was in over my head, but everything happens for a reason, supposedly, so I pushed out my best attempt for these characters and handed them over to my go-to gals, Toni Whitaker and Barb Dallinger, who did a marvelous job of simultaneously reassuring me and making this novel better. I am so thankful for their support and insight. Outside of the official beta readers, there are countless other friends, colleagues, and readers who have taken the time to encourage me on the long, doubt-filled days and nights required to write a novel. I hope I've thanked each one of you in person enough that you know who you are and how much I value you.

The day before I submitted the manuscript, it was still being referred to as "the life coach book." I'd tried every horrible play and pun on the word coach I could think of, when thirty seconds into a conversation about the story, my friend Andrew Cullison said, "What about LoveLife?" Thanks for making it look so easy, Andy. You can cross "title a lesbian romance" off your bucket list.

Finally, when I handed the results of my journey to the professionals at Bold Strokes Books, Len Barot once again entrusted my work to the very capable Shelley Thrasher, who gives me more tools and more guidance with each novel. I thank her profusely for both her steady hand and her willingness to work toward something we can both be proud of. While speaking of a willingness to work together, I'd be remiss not to thank my wonderful cover artist, Sheri, who turned out another great cover despite my meddling. Finally, thank you, Stacia Seaman, for being able to copy edit even toddler speak.

Now, I've come to the part of the acknowledgements where I try to put into words my thanks for the people who deserve the most credit and usually get the least of it. Jackson, you're the light of my life. You share me with my work more than you should have to, but some day I hope you're one-tenth as proud of me as I am of you. And, Susie, I'll never understand what you see in me, but you never falter as I spin from one crazy idea to another. You wait patiently when I need to go chase my muse, and you listen when I process the same circle of emotions for days. I know you don't always understand why I act the way I do, which makes it all the more impressive that you love and support me anyway. No matter what else I happen to be unsure of on any given day, I know that if everything has a purpose, you are mine. I love you, come what may.

Soli Deo Gloria

For Susie—Clearly, this one is all your fault,
perhaps even more so than all the others.

Chapter One

November 4

Joey glanced up from the table she was wiping down. Every time the little bell on the front door jingled between ten and eleven a.m., she held her breath, but the short, bald man rushing toward the counter wasn't who she'd hoped to see. She sighed and continued to scrub a small patch of dried coffee off the Formica.

"You're pathetic," Lisa said, her voice filled with amusement.

"I'm not pathetic. I'm a hopeless romantic, maybe a little obsessive."

"A little?"

"I have a compulsive personality."

"Is that why you've been washing that same table for five minutes, or did you just hope if you stood near the door long enough, super-hot new girl would breeze past you?"

Joey chuckled and flopped into a chair next to her. "It's not fair how well you can read me."

"Yeah, well, twenty years of friendship will do that," Lisa said, her eyes on Joey even though she never stopped tapping the keyboard of her MacBook. Aside from her height and her Rachel Maddow glasses, Lisa looked exactly like the lanky kid she'd met on their first day in Mrs. McEntire's second-grade classroom.

"Am I really pathetic?"

Lisa stopped typing and shook her head. "No. Mostly you're romantic."

"Mostly?"

"It's like eighty/twenty romantic over pathetic."

"Thanks." Joey laughed and threw her dishrag into Lisa's lap. She started to load a mismatched stack of coffee cups into the heavy plastic bussing bin but stopped when Lisa made a giddy little squeak behind her. Before she could turn to see her expression the door's bell chimed again. Joey froze in mid-reach for a cup.

Even in her stupor she knew the striking woman was walking toward her in real time, not slow motion. Still, her blond hair did blow back slightly from the breeze of her stride, like in the movies. Joey didn't feel any breeze. When had all the air left the room, or maybe only left her lungs? Either way, she didn't care. Such beauty made breathing a petty concern.

Three or four inches taller than Joey, the woman had legs that went on forever under flat-front khakis that hung perfectly on her hips' subtle curve. Her starched white oxford, impeccably pressed and tucked in, gave a clear line of sight up her torso. The top two buttons of the shirt, undone, allowed Joey a torturous peek at her delicate collarbones and the sinfully sweet tendrils of blond hair that snuggled against her neck. The woman's natural-pink lips were full and flawlessly formed under impossibly high cheekbones and the most devastatingly blue eyes imaginable. Joey almost swooned.

The woman didn't even notice her gawking as she strode casually toward the counter. She continued to stare at the woman as she decisively ordered chai tea without any of the silly requests that drove Joey crazy. Relaxed, comfortable, and secure, the woman vanished as quickly as she appeared, leaving Joey shaky and bereft yet thrilled and momentarily sated—a post-coital sensation.

"Sit down before you hurt yourself," Lisa said dryly.

Joey attempted to play it cool. "I'm fine."

"You've got some drool on your chin."

"Shut up." Joey rubbed the back of her hand across her mouth. She hadn't actually drooled.

"Why didn't you speak to her?"

Joey rolled her eyes.

"What?"

"She's out of my league."

"Don't do that, Joey. You're a doll. Plenty of girls would get as goofy over you as you got over Ms. Hottie Hot-Stuff."

"I do all right with girls, but she wasn't a *girl*. She was a full-grown woman. You saw her. She's sexy and stylish and cool and smart and—"

"You don't know if she's smart. She could be a complete airhead."

"She's not."

"You don't know that. You've never talked to her."

"Talk to her? She doesn't even know I'm alive."

"Whose fault is that?" Lisa shot back. "She's showed up for what, two, maybe three weeks? You've never even been behind the counter when she comes in."

"What would I say? Can I have your order, and your phone number?"

"Hey, that's pretty good."

"Yeah, well, I could never pull it off."

"Only because you'd never have the guts. You're such a chickenshit when it comes to stuff like that. You'll pine over her from afar forever."

Joey folded her arms across her chest. Lisa was right, of course, but she could be more sympathetic. "Stop bullying me. I'm allowed to have a crush."

"Don't sell yourself short. She could be more than a crush."

Joey shook her head. What was the point of arguing? She'd never have a woman like that except in her dreams.

❖

Elaine Raitt cradled the phone between her chin and shoulder as she sipped her chai tea. She sat cross-legged on the couch, comfortable as the drink's physical warmth mingled with the emotional warmth of the voice on the phone and spread through her chest and limbs.

"I've been hoping for this job, Elaine—meaningful, creative, and ready for me to dive into."

"That's amazing, John. I'm happy for you. How are you feeling about the fast pace?" Elaine had been John's life coach for the last nine weeks. He'd started their sessions stuck in a rut, but afraid to jeopardize his career by chancing something more challenging. She had spent the bulk of their early time together questioning him about his values, goals, and purpose to show him the incongruities between his dream life and his actual life. He had done a lot of soul-searching and seen a major payoff. Such sessions didn't always come together so neatly or concretely, but Elaine hoped her clients would gain the confidence and hope John expressed now.

"It's a whirlwind, but it's been better that way. I haven't had time to worry whether I'm capable. I focused so much on getting my portfolio together before our sessions ended, I didn't let myself listen to my inner critic."

"Good. You can usually silence it by refusing to give it the time of day."

"When I got the interview I started to wonder if I was good enough, but I told myself, 'Hey, I made it into the final four. I must have something going for me.'"

"Excellent. I'm proud of you. I knew you could do this." Her belief that her clients could successfully navigate any challenge formed the bedrock of her professional value system.

"I couldn't have done it without you, Elaine." He practically gushed.

"You did all the work," she said calmly. "You had everything necessary to succeed already inside you."

"But you helped me see that. I've grown more in the last ten weeks than in the last twenty years. You should bill yourself as a miracle worker instead of a life coach."

She laughed, pleasure, happiness, and relief melding into one lovely emotion and pouring from her. "Thank you, but I merely acted as a mirror for you."

"I know, I know. You won't take any credit, but without you I might never have found the confidence to search for more. Thank you for helping me find my path."

Her chest swelled with pride. "That's all the thanks I need."

"I'm headed in the right direction now and promise to keep moving."

"You've reached your goal. You don't need me as regularly, but I'll check in on you, and if you ever need anything, you can always call."

John thanked her several more times before finally wrapping the phone call with a promise to meet next week.

She lay back on her couch, breathing deep cleansing breaths and focusing on the sensation of being aligned with her purpose. She'd been coaching for only a year, and she still doubted her new role occasionally. She wanted to do well because she found fulfillment in her work, but she also wanted to do right by her clients. Helping them connect to their own purpose was both a privilege and a responsibility. Maybe she was idealistic, but she took her work seriously, so she felt reaffirmed when she successfully connected with a client. Her own journey as a coach was far from complete, but she felt more like her true self than ever, at least in her professional life.

Her personal life was much more complicated. Her belongings remained mostly in boxes while she tried to decide where everything fit in her new apartment and where she fit in her new city. Though Buffalo was actually her old city, she'd been in New York long enough that this rust-belt jewel on the shore of Lake Erie hardly felt like home.

She was searching, content to enjoy a journey of personal exploration. She'd taken the first step on her path by trading her too-comfortable, too-isolated life for a new place filled with new challenges and more significant relationships. But for right now, she'd allow herself to bask in the warm feelings that came from coaching.

Chapter Two

November 7

Joey glanced at her watch for the third time in two minutes.

"I saw that," Lisa mumbled.

"How do you manage to see every pathetic thing I do? Aren't you supposed to be working?"

"I'm multitasking." Lisa tapped on her laptop keys extra quickly to prove her point.

Joey didn't know how she managed to type that fast, especially without looking at the screen, though she should be used to it by now. Lisa had to be the most extroverted computer programmer in the world. Usually tech geeks wanted to curl into a corner with their gadgets or with other geeks and be left alone, but not Lisa, who was brilliant and extroverted. When Joey'd begun working at the Eclectic Coffee shop in college, Lisa had taken up residence at a small table near the counter for at least two hours a day when Joey was on shift, and sometimes even when she wasn't.

"It's ten forty-five," Lisa said. "Maybe Sexy McSexerton won't come in today."

"She doesn't show up every day." The fact depressed Joey almost as much as being depressed about a complete stranger's nonappearance.

"She didn't come in yesterday either."

"Thanks for the recap. You sound as obsessed as I am."

Lisa shook her head quickly. “Oh, no, you don’t. I’m not guilty by association. She’s not my type. You’re the one with the addiction. I’m only your enabler.”

“You’re a shitty enabler if all you can do is remind me how pathetic I am.”

“Hey, if you want to go for more, say the word. I’ll cyberstalk her for you. I could probably even hack her dental records if you were into that.”

“Not necessary.” Joey sighed. “A name would be nice, though.”

“Done,” Lisa said resolutely.

“What?”

“I’ll get you her name.”

“How? When?”

Lisa hopped up and grabbed an apron from underneath the counter.

“Lisa…” Joey followed her behind the cash register. “You’re not supposed to be back here.”

“Shh, here she comes.”

Joey spun around to see her dream girl push through the door. She wore a long, hunter-green cotton skirt today. *Dear God, look at those calves.* Her long-sleeve cream blouse hugged her skin exactly the way Joey wanted to, all snug around her waist. A black clip held her hair, pulled up in a twist, tight enough to pull it away from her face, but loose enough to let a few stray tendrils curl around her temples.

“May I help you?” Lisa asked in a stage voice clearly too chipper to fit any real food-service employee.

“A tall chai latte,” dream woman said.

“Coming right up.” Lisa nodded but didn’t move to get the drink or ring it up. Joey quickly reached around her to tap a few buttons on the register, the price of the drink flashing on the screen for her to see.

“Oh, looky there. That’ll be three dollars and twenty-nine cents,” Lisa said. The woman held out a debit card, which Lisa accepted and promptly handed to Joey.

"I've seen you in here a lot lately. Are you new to the neighborhood?" Lisa's attempt at subtlety failed epically.

The woman gave her a quizzical look. "Actually, I'm old to the neighborhood. I grew up here. I recently moved back from downstate."

"Ya don't say." Lisa spoke loudly enough to make it clear Joey was meant to overhear, even though she was only three feet away fixing the chai. "What brought you back to Buffalo? You work at the college?"

"No, I'm starting a new business, or trying to."

Joey could practically feel Lisa's excitement radiate from her. That little comment was the opening she needed.

"Wow, an entrepreneur. What kind of business?"

"I'm a life coach."

"Fascinating." Joey could hear the unspoken giggle Lisa somehow managed to contain. Most computer programmers had little use for intuitive arts or impractical, unquantifiable entities like human emotion, but Joey found it fascinating.

"Why don't you leave your information? Maybe we could put it on one of our bulletin boards. That might drum you up some business."

"That'd be wonderful," the woman said, the hint of a smile playing at the corners of her perfect lips. "I got my new business cards yesterday."

"Did you hear that, Joey? She'd like to get her information out there. You can take care of her, right?"

"Um, yeah, no problem." Joey stammered, looking awkwardly away.

"Great." The woman fished through her purse while Lisa gave Joey a discreet thumbs-up behind her back. She would've strangled her if she hadn't been so enthralled with the beautiful woman on the other side of the counter.

Lisa handed the card to Joey without glancing at it. Then, as if she wasn't being obvious enough as it was, she added, "Joey will take care of you."

Joey, mortified, held out the cup of chai tea, but Lisa gave her a subtle nod toward the counter. Swallowing a golf-ball-sized lump of nerves and embarrassment, she stepped forward and extended the cup. "Here you go."

The woman accepted it, her long graceful fingers brushing against Joey's with a soft flourish. Then with a knee-buckling sweet smile she added, "Thank you, Joey."

She turned to go and Joey braced herself on the counter. As soon as the door closed Lisa began to giggle. "Who's the best friend ever?"

Joey stared at her.

"Come on, that was an Oscar-caliber performance. 'And the Academy Award for best depiction of a matchmaker goes to Lisa Knapp.'"

She shook her head. "I can't believe you did that, and I can't believe she said my name and actually touched my hand when she took the chai tea."

"Yeah, well, the latter was a direct result of the former, you know," Lisa said, "and on top of that, now you have her name, too."

"I do?"

Lisa pointed to the card in Joey's hand.

"Oh, yeah." The whole hand-touching and name-saying had made her forget the business card. She turned it over and studied the bold white print on the baby-blue background. "Elaine Raitt, Life Coach."

"What is it?" Lisa asked.

"Elaine." She grinned. "Her name is Elaine."

"Elaine, that's nice."

"Nice?" She scoffed. "It's classy, and beautiful, and lyrical. It's perfect. She's perfect."

"Oh, Lord, you're totally gone now, aren't you?"

"Maybe."

Lisa grabbed the business card and headed for her computer. "Let's research her before you fall ass over teakettle, okay?"

"No," she said forcefully. "No cyberstalking. I have some dignity left. I won't hack into her personal information."

"She has a website on her business card. I won't go any further than her public information."

"Public as in she wants people to see it, or public as in you don't deem it sufficiently encoded to consider private?"

Lisa smiled mischievously. "You know me too well."

"I mean it. No sneaking around online. I may be a sad sack of insecurities, but I have some standards."

"Fine." Lisa pouted. "I don't want to offend your sense of honor. I won't do any Internet matchmaking."

"Thank you." Joey went back behind the counter and started to clean the overflow tray on the cappuccino machine, just to have something to do with her still-tingling hands. Having a name to go with the stunning body, stellar smile, and bluest eyes in the world made her dream woman seem that much more real. Little starstruck crushes came and went, obsessions faded, and fantasies fell by the wayside, but it was harder to brush away personal touches.

Joey sighed heavily. *Elaine, what am I going to do about you now?*

❖

November 11

Elaine sat down in front of her computer, one leg curled under the other, and settled back before mousing over her Skype contact menu. The green Available icon popped up for several people on her contact list, but she didn't want to chat with just anyone. After her busy week of life coaching, she was eager to start her appointment with Marty Maine, her mentor coach. She began to relax as soon as she clicked the Call button under Marty's screen name and hoped her own clients felt this way when they sat down with her.

"Elaine," a familiar voice called even before the grainy video screen showed the image of the woman she was speaking to.

"Hi, Marty. How're you this evening?"

"Lovely, darling." Marty's slight Southern lilt hadn't faded even after years in New York City. A pixilated image formed then became exponentially clearer, revealing Marty's welcoming smile and dark, mischievous eyes. Three years younger than Elaine's own forty-two years, she'd always seemed older, wiser, more put together than Elaine felt. She'd certainly come to coaching a lot earlier in life. Marty was born understanding the human psyche.

"And how've you spent your first few weeks in your new border town?"

Elaine smiled at Marty's accurate characterization, though most people didn't think of Buffalo that way. Most Americans focused on the smaller border shared with Mexico—tense, dusty, and fraught with conflict. Elaine didn't want that type of transitional space. No, Buffalo constantly ebbed and flowed, but in subtler ways: the unexpected uniform of a customs worker, the accented *aboot* instead of *about*, the more noticeable flair of French filtering through conversations regarding nearby Niagara Falls. Industry was also shifting away from the steel belt to the rust belt; college students flooded in and out, and young people constantly left to look for work or education, while others arrived from smaller towns. Neighborhoods were revived while others fell into disrepair, and businesses failed down the block from thriving art houses and theaters. Buffalo was always on the brink of either total collapse or renewal. Elaine felt much the same way.

"I'm getting my sea legs, or my lake legs, as the case might be," Elaine said. "I'm almost unpacked and have gotten out in the neighborhood a little bit this week. Most important, though, I've found the cutest little coffee shop. It's funky, with all kinds of modern art, and they serve great chai tea."

"Well, yes." Marty chuckled. "That is the most important part of a move, isn't it?"

"I'm starting to connect to this place, which is a big relief."

"You were worried you wouldn't reconnect?"

"I was, and I still can't say this return feels like any sort of a homecoming, but I'm no less grounded here than I was in New York."

"But no more connected?"

Elaine frowned. "No, but that's okay. I don't need to have any great affinity for the land or the buildings or scenery. I connect with people. Speaking of which, one of my clients landed a big job this week. You should've heard the pride in his voice."

"You two have been working toward the job?"

"No, toward him recognizing his own potential. He wasn't even going to apply for it a month ago."

"And what does this breakthrough mean for you?"

Elaine exhaled heavily. "I'm relieved."

"Why?"

"It's our first big success together. I was honestly wondering if I was doing right by him. We talked for weeks before he gave the slightest indication he heard anything I said. For a while, I thought he might give up."

Elaine was careful not to use John's name or industry or any other identifying factors. Even though she and Marty honored the same ethics of confidentiality, Elaine took her responsibility to her clients seriously. When she spoke to Marty about her job, they generally focused on her own feelings and gave only enough details about the client to accurately convey the situation.

"Did you change anything about your approach with him over the last few weeks?"

"I tried not to panic. I wanted him to trust me, and I attempted not to go overboard because he was clearly suspicious, but I kept affirming that I wouldn't be disappointed in whatever decision was right for him. He worried about letting people down and needed the freedom to stop and consider what he wanted."

Marty nodded. "And how do you feel about your relationship now?"

"When he relaxed, I did too. It's amazing how our confidence levels affected each other. This was my first breakthrough since I got to Buffalo, and it felt like a good omen. I don't know. Maybe the move caused so much upheaval in my life I needed something to hold on to here, and that connection filled the need. Does that make any sense?"

"It does. Personal connections of any kind ground us to a place."

"Exactly," Elaine said. "I need that human connection."

Marty nodded. "Which makes me wonder why you've talked about your apartment, your job, and even chai tea, but you haven't mentioned your sister or your niece."

She blushed a little, which she hoped wasn't enough to show through the computer screen. "Ah, well, I have seen Brooke, and I got to meet my great-nephew, Taylor. He's a doll, by the way. He's got blond ringlet curls and big blue eyes."

"Sounds like someone I know."

"Yeah, it's obvious what side of the gene pool he sprang from. I couldn't get enough of him. I still can't believe I have a great-nephew, but I fell for him right away." She paused. "His grandmother is more complicated."

"Interesting that you see her as his grandmother and not as your sister."

"Amy's still my sister, but she's more his grandmother. You know we were never close. With our age difference, I was always closer with Brooke."

Marty nodded and remained silent.

"Amy was always too busy for me as a kid, and by the time I went to high school she had Brooke and all the drama that surrounded her. Now Brooke has Taylor, and she inherited most of her mother's drama with men."

"And what does that mean for your relationship with them?"

"I don't know. I'd like to see Brooke find some of the stability and confidence Amy never had, but I'm not sure she's interested in finding that for herself, and I don't know why."

"Right." Marty pushed gently. "But why is that relevant for you?"

"I'm a life coach, for God's sake. I connect with people for a living, yet I can't relate to my own sister."

Marty raised her eyebrows as Elaine dropped her hands into her lap, her shoulders slumping. "I can't believe I said that."

"Do you feel better now that it's out?"

She shrugged. "I'm not sure where it came from. I know it doesn't work that way. I know I can't coach myself or my family. I understand that personal dynamics aren't the same with everyone."

"Of course you do. But you also understand that what you know and what you feel are two different things."

"I suppose that'll give me something to consider before we talk next month," she said, granting her a grudging smile.

"That sounds wonderful, darling, but could you try to consider it with your heart and not your mind?"

"I'll try." Elaine signed off. She found her assignment easy to agree with but hard to execute.

❖

November 14

Joey flipped up her denim jacket collar and curled back into the hard plastic contours of her seat to protect her neck from the biting wind whipping around her. She refused to wear a scarf this early in the season. Winter was long enough on Lake Erie's shores, and she wouldn't hasten its arrival by capitulating to the chill a minute before she had to. Besides, it hadn't even snowed yet, and here in the rock pile of Ralph Wilson Stadium you didn't dare dress like a wuss until you had to. Wind chill be damned, in Buffalo natives considered anything above freezing balmy and distinguished themselves from tourists and transplants by their layers of clothes. A few rows down, two shirtless men had painted their beer guts into an unflattering Buffalo Bills jersey, or some hairy approximation, and while they weren't exactly what she considered role models, they proved that you could survive the swirling stadium winds without a scarf.

Lisa hopped down the concrete stairs in a Bills sweatshirt and jeans, her ponytail threaded through the back of a cap with a red buffalo stitched on the front. If she was cold, she didn't show it while she practically crawled across Joey's lap to kiss the man next to her on the cheek. "Hiya, Mr. Bruce."

Joey's father smiled broadly. Lisa always called him by both his formal title and his first name, a habit left over from spending her childhood largely at Joey's house. "How's my adopted daughter?"

"Ready for some football." Lisa beamed, then slugged Joey on the arm. "What about you?"

"You know it," Joey said. "No better way to spend a Sunday than taking in a game with my pop and my best friend."

"It'd be better if the Bills could actually win a game," her father grumbled, though he managed to smile.

"It'd be better if I had a beer or two in me," Lisa said.

He nodded. "That's my girl."

"First round's on me." Lisa would buy the second round, and they'd alternate buying drinks and food throughout the game. They would let Joey's dad buy them popcorn so they wouldn't hurt his pride by suggesting he couldn't afford to contribute, aware that six-dollar drinks and five-dollar hot dogs were extravagances on his meager budget.

"Two beers here," Joey shouted to a vendor starting up the steps in their section. As the salesperson lugged a square tray harnessed to slender shoulders, she noticed a subtle sway of hips and the less distinguishable curve of breasts under the thick straps of the cooler. Lisa must have realized this wasn't their typical hardscrabble stadium vendor because she said, "Holy smokes, it's a beer girl."

Their whole row turned to see the cute brunette bounce up to greet them. She couldn't be more than twenty-two, but she lifted the cooler easily. "What'll it be, handsome?"

Handsome? Joey blushed. "Two Labatts and a Coke."

"You got it."

"This your first time working the rock pile?" Lisa asked, referring to their section in the end zone.

"Yeah." The girl nodded at Lisa, then turned back to Joey. "Normally they make the women stay in the concession stands on the concourses, but we're shorthanded today, so they let me outside for a while. I'm Melissa."

Joey passed the beers to Lisa and her dad, then cracked open the pop-top on her Coke. "Well, good luck today, and don't let anybody give you any crap."

"You don't need luck when you've got skills," Melissa said with a hint of suggestiveness. "And if anyone gives me any crap, I'll tell them to come talk to you."

"Somehow I think you'll do fine on your own."

"Probably," Melissa said, "but I'll expect you to check in with me at least once a quarter just to be sure, okay?"

Lisa cut in. "We'll turn to you for all our libations this afternoon."

"You'd better." Melissa headed off toward another customer.

Joey settled back in with her drink and turned her attention to the player introductions on the field, but both her father and Lisa were staring at her.

"What?" she asked, not taking her eyes off the field.

Lisa slapped her upside the back of the head.

"Please tell me I didn't raise a dunce," Bruce said. "I may be an old, straight man, but even I recognize a mating ritual when I see one."

"Come on, she was flirting to sell more beers. I'm sure she talks to everybody like that."

Lisa rolled her eyes. "She didn't talk to me like that, and trust me, I would've enjoyed some of the attention she directed at you."

"You do like women, don't ya, Jo?" her dad teased her. "'Cause I'm getting too old for you to change your mind on that one again."

"Yeah, Dad, I still like women," she said. She didn't mind their ribbing. She was lucky to have family and friends who supported her.

"Well, if I was thirty years younger—"

"I *am* thirty years younger, and I play for her team, but I still don't stand a chance with Joey around." Lisa stuck out her lower lip.

"She's always been that way. Gets it from her mom. She never understood what a knockout she was either."

"Stop it." They were teasing, but they were embarrassing her. She wasn't anything special, and she was certainly nowhere near as attractive as her mother. "Melissa's not my type."

"Someday you'll have to explain how that works," her father said. "A pretty girl is a pretty girl in my book."

"But she's not *the girl*," Lisa said.

"Oh, no, is there another one of those in the picture?"

"No," Joey said.

"Yes. Her name's Elaine. She comes in the coffee shop, and Joey's got it bad for her."

"Well, what are you waiting for?" he asked.

"She's doing that 'she's way out of my league' thing again. She always thinks that about the ones she really likes."

"She *is* way out of my league." Why couldn't they understand that just because she'd had crushes on other women also out of her league, the facts of the situation didn't change? She was just perpetually prone to fits of awkwardness.

"Oh, Jo." Her father shook his head. "I know how you feel. I used to be the same way when I was your age. I didn't think your mom would give an old factory boy like me the time of day, but I managed to get her attention."

"How'd you win her over, Mr. Bruce?" Lisa asked, as if they hadn't heard the story a hundred times.

"She used to play piano at this real upscale lounge downtown where all the businessmen and their wives went for cocktails. I worked by the docks then, and I'd have to change busses down the road from there, so every night I'd stop in and sit in the back and just watch her and listen to her music." His eyes became a little dreamy as he spoke, and Joey got carried away too. She'd been raised on this story, but she never got tired of it. In fact, stories like this had made her the hopeless romantic she was today.

"Everyone else would mill around and talk, but I'd focus on her. Imagine me, covered in soot and smoke, sitting there with all those folks in suits and dresses. I obviously didn't belong up there with the rest of them. God, I felt so awkward, but I was the only one who ever made her feel like her work mattered, and maybe valuing her art showed her that I valued her."

"I'll be right back." Lisa hopped up and jogged up the stairs.

"Where's she going? She'll miss the kickoff. Was my story that boring?"

"No, Dad." Joey smiled. "We both love to hear it."

They got to their feet as the Bills took the field, excitement buzzing around them as the team sprang into motion. She had her eyes on the field, but she kept thinking about her father's story, searching for parallels to her own feelings for Elaine. The kick was quick and on target. The ball launched weightlessly into the air, beautiful as it soared. Everyone followed its arc as the ball hung seemingly suspended, like her heart, in hope and promise and fear of the inevitable crash. Could she show Elaine she mattered to her? Could she make her feel as cherished as her dad had made her mom, and if so, how? Then, as quickly as it had taken flight, the ball descended into a receiver's waiting arms a second before a bone-crushing hit leveled him, ending the play with a reminder that the brutal always tempered the beautiful.

Lisa returned, carrying a tray of cheese fries and wearing a goofy grin. She handed the fries to Joey.

"What're these for?"

"Just say thank you," Lisa said.

"Thank you," she replied skeptically.

"You're welcome. And I hope you remember that sentiment years from now when you and Her Royal Hotness need a godmother for your firstborn."

She examined the cheese fries carefully, struggling to find a logical connection between them and Lisa's most recent bout of insanity.

"I made you an appointment with Elaine," Lisa finally said giddily.

"A what?" Joey asked, still confused.

"A life-coaching appointment, for a free consultation with Elaine on Friday."

The words spun around in the wind, but she stared in shock, unable to process them.

"I called her while I was in line at the concession stand." Lisa continued, oblivious to Joey's stupor. "I told her I was you and that I'd like to try being coached. Isn't that brilliant?"

"Brilliant?"

"Yeah, now you can show her that what she does matters to you. And it's going to work too. You should've heard how happy she sounded. You made her day."

"No, I didn't!" she exploded. "I didn't do anything. I had nothing to do with this. You lied. I told you not to matchmake. I told you to stay out of this. God, Lisa, what's the matter with you?"

Lisa looked dejected. "I was trying to be there for my best friend, and you didn't say no matchmaking. You said no *Internet* matchmaking."

"Call her back and cancel."

Lisa folded her arms across her chest. "No. You wanted to make her happy. Canceling will disappoint her. If you want out of this, you'll have to disappoint her."

Joey shook her head and turned to her dad, but he held up his palms as if to say, "I can't help you out of this one."

Lisa had played her perfectly. She knew her history and her insecurities too well. Lisa understood it would kill her to disappoint Elaine. Only a best friend could use this kind of information against a person. "Damn it, Lisa. I can't believe you put me in this position."

"Might as well make the most of it," her dad mumbled, but when she turned to give him her best icy stare, he pretended to be absorbed in the football game.

"Come on. Don't tell me you weren't trying to come up with a way to show her you'd do anything to make her happy."

She slouched down in her seat, unwilling to give Lisa the satisfaction of admitting she was right.

"This is your chance, Joey. I promise I won't meddle again, but don't screw this up to spite me. You've got a free hour with the girl of your dreams. Go make her yours."

"Shut up," she snapped, but she sounded more resigned than defiant. She'd go to that meeting, and they all knew it. But what would she do when she got there?

CHAPTER THREE

November 19

Elaine had a crazy morning, with grocery shopping that took longer than she expected since nothing in Wegmans was where she thought it should be, then a haircut that should've been a trim, but the stylist her sister recommended chattered so much she took a couple of inches off. She topped it off with a typically frustrating trip to the DMV.

Returning home late and frazzled, she lugged several reusable groceries bags up the stairs to her apartment, then fumbled for her keys, dropping a few apples and a can of soup. She managed to stop the soup with her foot but refused to chase the apples back down the stairs. As she half carried, half kicked her purchases into the apartment, she blew a stray strand of her too-short hair out of her face and glanced at the clock over the kitchen sink. Three forty-five. She only had fifteen minutes until her next appointment.

Something inside her shifted, the calm instantaneous. Even though she continued to put away the groceries, she was already in life-coach mode, separated from the details of her own life. Elaine, the frazzled transplant in a new city, disappeared, and Elaine the calm and centered ally filled every space in her mind. She wasn't sure how she summoned such centeredness. She hadn't been able to find any for herself a few minutes earlier, but this wasn't about her. She'd received the capacity to carry the burdens of others while they sorted through their clutter and discovered a bigger truth about themselves. She felt no vanity or superiority, only a sense of responsibility to those she coached. She was happiest fulfilling her purpose and hoped she could foster the same sense of peace in the person she met today.

Elaine had wondered about Joey frequently in the week since her initial call. Usually those first contacts were tentative and awkward, but Joey had stated very clearly that she was interested in a consultation, and when Elaine offered to meet with her free of charge to see if they were a good fit, Joey enthusiastically said she was interested in exactly that kind of meeting. Maybe Joey was already highly motivated and wanted someone to act as a sounding board, or maybe she was familiar with life coaching and had been through this before. She wished she'd had more time to talk to her on the phone so she could better prepare for their meeting, but Joey had been in a hurry.

It'd sounded like she was in a crowd too, which was odd, since most life coaching occurred in private under strict confidentiality. Elaine had clients call her on recommendation from friends, on referrals of a colleague, or even through her website, but she'd never had anyone jump in this fully and without explanation. Yet despite the unusual introduction, she felt good about this appointment, like she and Joey Lang were meant to meet this afternoon.

She smiled when she heard footsteps on the landing outside her apartment door at two minutes till four. So Joey was prompt, another sign of eagerness, but she must also be a little nervous because, instead of a knock, rubber soles shuffled on the tile of the hallway floor. She couldn't be certain because the door muffled the sounds, but she thought she heard Joey sigh heavily, then tromp back down the stairs. Maybe Joey wasn't so certain after all. The footsteps were almost out of range when they stopped again. She stood but fought the urge to throw the door open. If Joey was battling something, she didn't need Elaine to scare her off. Then again, she didn't want to lose her.

"Come on, Joey, you can do this," she whispered, and waited with her hand on the doorknob.

Slowly the footsteps neared again, one deliberate stomp at a time. Was Joey wearing boots, or was she really making an effort to put one foot in front of the other? Then came a quick but light rap on the door, as if the person knocking had forced herself to act before she fled. But Elaine wouldn't allow that to happen without offering Joey another option. She smiled automatically as she opened the door. She didn't have to see the woman in order to feel an affinity for her. She genuinely cared for all her clients, but first she understood every person's human value, then over time developed a unique affection for each individual. That deeper bond usually took time to nurture, but the instant she met Joey's deep brown eyes, their connection cemented.

The surge of affection she immediately experienced caught her off balance. Joey had her hands jammed in the pockets of cargo khakis and a long-sleeve baby-blue polo tucked in neatly. Her chestnut-brown hair, trimmed short on the sides and longer on the top, wisped lightly across her forehead, but it fell short of the eyes that held her captive. Expressive, dark, and deep, they resembled shimmering portals to some inner recess of her personality. She had never before understood the expression of getting lost in someone's eyes. Something comfortable, familiar, yet still alluring dwelt there.

Joey shifted awkwardly from one foot to the other. "I'm Joey Lang. I had an appointment."

"Yes." She shook herself back into the moment, a little embarrassed to be almost speechless. She extended her hand. "I'm Elaine."

Joey's fingers slid along Elaine's palm and clasped it firmly, but the nervous shuffle of her feet and the way her gaze kept drifting back to the floor undercut the confidence in her handshake. "I know, we, um, met, kinda. I work at the coffee shop. You probably don't remember—"

"That's right. Of course I remember now. I couldn't have survived the drudgery of unpacking without your amazing chai tea. You're a lifesaver."

Joey grinned, and her cheeks flushed an endearing shade of pink. "Not really, but it is a nice little coincidence."

She shook her head. "No, I don't believe in coincidences. That cup of chai I needed and you made perfectly led us to this moment. Everything happens for a reason."

Joey's eyes grew round. "I've never, I mean, wow, that's a nice thought."

It was nice, and a belief she held dear, but she relished the idea even more than usual with Joey. Anticipation buzzed through her veins as she considered what purpose this relationship could hold, but she was getting away from herself.

"Please come in." She motioned to her small living room. Joey nodded for her to lead the way, and she did, sitting in a large, overstuffed chair and crossing her legs. Joey tentatively perched on the edge of the couch, her feet flat on the floor, knees together, back rigid and upright like she might flee. Elaine had a hard time reconciling this body language with the confident, eager woman she'd spoken to on the phone.

"Why don't you tell me a little bit about yourself, Joey."

"Not much to tell. I'm an average blue-collar Buffalo boi. I work at the coffee shop. I've lived in Buffalo my whole life. I like sports, and…" Joey tilted her head to the side slightly like she needed to ponder the question. Her innocent, pensive expression made her appear shockingly young.

"Do you mind me asking how old you are?"

"Twenty-eight," Joey said, then shifted uncomfortably. "Is that okay?"

"What? Of course it's okay. It's your age," she said, but even as she reassured Joey, something inside her head reminded her that twenty-eight was very young compared to forty-two, not that the comparison mattered in a professional context. And since their professional context meant they couldn't have a social context, she wasn't sure why their age difference mattered. "What about your family?"

"I'm close with my dad. I have dinner with him a couple times a week and try to help him out a little financially, since my mom died."

A flash of pain crossed Joey's youthful features at the mention of her mother. Her jaw tightened, and a frown creased subtle lines across her smooth complexion. Elaine hoped Joey wasn't fond of playing poker, because even though her voice remained steady in her recitation of the facts, her face clearly showed the emotion she tried to gloss over. "And my best friend Lisa is more like a sister. She's a blast. We've known each other forever. We live together on Granger, off Elmwood."

"That's not too far from here. Do you like the area?"

"Yeah, we're off the beaten path so it's not too loud, but we're close to all the restaurants and the coffeehouse. I moved in when I started at Buff State, and Lisa joined me when she moved back after college."

"What did you study?"

Joey stiffened again. A casual observer might not have noticed the response, but she was highly attuned to people's reactions. Joey looked out the window, and her breathing became more labored. Her voice also registered an uncertainty absent in her tone when she talked about her friend. "I, um, I started out in education, but didn't finish. Life, you know, it…" Joey shrugged and made a feeble attempt to smile. "It is what it is."

Elaine nodded. She wanted to move closer to Joey, to lay a hand on her shoulder and tell her it was okay to talk about whatever was on her mind, but she didn't make a habit of touching her clients, and she didn't sense that Joey was ready to dig deeper yet. In fact, she was still uncertain what Joey was so eager to talk about when she'd called her.

"You didn't mention much on the phone. Would you like to discuss something specific today?" Joey shifted on the couch like she wanted to stand, and Elaine quickly tried to reassure her. "It's fine if you're not ready to jump in, but you can talk to me about anything and it will never leave this room. I'll never betray your trust. I'll never judge you. I'll be your sounding board, your cheerleader, your mirror, whatever you need."

Joey's lips parted slightly and her eyes grew wider. Then she smiled, her reserve disappearing, and a piece of Elaine's professionalism melted just a little along with it. Joey tugged her heart in directions she found more than a little distracting.

❖

"There's a girl," Joey blurted, then immediately regretted her words as Elaine blinked back her surprise. What in God's name had possessed her to say something so personal, so stupid, and so true? She'd done okay. She hadn't been suave or charming, yet she hadn't made an ass of herself until now. She'd intended to show up, make conversation, maybe find some common ground, then politely excuse herself. Sure, part of her had hoped they'd hit it off and Elaine would want to date her, but she would've been content to continue admiring her from afar. She hadn't wanted to say or do anything to get her in any deeper. She had been prepared to be nervous and a little awestruck, even act a little silly, but she hadn't expected to be so drawn to Elaine. She hadn't thought she'd want to tell her things she'd never told anyone and was unprepared for how at ease she felt.

Now she'd not only opened herself up to being coached, she'd stepped into exactly the type of deception she'd been afraid of when she agreed to Lisa's crazy scheme. Damn it, if Elaine hadn't been so perfect, she could've gotten out of here with what was left of her heart and her pride. But when Elaine leveled those beautiful blue eyes on her and said she'd be whatever she needed, the words just rumbled out.

"Okay," Elaine said, "tell me more about what that means for you."

"I don't know," she said, trying to back out of the situation. "I don't even know why I said that. It's nothing."

Elaine pursed her lips, causing little lines around her mouth and a deep crease between her eyebrows. Joey's heart clenched. "You don't have to tell me anything you don't want to. I understand that you may not trust me yet."

"No, it's not that. I do trust you." That was true. She trusted

Elaine completely, but not herself. She'd never been able to deny a beautiful woman, and if Elaine asked her for an honest answer, she'd end up giving her one. "It's complicated."

"Women usually are," Elaine said, her conspiratorial smile making the bottom drop out of Joey's resistance.

"You say that with authority." Elaine's full, easy laugh sent Joey's heartbeat skipping. "Is that because you *are* a woman, or do you have this specific kind of experience with them?"

Elaine leaned forward as if to pass a secret between them. "If you want a life coach who's seen both sides of that coin, you've come to the right place."

She blushed again, unsure why. Maybe her sudden shot of boldness or her thrill at Elaine's answer. Sitting in her living room laughing, teasing, sharing a common thread made her feel she was right where she needed to be. Of course, Elaine was stunningly attractive, even more so as she relaxed into their conversation. And her blue jeans stretched tight against the curve of her hips when she crossed her legs while her long-sleeve red tunic accentuated her pink lips and hint of blush, though maybe the color in her cheeks was natural. Either way, Joey stared.

"So this woman of yours—"

"No, no, she's not mine," she said. "Not mine at all. She barely knows I'm alive."

"But?"

"But…" She hesitated. She could turn this conversation around, put a stop to everything. She could shake Elaine's hand, thank her for her time, and walk out the door. She needed to get up off the couch. She couldn't sit here and talk in hypotheticals about Elaine to her face. That would be dishonest and crazy.

"I'm crazy for her."

Elaine's broad, genuine smile expressed support and understanding. Joey felt so comforted and bolstered she would've done or said anything to keep Elaine looking at her that way. So she kept talking, fully aware of sliding into an oblivion from which she might never be able to return.

"She comes into the coffee shop a lot. She's stunning. She makes me all wobbly, and I can hardly say a word when she's around. I've never really been able to talk to her, but she's talked to my friend Lisa. And she's smart and seems sweet, with this smile that makes my knees go out from under me."

"She sounds wonderful."

"Too wonderful." Joey sighed. "She's way out of my league."

"Is that why you called me?"

She didn't want to blatantly lie about having called Elaine, though at this point she couldn't distinguish between Lisa's deception and hers. "I suppose I'm here because I want to get her attention, yes. God, it's pretty pathetic to go to a life coach because I'm all loopy for a woman who totally outclasses me."

Elaine's brow furrowed again, causing that V-shaped crease between her eyes. "I don't think you're pathetic, and I seriously doubt she outclasses you. You apparently have a strong critical voice talking through you right now, though. That might be a good place to start with our next session."

Next session? Joey sat back and exhaled. What had she done? What happened to getting in and out gracefully? She'd been sitting on Elaine's couch for an hour, and not only had she allowed herself to be coached, she'd actually expressed her insecurities about the woman of her dreams *to* the woman of her dreams. Now Elaine was talking about another session, and why wouldn't she? Joey had done absolutely nothing to indicate she was uncomfortable with the direction of their relationship. She'd wanted to be polite and supportive, interested in Elaine and what she did for a living. She hadn't intended to become a client, and this was her last chance to stop that from happening.

"You should probably know some things before we talk about another session," she said, then faltered.

"It's okay." Elaine rose, leaving her looking up into those dreamy eyes. "We don't have to cover everything in the first session. The conversations will flow more naturally as we get to know each other."

That's what I'm afraid of. She couldn't imagine getting any more attached to Elaine. She'd spent only an hour with her, and already she didn't have the strength to walk away. "It's just that I don't know what I'm doing here, and I don't want to waste your time."

"Joey, please," Elaine said quietly, "you're not a waste of time. You're precious, and I see so many beautiful qualities in you. I'd like to help you see them too, if you'll let me."

She was dizzy. No woman had ever said anything like that to her, and she wasn't sure how to respond. When Elaine asked if she'd like to meet at the same time next week, she simply nodded.

Chapter Four

Amy couldn't be bothered to put her phone conversation on hold long enough to say hello, so Elaine made herself comfortable in the living room while Taylor watched *Go, Diego, Go!*

"Hi, Anwainie." She translated that into "Aunt Lainie."

"Hi, buddy," she answered as he crawled onto the couch next to her. "How was your day?"

"Good." He gave a curt nod. "I eat macaroni."

"That is a good day."

"How your day?"

No one had asked her that in a long time, and she hadn't expected a three-year-old to. "Pretty good."

"You eat macaroni?"

"No. But I made a new friend." She rethought her words. Joey was a client, not a friend, and she needed to keep those things separate.

"A kid friend?" Taylor asked excitedly.

"Well, no, but she's young. Sometimes she seems very young, actually, but not a kid. Definitely a woman."

Taylor frowned, then shrugged before he turned back to his cartoon, reminding her that she was talking to a toddler, not a colleague. She didn't know how to talk to kids. She hadn't been around anyone this young since she'd left for college almost twenty-five years ago. What had made her think she could move back to Buffalo and suddenly remember how to relate to people she knew when she used to be someone else? Had she even related to them back then? She'd enjoyed baby-sitting Brooke, but they hadn't understood each other or connected on any lasting level. Clearly they hadn't bonded, because here she was, decades from her last meaningful interactions with her family, a stranger in the home of her closest relatives. Surely that didn't have to be the end. She had another chance and she wanted to seize it.

She put her arm around Taylor's tiny shoulders and kissed the top of his curly blond head. "I want to know you, Taylor."

Taylor cocked his head to the side as if seriously considering her words. The move reminded her of Joey. They were both so sweet and innocent, and serious beyond their years. Joey would be great with kids. Despite her terrible insecurities, Joey would be impossible to dislike. She was innately relatable. How surprising that she thought herself unworthy of some woman's affections. Surely any right-thinking lesbian would gladly receive such adoration from someone as loving, sincere, and attractive as Joey. *Oh, come on, Elaine, what's gotten into you?* She sometimes thought about her clients between sessions but generally focused on their problems and ways to help them, not their cute smile or devastating eyes. She'd never had to remind herself about her professional responsibility before. Still, no amount of professionalism could blind her.

"So, all moved in?" Amy asked as she entered the room without explaining or apologizing for her extended phone call.

"Yes, I'm settled in. I had my first local client over today."

"You had a client in your apartment?" Amy asked with more disdain than concern. "Is it a good idea to tell the crazies where you live?"

"She's not crazy," Elaine said, immediately defensive on Joey's behalf, even though Amy was questioning her sanity more than Joey's.

"If she's not crazy, why go to therapy?"

Elaine bit her lip until she could control her tone. "I'm a life coach, not a therapist."

"Right, you call it something different, but it sounds the same to me."

She had already explained that she didn't diagnose people

or conditions and she remained neutral to any outcome her client chose, but damned if Amy cared. She'd clearly put Elaine and her clients into neat little boxes she could easily label.

"I don't know why anyone would want to sit and listen to people complain all day. Lord knows I've got enough troubles. I don't need to get involved in other people's messes."

That was true. Amy had more than her share of issues and wasn't in a position to help anyone. Elaine internally chastised herself for harboring negativity toward her sister, but how could two people who looked so much alike see things so differently? She tried to direct the conversation to a topic Amy would enjoy. "Tell me something new about you."

"This guy came into work yesterday, and we started talking like we were old friends. He asked me out for Saturday night. He might be future ex-husband number four." Amy laughed at her own joke.

I asked for something new, not the same story I've heard since I was fourteen, Elaine thought as she smiled and nodded. Amy had always been beautiful in the most conventional, Barbie-doll ways. Time and stress had left her less firm or fit and added lines around her eyes and mouth, but she was still attractive, and men still responded to her. Apparently she still reacted to their attention with the same reckless self-abandon. Elaine gave it two months before the inevitable crash and heartbreak would consume her again.

Geez, what was with her? She'd come over here in such a good mood after her meeting with Joey, and now she couldn't control her negativity. Why did spending an hour with a stranger make her feel alive, valued, and purposeful, but five minutes with her closest relative have her ready to strangle someone? What type of person extended her heart and affections to someone she'd just met, but silently mocked her own sister's genuine excitement? She was the most hypocritical life coach in the world, not to mention a horrible sister and an all-around bad person.

"Crap," Elaine said aloud, startling Amy, Taylor, and herself.

"Crap's a bad word," Taylor said, causing Amy to let out a deep, reverberating laugh.

"I'm sorry." She flushed. "I shouldn't have said that. Aunt Elaine just remembered I forgot something."

"What'd you forget?" Amy asked.

That I'm not a horrible person or a terrible life coach, that you bring out my inner critic... "An appointment."

"Oh, well, don't let us keep you." Amy seemed relieved to have her go.

"Thanks. Maybe we could get together for coffee sometime?" she said, feeling guilty for needing to get away from the person she was trying to connect with.

"Oh sure, I'll call you," Amy said, but Elaine knew she would be the one to call.

"Good-bye, Taylor."

"Bye-bye, Anwainie," Taylor threw his tiny arms around her thighs. "I wuv you."

Her voice caught in her throat, but she managed to squeak out "I love you too" before heading to the door. When she ran away from Amy, she also ran away from her chance to do better with Taylor than she had with Amy and Brooke. *Maybe I am a terrible person.*

❖

Joey must have looked as disoriented as she felt as she trudged up the steps of her old Victorian home because Lisa met her at the door and looped an arm around her waist to help her to the couch. She was cold and tired from the walk in the frozen Buffalo dusk, and emotionally zapped from her session with Elaine as well as the subsequent questioning and second-guessing she'd done while taking the long way home.

"Dare I ask how it went?"

"I plan to kill you as soon as I regain some strength," Joey said, lying back and kicking her feet onto the armrest.

"That good?" Lisa grimaced. "So Ms. Perfect wasn't, well, perfect?"

"No, better than perfect, whatever that is. Sweet and warm and smart and so damn captivating. She was even more amazing than I expected."

"So what's the problem?"

"I'm the problem." She threw her arm over her eyes. "I told her I was all hung up on her."

"That's awesome," Lisa said, bouncing up and down.

"It would've been awesome, except I didn't use her name."

"You called her someone else's name?"

She peeked out from under her arm. "No, you moron. I didn't use anybody's name. I just said I was hung up on a woman who was out of my league."

"Geez, what did she say?"

"She thinks I need life coaching. Apparently I've got some inner voices we need to examine."

"Uh-oh."

"Yeah. She asked me to come back next week."

"And that's when you told her you didn't want to be a client?"

She covered her eyes again.

"Oh, Joey, you didn't."

"I'm going back next Friday."

"Shit." Lisa flopped into a recliner.

"And I assume I'll pay for her company."

"Joey, I got you into this. The least I can do is pay for the session."

She shook her head. "No. Your paying a woman to hang out with me is more pathetic than my paying a woman to hang out with me."

"Is she even any good at this coaching thing?"

"Damn good. I went in determined to be strong, and you know I'm stubborn when I set my mind on something."

Lisa nodded. "But?"

"I didn't even last twenty minutes until I cracked. I went on and on about this mystery woman and what I loved about her and how she'd never go for someone like me, and the whole time the woman I was talking about nodded and smiled sympathetically. Oh, and she came out."

"What? Wait. She came out to you?"

"Totally, and you should've seen her when she did. She gave me this cute little grin and said she knew exactly what I meant about women, like she wanted to give me the secret handshake. I almost came unhinged."

Lisa slapped her knee resolutely. "She's into you."

"You're nuts."

"No, follow me for a second." Lisa hopped up and paced in front of the couch.

"She just met you, and she's supposed to be all professional and therapisty."

"*Therapisty* isn't a word."

"Shut up. You know what I mean. She's not supposed to tell you she's gay."

"Why not?"

"I don't know why. She's supposed to be neutral or something," Lisa said confidently. "She came out to you because she felt close to you. She wanted to connect to you, and the way you tell it, she was even a little flirty."

"I don't know." Joey deliberately ran through the images in her mind again, searching for any hint Lisa's theory wasn't a wild fantasy.

"What else did she say, about you?"

"Um, she said I wasn't pathetic."

Lisa shrugged. "It's a start, I suppose."

"Oh, wait. She said she doubted the woman outclasses me. Then again, she didn't know who I was talking about. She might change her mind after she hears that."

"Good point, but she surely said something else."

Joey blushed. "She did say I was precious and she saw so many beautiful qualities in me."

Lisa stared at her wide-eyed. "Seriously?"

Joey nodded.

"Oh. My. God."

"Yeah, that's when I caved and made another appointment."

"Wow, I would've too," Lisa said.

"What should I do? I can't keep seeing her, but I can't tell her no either."

Lisa sat back down and rested her chin on her fist, like *The Thinker*. "You're headed down a dangerous path, my friend. You're headed for the client zone, and if she's as good a life coach as you say, there's no way she'll date someone she's coaching."

She groaned. "I know."

"But all is not lost. She's opened up to you, and she's said some pretty nice things about you too. I think you've got an in."

She didn't want to believe Lisa. She wanted to stay levelheaded and write off Elaine's compliments as her being polite and supportive as part of her job, but her hopelessly romantic side surged a little at Lisa's logic. Surely she wasn't the only one who felt the connection she and Elaine had shared.

"Here's the way I see it. You've made another appointment, and you and I both know you won't cancel, so you've either got to settle for being her client or you've got to turn it around before the end of your next meeting."

"How can I turn it around?"

"Go in there and charm her pants off."

Joey arched her eyebrows.

"Well, she can leave her pants on for a few more dates, but you know what I mean. Open up to her. No more moping around. No more trying to be stoic. You can't pull that off. You need to show her you're a loveable muck. Be sweet and smart and sincere."

"I can't."

"You can, Jo. You're all those things and more, and if you let her see that, it'll be harder for her to turn you down when you ask her out."

Joey sat up. "Wait, when do I ask her out?"

"Soon. You can't get any further into the client zone. You gotta jump into the dating zone by the end of your next session. So long as you do it before the session ends you won't have paid her, and you're not a client until you pay her."

That made sense. The payment made the relationship so seedy. People talked about their problems and hopes and plans all the time.

The coaching part was actually pretty wonderful. "What if I chicken out?"

"You'll have a good life coach to dissect your cowardice."

"Gee, thanks."

Lisa sighed. "Come on. There are worse things than having your dream girl give you her undivided attention for an hour every week."

Joey could think of a lot less enjoyable ways to spend an hour than staring at the most beautiful woman she'd ever seen, and if she could actually convert the appointment into a date, that would be downright magical.

❖

November 25

"Marty, she's so frustrating. It's like she can't see beyond the tip of her nose. Or maybe she doesn't want to." Elaine sighed.

She'd just finished another disastrous meeting with her sister. Both Amy and Brooke had brought their boy toys of the week along for Thanksgiving dinner. "You know it's bad when Brooke's tattooed and pierced punk rocker seemed like a lovely father figure sitting next to the smarmy used-car salesman Amy swears is great husband material, but judging by the pale white circle on his ring finger he might actually be someone's husband."

"How was the food?" Marty asked cheekily.

"Fantastic." She sighed again. "I suppose that's one thing Amy's got going for her. She can cook a lot better than I can. She's like our mother in the kitchen. I wish I'd inherited that skill."

"Excellent, darling. You saw something human in your sister. How you do feel about that?"

"Ugh, I'm terrible. I know she's human, and I love her. I want so badly for this to work out. I don't mean to go on these tirades." She had set unrealistically high hopes for her first holiday at home with her family, only to end up at a table full of strangers. Aside from a couple of big hugs from Taylor, she'd wasted her holiday floundering in awkwardness. The exchange made her feel less grounded than ever and sent her running to an unscheduled call to Marty. Instead of sharing her holiday with family and friends, she sat alone in a tiny apartment talking to her life coach through a computer screen. "Maybe they aren't interested in the type of relationship I moved back to Buffalo to establish."

"I can't coach your family. I'm here to coach you. What do *you* want to see change about that relationship?"

"All of it," Elaine said quickly. "I want to actually have a relationship. Amy just wants to cut me out of her life while she repeats her mistakes—until everything crashes down, and then she calls wanting help or money or sympathy. I hate that."

"So you have a problem offering your sister help, money, or sympathy?"

"No, of course not, but for doing the same thing over and over?"

"So you want her to learn from her mistakes?"

"Yes," she answered, then listened harder to her heart. "Maybe it's not even that."

Marty sat quietly, her image calm and serene on the computer screen. Her cream-colored sweater accentuated her long dark hair and almond-colored skin. Her eyes remained steady and filled with patience as Elaine tried to process what she was saying.

"Maybe I want her to try."

"Why does what she's willing to work for or let go have such a profound effect on what you're willing to work for?"

"I don't know," she said. "I honestly don't know why it bothers me. I wonder if I should have moved back here."

"Really?"

"I tell myself that everything happens for a reason, but I thought I wanted to build a meaningful personal connection."

"Right, and we both agreed that was an admirable goal, but we never said the connection had to be with your sister, did we?"

"If not my sister, then who? I moved for her and Brooke. If I wanted to connect with a random stranger, I could've stayed in New York. I had a lot more random strangers to choose from in a city that size."

Marty didn't have to say anything. Elaine was deflecting from the central issue. Why fight so hard for Amy? Why not a friend, or a colleague, or a lover? She didn't have the answer.

"I met with a new client," she finally said, "my first local connection."

Marty nodded. "That's important to you, right?"

"I've got a good feeling about her. She's fragile and strong all at once. Such a loud critical voice, but she's so open. I've only met with her once, but I could see pain covering so much strength in her."

"Sounds like you feel a strong connection." Marty sat forward, like she'd seen something on the computer screen she wanted to examine. "What about this client feels different from the others?"

"I'm not sure," she said honestly. She didn't know what had kept Joey on her mind long after their session had ended. "I think I'll really be able to help her. My thoughts about her have a sense of purpose, even more than usual. Like some bigger plan is driving our interactions."

Marty smiled. "And that sense of purpose might help you find your own path."

She nodded. By reaffirming Joey, she'd also reaffirm herself, and she could use a little of that right now.

Chapter Five

November 26

"What're you doing?" Lisa asked, leaning over Joey's shoulder.

"Homework from Elaine. It's a character-strengths assessment." Joey clicked her mouse on the "Like me" option under the statement "I never miss group meetings," then scrolled to the next statement.

"What do you mean?"

"It asks questions about me and my values, and it's supposed to calculate them and determine my character strengths."

Lisa pulled up a chair. "What's it asking?"

"A boatload of stuff. There are over two hundred questions like 'Is the world interesting?' 'Do I have good friends?' and 'Am I willing to take risks to establish a relationship?'"

"I guess we know how you answered the last one."

"Yeah, I suppose I've taken some pretty big risks, but only under duress."

"Come on." Lisa laughed. "I gave you a little nudge, and who knows you better than I do? I could probably fill that out for you. Hell, I might even make you look better for Coach Hottie Hot-Hot."

"No." She slid the mouse out of Lisa's reach. "No more games, no more lying. I'm going to answer this honestly. Elaine can take it or leave it."

"Wow, that's very ultimatumish of you."

"I know it is, and I doubt I'll have the courage to pull it off once I get there." She clicked on another answer. "But I don't like being dishonest."

"I know you don't," Lisa said, tussling Joey's hair. "You're a good boi, and she'll either see that or she won't, in which case it's her loss."

She rolled her eyes. "Thanks for the pep talk, but we both know how this'll end, and Elaine won't be the one who ends up devastated."

"Geez, Eeyore, I hope she's at least a decent life coach. You've got some major self-esteem issues. If you don't have the chutzpah to ask her out, maybe she can help you find your spine."

"Ouch." Joey pouted. "That'll give me something nice to think about on the walk over."

"Are you done with the quiz?"

She clicked on the Finish button and pushed her chair back from the desk. "Yup, it's tallying my results."

"You get to see them?" Lisa leaned closer to the screen.

"Yeah, I'm supposed to take them to Elaine's for our appointment." She tried not to sound like the prospect terrified her. She'd peeked at the questionnaire earlier in the week and then promptly closed it. She dreaded having to open herself up in front of the woman she was later going to ask out. She'd put off answering until the last minute. If she were smarter or stronger, she wouldn't have answered them at all. Who airs all their weaknesses to the woman they want to woo? Of course, the exercise was supposed to focus on the good, but surely this survey would broadcast to Elaine all the ways Joey was unworthy. What if she didn't really have any strengths?

Her results popped up on the screen. Lisa and Joey both scanned them silently, nervousness segueing into awe. According to the questionnaire, her top five strengths were the capacity to love and be loved, bravery and valor, humor and playfulness, kindness and generosity, and love of learning. There was a paragraph under each title, but Joey only made it to the first one. *Capacity to love and be loved—You value close relations with others, in particular those in which sharing and caring are reciprocated. The people to whom you feel most close are the same people who feel most close to you.*

Lisa let out a long, low whistle. "Holy smokitos, you're a fucking personality superhero."

Joey continued to stare at the screen, waiting for the bad news to pop up. "There's gotta be a mistake. Look at this." She pointed to the next paragraph that read, *Bravery and valor—You are a courageous person who does not shrink from threat, challenge, difficulty, or pain. You speak up for what is right even if there is opposition. You act on your convictions.* "That's not me. I'm a nervous wreck."

"Yeah, but you act on what you believe in. Think about what you've done over the past five years."

She shook her head. "This stuff isn't like me, not even a little bit."

"Dudette, that's you to a T. Loveable, brave, fun, kind, and smart." Lisa hit the Print button. As the paper emerged, Lisa quickly grabbed it, folded it into quarters, and tucked it into the front pocket of Joey's gray button-down shirt. "Now go woo your girl."

Joey nodded. She didn't agree with Lisa or the questionnaire at all, but a little ego boost to help carry her on her mile-long trip through the streets of Buffalo didn't hurt.

The fall chill had shifted to a winter wind stirring paper-thin leaves in circles across bare ground. The traffic along Delaware Avenue blew clouds of visible heat from overtaxed exhaust systems. Translucent shards of ice lined the edges of gutters. The gray dusk under cold, cloudy skies would've surely made her trek seem like a metaphorical death march without the list that covered her heart. Even now she couldn't muster much hope for a happy ending, but at least she'd moved into a neutral space, where a possibility of something other than ego-killing rejection existed.

This time when she reached the top step of Elaine's apartment, she wasn't shaking with nerves. Her heart rate accelerated, but she didn't feel like a faint was imminent until Elaine opened the door and flashed one of those mind-blowing smiles that caused her to melt all over again. The resolve and fortitude she'd spent all week cultivating disintegrated. Elaine's loose-fitted khakis and brown sweater over a navy turtleneck made her look downright snuggly, but her blond ringlets were down, disheveled, and slightly damp, like she'd recently gotten out of the shower, adding something sultry to her appearance. One of the curls fell across her forehead, and she casually blew it out of her face. Elaine was so beautiful Joey could barely absorb the striking image.

"Hi, Joey." Elaine swung the door open wide. It was a simple invitation, the only kind needed, and Joey couldn't have resisted even if she'd wanted to.

She grinned in spite of all the warnings sounding in her ear as she stepped across the threshold. *Here we go again.*

❖

Joey tentatively perched on the couch, her deep brown eyes watching Elaine carefully as she curled into her chair.

"How was your Thanksgiving?" Elaine asked, hoping Joey would relax a little before they broached heavier topics.

"Pretty much the same as always. I worked in the morning, then had dinner with my dad and Lisa. We all fell asleep watching football."

"That sounds wonderful." Elaine wished she'd had such an easy, natural camaraderie with the people who'd shared her holiday.

"I don't lead an interesting existence."

The comment was probably meant to be light, even a joke, but Elaine heard the insecurities in Joey's voice. She'd used the same tone last week when talking about how she wasn't good enough.

"Did you get to do the character-strengths assessment?"

"Um, yeah, I did." A light blush colored Joey's cheeks, piquing Elaine's interest. Joey pulled a paper from her breast pocket and unfolded it, her hands trembling slightly as she tried to smooth the creases. What about those results made her nervous? People usually found a list of their strengths empowering, but Joey looked embarrassed as she extended the paper shakily.

Elaine quickly scanned the printed list and, though her heart beat faster, she fought to remain objective. She wasn't sure why the top item on the list sent a thrill through her, but having a personal foundation for the capacity to love and be loved was certainly a good place to start working with someone who needed to boost her self-image.

It wasn't uncommon for clients to experience a conflict between their values and their way of life, but it did strike her odd that Joey, who seemed so loveable and clearly had the capacity to be loved, was completely unable to see that about herself. It made her sad to think about such a beautiful trait beaten and bruised under so much insecurity.

"Is something wrong?" Joey asked, her voice wavering.

"No, of course not. Why?"

"You frowned."

"I did?" Elaine was surprised. She usually remained neutral in front of clients.

"Just a little frown," Joey explained almost apologetically. "I thought maybe you didn't like something on there."

She sat forward, wanting to be close to Joey. "I'm impressed. You're creative, resourceful, and whole. You have everything you need to be successful and fulfilled. If I gave you any indication I saw anything less in you, I'm sorry, because the opposite is true. I'm only sad you don't seem to see what I do."

"Oh." Joey blushed.

"I find it interesting your top strength is the capacity to love and be loved, and yet you're here because you don't think you're worthy of a woman you barely know. It's even more intriguing you haven't approached her when you're so strong in bravery and valor."

"It's not that easy."

"Why not?"

"I talk to girls all the time, but like young, fun party girls. This woman's not a fling sort of person. She's happily-ever-after material."

"And that's not what you want?"

"No," Joey said emphatically. "I've been waiting for someone like her ever since I was a little kid watching my parents dance in our kitchen or hearing my grandparents whisper little I-love-yous to each other. They were made for each other. I really believe in that, you know?"

Elaine nodded, captivated by the spark that flashed in Joey's eyes. She was a completely different person. Her shy, downtrodden shell harbored a passionate romantic. "And you don't think you deserve all that?"

Joey wilted again. "I don't know if I don't deserve it…it's that this girl, this woman, she's the total package. She's beautiful and classy and educated, and I'm none of those things. I can't even approach her."

"When I hear the word 'can't' a red flag goes up in my mind, Joey. It's a sign your critical voice is talking, not your authentic self."

"I don't know what that means."

"You have two voices in your head right now. One is your authentic self. It's the voice talking about love and soul mates and your dream of finding yours. The other voice is a critical one. It's the mean voice saying you're not good enough for love, that you can't approach someone you're interested in."

Joey still looked skeptical, so Elaine elaborated.

"That critical voice starts as a survival tool. It's supposed to keep you safe. But somewhere along the line you got hurt or scared or separated from your path and let your critical voice take over. It became restrictive, like a bully. Now it's choking your authentic self."

"How do you know the critical voice isn't right? It's pretty hard to argue with."

She hurt to hear Joey identify with her inner critic. Fighting a voice that strong was hard even when a client recognized its destructive properties. Without that understanding it was more difficult to separate the critical and the authentic. Still, at least Joey was engaging her now, which was a good step. "What aspect of your critical voice do you agree with?"

"All of them." Joey sighed. "She's graceful, and I'm so bumbling every time I'm around her."

"Are you always bumbling, or is it just around this woman?"

Did the mystery woman have a name, or was Joey simply more comfortable with hypotheticals? She wouldn't let her own curiosity undercut the tenuous balance of trust they were establishing.

"Mostly around her. I guess it's like a self-fulfilling prophecy. With other women, the stakes aren't as high, so I'm more relaxed. But I expect to make a fool of myself in front of her, so I'm a nervous wreck and get all bumbly, which assures I make a fool of myself."

She tried to remain objective about the connection Joey had made on her own, but being able to recognize a pattern like that was important. "So that's the critical voice telling you you're insufficient. If you're not generally an inept person, what else sets you apart from her?"

"She's smart, really smart, like educated and refined. She's got a master's degree, and I'm a college dropout."

"It's interesting you see yourself as less than another person because of something like formal education. Is that consistent with your values to discount a partner because they have more schooling?"

"I'm not discounting her because of her schooling," Joey said. "I admire her education."

"But you see people as inferior as partners if they don't have a college degree?"

"No, of course not. My dad never made it to college, and my grandparents never graduated high school, and they all had amazing marriages. They didn't need a degree to love, honor, and cherish another human being. If I'm half the spouse they were, I'll be thrilled."

She smiled. With an attitude like that, Joey would indeed make some woman very happy. "You're quite eloquent when you talk about things you're passionate about, Joey."

Joey blushed, but Elaine continued. "If you met someone who believed in eternal love, someone dedicated to a partner, who was sweet and smart enough to support herself even without a formal education and whose only fault was that she cared so much it made her nervous, would you judge that prospective partner as harshly as you're judging yourself right now?"

Joey's cheeks were crimson and her eyes firmly riveted on her work boots. Elaine pleaded with her internally. *Come on, Joey. Try to see what I see.*

"Maybe my standards are a little high," Joey mumbled.

She nodded and pointed back to the list of Joey's strengths. "This is an impressive list. You've got a lot to offer a partner, and deep down you know these things about yourself, but you've got to learn to believe them, to harness them, to pull from them in your daily life."

"You think I could ask her out?"

"That's not for me to decide, Joey."

"She's a real knockout," Joey said, then her eyes widened. She stood up and faced the window, hiding her expression. "I can't believe I said that."

Why would a simple expression of attraction spark such a dramatic reaction? Why was Joey embarrassed? They'd already come out to each other. Surely she didn't worry about offending her. Maybe she was insecure about her own looks, but that was even sillier. Joey had to know she was beautiful. How could she not? Those eyes, that chiseled jawline, her fit physique. She didn't care how beautiful Joey's dream girl was. She was lucky to have someone as cute and passionately devoted as Joey pining after her. If Elaine were ten years younger, she'd…she'd still be Joey's coach and therefore not allowed to let her mind go where it had started to.

What should she say now? She never wandered off track in her sessions. That little lapse of her own feelings overflowing into something more personal disconcerted her, but even now as she regained her professional composure she wondered how to respond to Joey.

Thankfully, Joey seemed to move past whatever had sparked her withdrawal because she turned around, more composed and purposeful. "I'm running out of time, and everything's already muddled up."

Elaine's confusion melted fully back into life-coaching mode. "We don't have to solve everything today. We've got plenty of time."

"No, we don't," Joey said, calmly picking up her list of strengths. "I'm not sure if everything you said was true, but bravery and valor better not fail me now. But I guess if they do, I'll have a sense of humor to fall back on."

Joey was obviously trying to draw strength from her list of strengths, but Elaine wasn't sure why. The boi who'd slumped and hidden her eyes since arriving straightened her shoulders and leveled a steady gaze at her, pulling her into those deep brown eyes. It pleasantly unsettled her.

"Thank you, Elaine," Joey said. "I'm a mess, but you're amazing. You're sweet and attentive and genuinely caring. I'm not sure what'll happen here in a minute, but if nothing else, I'm grateful for everything you've said today."

"Joey, I don't know where you're going with this, but I didn't say anything I didn't believe."

"Okay, then please remember that too when I muck this up. Remember that you're the one who gave me the fortitude to ask you out. Okay?"

"Okay…wait. What?"

Joey's words ricocheted through Elaine. So many thoughts pounded through her confusion, but she couldn't single out any one worth giving voice to, so she continued to sit mutely, looking up at Joey. She wasn't afraid of the silence. She used it to sort out the tangle of emotions surging through her. Joey was clearly less at ease with the quiet and struggled to fill it.

"I probably haven't sold myself as an ideal date after all the stuff I told you, but I'm a good person. I try, anyway." Joey paced around the small living room, and Elaine eyed her movements but stayed firmly planted in her chair. She felt flattered and wanted to soothe Joey's clear torment and uncertainty, but her ethical code wouldn't let her forget a client had crossed the line.

Finally the ethical side won out, maybe not because it spoke the loudest, but because it showed her the most clearly delineated path.

"Joey, I can't date a client," she said firmly. "My profession doesn't allow me to have a personal relationship with someone I'm coaching."

"I understand. I'd never ask you to compromise who you are. You're an amazing coach, which I admire, but that's not all I admire about you." She exhaled forcefully. "I'm not even making sense now. I meant to say from the beginning that I'd like to date you."

"From the beginning? I thought you had a woman that you… Joey?"

Joey smiled weakly. "It's you. It always has been."

Her thoughts clouded over again. She'd felt complimented when Joey had asked her out, but knowing that she was Joey's dream woman flattered her so much she blushed. It also creeped her out and made her suspect Joey's motives. Had their entire interaction been an elaborate plan to get a date? That their connection hadn't been genuine hurt on multiple levels.

"I know it probably seems like a set-up," Joey said.

"It does, and I'm feeling a little foolish for falling for it. I guess that's one of the downsides to trusting people the way I do. Sometimes you get played."

"No, oh, God, it's not like that at all." Joey roughly shoved her hands through her hair. "I got played. Lisa played me like a fiddle. I wasn't strong enough or smart enough to stop, and I've let us all down now."

Elaine arched an eyebrow.

"When Lisa made the appointment, I should've called right back and canceled."

"Lisa made the appointment?" That explained why the person on the phone had seemed so confident when Joey was actually a mess of nerves.

Joey sighed. "She did. I saw you in the coffee shop all the time, but I was too nervous to talk to you. She wanted to help. She didn't mean any harm, and I didn't either, but I needed to be better, stronger. I don't know what's wrong with me sometimes. I meant to tell you right away."

Elaine fought to remain neutral, even as Joey unraveled in front of her. The picture of Joey as willfully manipulative was hard to bring into focus now. This beautiful boi's insecurities were clearly tearing her apart, but she had already pulled Elaine in and caught her completely off guard. Joey didn't seem capable of that level of deception, but she was. She'd been misleading before and might not be telling the whole story now either.

"Anyway, when I showed up here, you seemed happy to see me and were so sweet, I didn't have it in me to disappoint you. I wanted to make you happy. I know I got off track, not that I'm probably your type to begin with."

"Joey, I want to believe you, but we've got a bigger conflict than that. I'm not sure I can trust you."

All the color, a lovely mix of tan and blush, drained from Joey's beautiful face. "I'm sorry. I worried I'd never find the courage to ask you out and would end up being a client forever. That was probably the best I could've hoped for."

Elaine looked at her questioningly

"I clearly need coaching." Joey continued to babble. "I manage to mess up every situation I let myself get dragged into. Now instead of thinking I'm pathetic, you think I'm a liar."

She struggled against the impulse to comfort, to nurture, to soothe. She had to set her jaw against the words that pushed up from her heart. Was Joey desperate enough to fake an anguished need for coaching? She'd done it before. Elaine needed to protect herself from another set-up, another ploy, but as a life coach she needed to listen to her heart, to her gut, her true feelings, which were harder to sort through.

"Could we possibly pretend none of this ever happened?" Joey asked.

"No." She was resolute yet longed to return to their previous relationship. No matter how comfortable she had felt talking to Joey earlier, everything had been a lie, the antithesis of the authenticity she strove for.

"Okay, I'll go. I'm really sorry. If I could somehow undo everything, I would." Joey stepped toward the door, then turned around again. "No, I wouldn't undo it. I'd do it differently. I'm sorry I wasn't up front with you, but I'm glad we talked. I don't regret the coaching sessions. Even if I'm not right for you, you were the right coach for me. I'm sorry I didn't see that until I'd already messed up."

Joey hung her head. "I'm making this worse, aren't I?"

No, you're breaking my resistance. Elaine sighed and stood up. "I can refer you to another coach."

Joey's short shot of a laugh suggested disgust or disbelief. "No. Thank you, but I'm going to lock myself in a dark room for a while. The last thing I want to do right now is relive this massive crash and burn with someone else."

Elaine bit her lip to keep herself from offering something she shouldn't. She wanted to see Joey again, and Joey clearly needed more coaching, but their relationship was too complicated, too messy, too personal. "Do you want to talk to a coach about anything else?"

"Sure, I'd love to get to the bottom of all my junk, to learn to be better, or stronger, or to tap into some of the strengths we talked about. I felt good right until I blew it." Joey shrugged, as if trying to pretend she didn't care as much as her words clearly conveyed. "Who wouldn't want to learn how to live that way all the time, but I just can't, and you can't work with me either."

"Can't," Elaine repeated. "I hate that word. That's the inner critic's realm. I don't like to hear that you can't, and I don't like to hear that I can't do something either."

Uncertainty and confusion filled Joey's eyes.

Elaine sighed. "I need more time."

"More time?"

"To think, to consider things, to come to a decision. Not about the date. That's definitely a no, but I take the coaching relationship very seriously, Joey."

"I understand." Joey nodded solemnly.

"I'll call you in a few days," she said, and opened the door. "I'll think about all this and let you know what I decide by early next week. That's the only promise I can make."

"Thank you," Joey said sincerely. "And in case this is goodbye, thank you for everything else too."

Elaine closed and locked the door, attempting to somehow barricade the turmoil that roiled through her mind and body. She slid down the wall and braced herself with both hands flat against the cool hardwood floor. Closing her eyes, she attempted to breathe deeply, but no matter how much she tried to focus on things that anchored her to the present, she could only wonder, *What the hell just happened?*

CHAPTER SIX

A flurry of thick snowflakes swept through the air as Joey trudged across the pedestrian bridge over the Scajaquada expressway. Winter was here. They'd been blessed with an Indian summer by Buffalo standards not to have a real snowfall until the last week of November. She got swept up in it along with the hope she'd had in Elaine's presence, but as the snow settled heavily against her shoulders, so did a cold melancholy. She was a blue-collar Buffalo boi, and she'd survive the cold, she'd even thrive in it, but it was harder to handle the change of the seasons inside herself. She'd seen spring in Buffalo, but she had no such visual for who she'd be post-Elaine. She scanned her surroundings now, trying to anchor herself to the present, the familiar, the unchanging.

Normally she loved this view of Buffalo. To her right stood the colossal columns of Albright-Knox Art Gallery, to the left the picturesque expanse of Hoyt Lake with Delaware Park stretching off behind it. The scene was damn near idyllic in the summer, and in the winter carried a certain amount of peaceful quiet in the midst of a bustling city, but today she couldn't summon peace. It was almost a mile exactly from Elaine's apartment to the Victorian that she shared with Lisa, and every step sparked a new question, a new doubt, or a new insecurity. Did Elaine pity her? Fear her? Hate her? Clearly she had no interest in dating Joey, and who could blame her? Not only was Joey dull, uneducated, and weak, she was now also manipulative and deceptive.

If only she'd been stronger sooner, things might have gone

differently. What would've happened if she'd been honest with Elaine during their first session, or better yet, what if she'd struck up a normal conversation with her in the coffee shop? Surely Elaine wouldn't have been attracted to her, but maybe they could've connected in some other way. Maybe even as friends. Then again, if she hadn't asked Elaine out today, maybe she could've gone on being coached. That wasn't a perfect scenario, but maybe she could've learned how not to suffocate under all the "what-ifs" burying her now. She could obsess over this disaster all night, and probably would, but no matter how she should've handled the situation, she was too late. Elaine would never be a lover, or a friend, and the chances of her continuing to coach Joey seemed bleak.

Her front steps were already slick with wet snow and she paused to scoop a cup of salt from a bag on the porch. The simple act had tangible, predictable results and she took comfort watching the tiny crystals sink into the thin layer of fluff and melt in a scattered pattern. Did life work like that? Did we land somewhere at random and then bleed out, or was Elaine right about some pattern we simply weren't big enough to see in full? She must have zoned out, because Lisa stuck her head out the front door. "Do you plan to stay out here all night? I made hot chocolate, in case you want to mope inside."

Joey managed a small smile. Lisa always cut through the metaphysical crap. "I'm coming in."

Warmth emanated from the cast-iron fireplace in the living room, and Joey gravitated toward it. Lisa handed her a steaming mug, and she curled up on the couch, patting the cushion next to her.

"It didn't go as well as you'd hoped?"

She snorted and rested her head on Lisa's shoulder. "Dismal."

"That bad?"

"Yep. Not only am I a pathetic loser who can't get a date, I'm a liar and a user who has to manipulate a woman to get her attention."

"Jo, you know that's not true, right?"

"What does it matter if it's true? It's how she sees it, and I can't blame her. My intentions don't matter. I misled her, and I showed us both how weak I am. I'd totally understand if she never wants to see me again. It'd hurt, but I'd understand. Hell, I expect it."

"What do you mean, you 'expect it'?" Lisa asked. "That's not what she actually said, is it?"

"No. She said she'd call me."

Lisa stood up abruptly, causing Joey to lose her balance and spill her hot chocolate.

"Ouch. Damn." Joey licked the scalding drink off the back of her hand.

"She'll call you?" Lisa asked, astonished.

"Not about a date. She was very clear she doesn't want to date me."

Lisa eyed her suspiciously. "Really? What does 'very clear' mean in your world?"

"She said it would be completely unethical, and before I left she said the question about dating was, and I'm quoting here, Lisa, 'a definite no.' Could she be much clearer?"

"It's pretty clear she doesn't think she *should* date you. It's not clear she doesn't *want* to date you."

"Damn it, Lisa. You're always finding these little things for me to hold on to. It's a fantasy."

"Did she say you weren't her type?"

"No, but—"

"Did she say she wasn't interested in you?"

"No, but—"

"Did she say she thought you weren't compatible?"

"No means no, Lisa," Joey said sternly. "What are you, a frat boy?"

"Well, then, what's she going to call you about?"

Joey sighed and flopped back onto the couch, kicked her feet up, and stared at the ceiling. "She might continue to coach me."

"Really? You into that, or do you just want be close to her, 'cause you know that's not cool, right?"

"What's not cool, having a life coach or paying a woman to talk to me?" Joey shook her head. "Never mind. I'm sure you find them both equally pathetic."

"No. I'm just surprised. Current position aside, you don't strike me as the lie-on-the-couch-and-bitch-about-your-problems kind of person."

"You know me better than that. Do you think I'd want to sit around and whine about my inner child, or complain about my horrible parents?"

Lisa shook her head. "Then what do you do?"

"Honestly, it is a little like school, but instead of learning about other people, I'm learning about me."

"You did like school," Lisa said softly. Joey knew they were thinking the same thing. She had loved school. The only thing more painful than dropping out was why she'd had to, but she didn't want to dredge that up again.

"It's not structured like school at all, but I always loved that moment when things connected and opened me up to a whole other set of ideas I'd never considered. I loved feeling that the possibilities could stretch out infinitely, and I had a moment like that today."

Lisa sat down on the floor cross-legged, like a child waiting to hear "once upon a time."

"She was talking about the critical voice and my authentic self, and how when I got hurt and wanted to protect myself from feeling that way again, I let the critical voice take over, but now it's keeping me so safe I can't take any chances on anything."

"So you told her about Serena?"

She grimaced at that name. She thought about her ex often, but no one talked about her. Hearing her name aloud was jarring. "No, that's just it. Elaine knows virtually nothing about me, and she still knew what was going on inside me."

"She sounds good."

"Yeah, and if she's that good about knowing what I'm thinking, maybe she can help me learn to approach life differently."

Lisa nodded. "It's not a huge jump. I didn't know you were interested in counseling."

"I didn't know either until I met Elaine." She sat up. She needed Lisa to understand her, or maybe she needed to understand herself. "She doesn't make me feel like a loser. I mean, I still feel like a loser about how I botched things up, but for the first time in a long time I felt like I had new possibilities."

"You know you're not really a loser, right?"

"Thanks." Joey smiled. "But what I know and what I feel haven't matched up for a long time now."

"Then you should keep seeing Dr. Sweet and Sexy."

"Her name is Elaine, and she's not a doctor, but I'd like to keep working with her too. I only wish I'd realized that before I tried to put the moves on her."

"Yeah, stud muffin, you came to that conclusion a little late."

Joey remembered Elaine's beautiful features etched with confusion and betrayal, and her stomach clenched. She wanted a do-over. She needed to make it up to Elaine, and she had to try to get to the bottom of her own issues in order to ensure she never did this again. She wouldn't blame Elaine for never wanting to see her, but if that was the case, Joey didn't know how she'd face herself in the mirror. "I just hope I'm not too late."

❖

November 29

Elaine watched snowflakes fall outside her window. It had snowed for three days. Mother Nature had given them a break by waiting until the end of November before unleashing winter, but now she was making up for lost time. The snow soothed her so long as she didn't have to actually go out. She loved to watch it float downward in little drifts and settle lightly on tree branches and rooftops. The previously gray, rusty, or dirty now shone bright white. The transformation the snow brought entranced her. She especially enjoyed the way the snow swirled and settled in its own delicate dance, blanketing the world outside her window, softening harsh edges and muting the sounds of traffic until only a gentle, peaceful serenity remained.

Serenity was precious, and she wanted to wrap herself in it like a warm blanket, especially now while she struggled against the turmoil that threatened to envelope her from the inside. Three days had passed since she'd seen Joey, and hardly an hour had gone by without memories of her invading Elaine's thoughts. Rarely had she experienced a situation in which the hard facts clashed so drastically with the emotions they sparked. She had been a coach for less than a year, but she didn't need experience to know romantic attachments in any configuration between a coach and client were completely off-limits. Not only was it unethical to allow those feelings to go unchecked, but a relationship of that nature directly opposed the neutrality and objectivity essential for her to do her job effectively.

As a coach and not a therapist she didn't diagnose or prescribe, offer advice or judge. She listened, encouraged, and asked questions. She couldn't have a stake in her client's decisions. She couldn't afford to worry about where a question would lead or hesitate to offer enthusiastic support. Could she maintain that sort of impartiality with Joey, or would she always have reservations? Would she wonder if she could trust her? Was Joey even capable of being trustworthy or merely a lovely performer? Coaching sessions couldn't become a performance space for either of them. Authenticity was essential. She had to maintain a steady state of positive regard for Joey. There was no room for skepticism.

Was she skeptical of Joey? Maybe on an intellectual level, but she couldn't summon the gut reactions to go with that. When she closed her eyes and focused on her own visceral connection, compassion overwhelmed her. She saw the torment in Joey's deep brown eyes, heard the anguish in the crack of her voice, felt the dejection emanating from her, and ached to soothe her. As hard as she tried to remain logical and objective, she couldn't consider Joey manipulative. She might be naïve, but Elaine saw Joey's intentions, while misguided, as ultimately good. Even when she'd crossed the line into Elaine's personal space, Joey hadn't been predatory or disrespectful, but apologetic, as if her affections were somehow an imposition or an embarrassment. Surely someone who'd masterminded an elaborate scheme to win her good graces wouldn't have crumbled so quickly and completely. It didn't make sense to see Joey as anything other than a very sweet, very confused, very dejected person, and no matter what Elaine's head said she should do, her heart ached to reach out to her.

Didn't Marty always say she needed to focus less on what she thought and more on what she felt? The head was the realm of the critical. The gut, the heart housed the authentic. She encouraged her clients to think less about the restrictions society or culture or even their own experiences placed on them and focus more on their purpose, their passion. Her passion, the reason she existed, was helping people. She could help Joey. Wasn't that enough to make her decision for her? She'd connected instantly to Joey. Could she throw that away based on protocol or surface doubts? Joey's sincere desire to respect Elaine's decisions and her need to get in touch with her authentic strengths were genuine, if not from the beginning, then at least by their last session. She believed Joey honestly wanted to be coached and would continue to respect her boundaries, so the only problem would be Elaine's ability to remain unbiased. Judging from the continued strength of her connection to Joey, it shouldn't be hard to muster goodwill toward her.

If anything, she feared feeling too connected to Joey, as though the internal battle she'd waged on her behalf solidified the importance of their relationship. The residual tinge of pleasure at Joey's massive dose of flattery concerned her too, but who wouldn't appreciate being seen as smart, beautiful, and classy? It was impossible not to be honored by Joey's affections, and of course she was easy on the eyes too. But that didn't have any bearing on their coaching relationship, so she made sure not to dwell on those thoughts. She'd made her decision, and while unconventional, it fit her values and sense of purpose.

She'd call Joey tomorrow, or maybe she'd go down to the coffee shop and speak to her in person. It made more sense to meet with her face-to-face, not because of any desire to see her or to assure herself Joey was safe and steady and smiling again. No, it simply made more sense to see Joey so she could read her body language and establish a new tone for their interactions.

❖

November 30

Joey handed a customer his tall skim mocha, no whipped cream. “Thank you, sir. Have a nice day.”

The man, in a fancy suit and over-gelled hair, was apparently in too much of a hurry to acknowledge her comment or even her existence as he rushed out the door. She stared after him until the door shut. “If I ever get that self-important, you have my permission to smack me.”

Lisa laughed without looking up from her computer. “I’ll hold you to that.”

“How much time does it take to say ‘you too’ when someone tells you to have a nice day?”

“About a second.”

“How freakin’ hard is that?” She started scrubbing the grooves of the wood counter. It wasn’t dirty, but if she had time to lean, then she had time to clean, though she actually found that particular phrase pretty annoying. She liked to stay busy. The day went faster if she had something tangible to focus on. She’d told her new clerk, Franklin, to take his break. The morning rush had ended a while ago, and people wouldn’t start coming in on their lunch breaks for another hour. She could’ve had a break too if she’d wanted one, but constant motion was her default position, especially when stressed out. She didn’t like to dwell on her problems. She was a doer. She’d reacted to all the major conflicts in her life by simply working harder. When her mom got sick, she’d dropped out of school to work full-time. When her dad had been laid off, she’d worked overtime. Sure, she wished her work had more meaning. She wanted to help people or build things or fix things, but if all she could do was pour coffee and bus counters, then that’s what she’d do, and she’d be damn good at it.

Cleaning made her feel less helpless. She could clearly see her progress. It helped her to feel like she could control something, and she hadn’t had much of that lately. She wasn’t good at waiting, and waiting was all she’d done over the weekend. She’d waited for Elaine’s call, constantly replaying their conversation in her mind, always alert, ready for her chance to make it right, to handle herself differently, to be strong and brave and composed. Even when Lisa dragged her outside to play in the snow, she'd listened for the phone to ring. The longer she waited, the more she worried the news would be bad. If Elaine felt that conflicted about coaching her, surely she'd decide against doing so, and she didn't blame her. She blamed only herself and the guilt suffocated her, so she resorted to her only remedy and grabbed a mop.

The bell on the door chimed while she was in the back room filling a bucket with hot, soapy water. She'd spent all weekend waiting, whoever had come in could wait thirty seconds, but Lisa skidded around the corner. "Jo, it's her."

"Who?"

"Her," Lisa repeated with exaggerated emphasis. "Lovely Life Coach."

Joey's heart accelerated, but she tried to keep her hands steady as she turned off the water.

"She looks hot."

"Thanks."

"I don't think she's breaking up with you," Lisa whispered.

"There's only one way to find out." Joey forced her feet to move despite her own fear about what she had coming. She didn't share Lisa's assessment. Surely Elaine had come to say good-bye, but she could've done that over the phone, couldn't she? Either way, she'd know for sure.

Lisa was right. Elaine did look hot, more like stunning, actually. She was bundled up in blue jeans and calf-high boots. A red turtleneck peeked out beneath a navy-blue pea coat. She had a brown leather satchel slung across her shoulder, and her hands were covered in a sleek pair of brown gloves. Her cheeks were pink from the cold and her blue eyes crystal clear. Most appealing, though, was the smile that crossed her face when she saw Joey.

"Tall chai tea?" Joey asked sheepishly. She didn't want to assume Elaine was here to talk to her even though that smile set her body humming.

"I'd love one," she said, then added, "and I'd love to talk to you, too, if you have a moment."

"Of course. Have a seat and I'll join you." She turned her back to Elaine, hoping she couldn't see her hands tremble as she poured three shots of chai into a tall mug. She grabbed a bottle of water from the cooler on her way around the counter to soothe the sudden dryness in her throat.

Elaine had chosen a table in the front part of the coffee shop opposite where Lisa sat. The location gave them maximum privacy for a public place. Joey sat across from her but couldn't bring herself to meet Elaine's intense eye contact.

"How're you doing, Joey?" she asked, her voice clear but soft.

Joey shrugged. "I'm fine."

"I've thought a lot about you this weekend..."

Joey stared out the window. The sun shone brightly in a pale-blue sky. Snow was melting rapidly, causing little rivulets of runoff to shimmer in the street. The colors reminded her of the eyes she was currently avoiding. *Here comes the big "I care about you but..." portion of the conversation.*

"Are you still interested in working together?"

Joey whirled to face Elaine. Her breath caught painfully in her chest. She nodded.

"I'd like that too," Elaine said resolutely, a flash of a smile playing at the corners of her mouth. Then she quickly switched into professional mode. "But we need to do this by the book, Joey."

She nodded again, still unable to speak. She could keep working with Elaine. It wasn't exactly what she'd dreamed of, but she was grateful for a second chance under any conditions.

Elaine lifted her satchel from the chair and pulled out a stack of papers. "Here's a coaching contract I've used in the past. It's not a legal document, but it should help assure we're on the same page as far as our expectations go."

Joey continued to nod like a bobble-head doll. *Say something, you idiot,* she screamed internally. She hadn't expected to see Elaine right now. She'd barely hoped to see her again at all. Now she was sitting across from her, close enough to smell the sweet, understated scent of jasmine in her perfume. Elaine was giving her another shot, and she wanted to accept it fully and graciously, but she couldn't speak.

"The other form is a discovery questionnaire. I use it to help gauge where a client is in her life and where she ultimately wants to go. It covers things like motivation, personality, and most importantly, the goals you want to achieve through our coaching relationship." She slid the papers across the table to Joey.

"Are you okay, Joey?" she asked softly.

"Yes," Joey managed to squeak out.

Elaine searched her eyes. The intensity of the connection made Joey blush, but this time she didn't turn away. They were turning a corner, and she needed to acknowledge that fact. "I want to be better."

Elaine smiled. "We'll work on helping you see you're already creative, resourceful, and whole."

"Thank you." She hoped her simple words somehow conveyed her sincerity. "I really am sorry about—"

"No." Elaine shook her head. "You've apologized enough. There's a reason for everything. It all serves a purpose, but now we're moving forward."

"What about the things I said before? I mean, can we…I don't know…"

"I'm your coach, Joey. I'm not your judge. I promise I'll never judge you. I believe in you, and I'll be your champion."

"I'm going to be worthy of the faith you're showing in me," she said. "I promise I'll never lie to you. I'll honor your commitment and be equally committed to my end of this contract."

Elaine's smile sent Joey's nerve endings buzzing. "I'm looking forward to working together."

Joey returned to nodding again, but this time the words came easily. "Me too."

CHAPTER SEVEN

December 1

Joey sprawled out on her living room floor with the paperwork Elaine had given her. The fireplace was ablaze, she had a pencil and a pen beside her, and she'd brought water and potato chips with her, trying to make a preemptive strike on possible distractions. It should be easy to examine her life and her goals without the prospect of dating Elaine, but she couldn't ward off her own insecurities.

Would she be able to live up to her promise to Elaine? She would have to do more than simply not lie again. To be worthy of the trust Elaine had placed in her, she'd have to be completely open about herself and what she wanted. She wouldn't settle for a lie of omission. Half-truths weren't fair to either of them. She had to do some serious thinking about who she wanted to become.

After taking a few deep breaths, she opened the client agreement. The contract seemed standard, stating the names of both parties, along with an explanation of the meeting schedule, weekly for ten weeks, directions for terminating the relationship, two weeks' notice, and a confidentiality statement. Elaine wouldn't reveal Joey's identity or share any personal information with anyone. Only the end of the letter truly caught her attention.

> *Throughout the working relationship, the coach and client will engage in direct and personal conversations.*

> *The client can count on the coach to be honest and straightforward in asking questions and making requests. The client understands that the power of the coaching relationship can be granted only by the client, and the client agrees to do just that: have the coaching relationship be powerful. If the client believes the coaching is not working as desired, the client will communicate that belief and take action to return the power to the coaching relationship.*

She sat back. Putting that much responsibility on the client was a little daunting, but as she mulled over the concept of holding and granting power in the relationship, she found it awe-inspiring too. She would've thought Elaine held all the power. She had the education, the skills, and right to be paid, but none of that meant anything unless Joey opened up. She shared the control. It was up to her to get what she needed from the coaching process, and that terrified and exhilarated her. Her promise to live up to Elaine's faith in her took on new meaning. She wouldn't just have to listen to Elaine. She'd have to play an active role.

She opened the discovery questionnaire and scanned the nearly three full pages of questions. The first on the list read, *What motivated you to hire me as a coach?*

"The fact that I screwed up at getting you as my girlfriend," she said aloud, then shook her head. No, that would be rude and not even true. Why had she wanted Elaine to keep coaching her? Because she was missing something in her life or in her mental makeup that kept her from feeling whole? Because she didn't feel incomplete when she was talking to Elaine? Because she wanted a better life? Or a better future? All of the above. She wasn't sure she knew the full answer, or maybe she was just having trouble articulating it.

She wrote in pencil so she could go back and refine her answers later if she needed to. *I hired you as a coach because you saw strength and love and worth in me, and I want to learn to see myself that way.*

The answer wasn't suave or eloquent, but it was true. Would Elaine find such a simple answer pathetic? It shouldn't matter what

Elaine thought. She wasn't trying to win her over. She needed to focus on being a good client, which meant giving power to the coaching relationship. Truth was power, right?

"Now you're being dramatic." She turned to the next question.

What primary short-term goals do you want to focus on in the next ninety days?

There was space for ten goals.

"Oh, dear Lord." She continued to talk to herself. "Ten goals? I can't even think of one. I'll come back to that."

What long-term goals do you want to focus on in our coaching? (Only choose things you really want, not what you feel you should do!)

Geez, weren't there any easy questions on here? Joey scanned farther down the list, searching for something she could actually answer.

What are your favorite pastimes (name at least five)?

"Okay." She wrote, *Hanging out with Lisa, visiting my dad, sports (baseball, hockey, football, tennis), cooking, and reading.*

She could've kept writing all day. She searched for another easy question.

What motivates you or gives you energy? (e.g.: deadlines, caffeine, your values, meditation, exercise, nature, status, adrenaline, etc.) Not as fun as the last one, but easy enough to answer. She didn't need caffeine or adrenaline. She hated exercise and couldn't imagine meditating, but her values and the people she valued motivated her in most situations.

She grabbed her pencil again. *I'm motivated by my personal connections. My relationships with my friends and family are the most important things to me. I want to be a good person, a good friend, a good daughter, and a good partner.*

She read through the rest of the questionnaire, hoping for another easy question, but she didn't find one. She returned her attention to the questions about her goals, then rolled onto her back and stared at the whitewashed ceiling. She hadn't thought about where she wanted her life to go for a long time. She'd spent the last few years in survival mode, without time or energy to think about anything other than how to keep herself or her family from going under. Could she let herself want more? Did her old dreams still fit the person she'd become, or would she have to start over?

She continued pondering those questions until Lisa came home and plopped down on the floor beside her. "Whatcha doing?"

"Working on this questionnaire from Elaine."

"Like a *Cosmo* quiz? I love those."

"No, it's actually pretty hard. She wants to know about my goals."

"Speaking of goals, the Sabres scored three tonight and shut out the Lightning."

"The Lightning suck. They're about as good with goals as I am."

Lisa read over Joey's shoulder. "You don't have any goals?"

"I don't know. I used to, but then everything got off track."

"You want to go back to get your degree someday, right?"

"Sure, but the longer I've put it off, the more it feels like a pipe dream."

"A dream and a goal aren't that different. Maybe it's a long-term goal."

Joey sighed. "If I write it down, I'll feel obligated to try."

"Aren't you doing the whole coaching thing because you want to move forward?"

"I suppose." She still hesitated before writing it down. She wasn't sure she was ready to admit how much she wanted to finish her education. It would be a huge step to try to go back to school. Could she be a student and still uphold her responsibilities? The prospect of that kind of workload was daunting, and even if she could pull it off, was she smart enough to go back into the classroom after all this time? She'd be at least five years older than her classmates, and ten years older than some of them.

"What are you waiting for?" Lisa whispered.

"The inner critic to shut up," Joey whispered back, then smiled and wrote down *finish college.*

She sat back and stared at the page. The simple act of writing those two words gave them power, but could she learn how to wield that power?

❖

December 2

Elaine hurried into her apartment building, trying to escape the wicked winter wind whipping in from Lake Erie. It hadn't snowed anymore, but she wished it would. At least the snow was pretty compared to the dingy gray slush left on the side of the road. Plus the snow hadn't been replaced by warm weather or sunshine. If nothing else, the snow would give her a good excuse to stay inside. As it was, she felt like she'd better do her errands before the next storm hit. She'd forgotten about the unpredictability of the weather in Buffalo. People in New York City always had considerable warning of storms, which moved along the radar, crossing the country in computerized blocks of green or white. In Buffalo weather materialized over the lake and pounded the shore with spontaneous brutality. Lake-effect snow burst into violent, concentrated bands that pummeled one neighborhood while sparing another less than a mile away. That lack of predictability hammered home the old adage of never putting off until tomorrow what you could do today.

As she jogged up her stairs, she noticed a large document-size envelope leaning against the door of her apartment. She wasn't expecting anything, but she'd never lost the childlike excitement that came from getting a package in the mail. She carried it inside before opening it. She slid out the stack of papers, saw a cover letter, and glanced to the bottom, her smile automatic at the sight of Joey's name scrawled in broad, neat print. She wrote in all capital letters, with the first letter in each sentence taking up the full height of the line and the others miniature uppercase, clean, efficient, and not flashy, but with a charming edge.

The note read, *Elaine, I thought you might like to go over this before our session tomorrow. I hope you don't mind me bringing it by. Not everything is filled out, but I did my best. Joey Lang.*

She ran her fingers over the name. The simple note said so much about its author. Joey was thoughtful and dedicated but also uncertain. Elaine wanted to help her learn to see the wonderful parts of herself the way she saw them.

She flipped through papers, seeing Joey's signed contract and her completed discovery questionnaire, but stopped herself from actually reading any of her answers. She wanted to give the document her undivided attention. It was only professional to focus fully on something a client had put so much time and thought into. Yes, her professionalism made Elaine stop and change into a more comfortable long-sleeve T-shirt and trade her blue jeans for sweatpants so she wouldn't be distracted. It was harder for her to explain why she chose to curl up on the couch instead of sitting at her desk, and the steaming cup of tea she brewed may've added a personal touch, but no one was there to notice she looked less like a professional about to evaluate a client and more like someone settling in to cherish a good book. She didn't have anyone around to judge her, and she'd learned not to judge herself too harshly either.

She flipped open the discovery questionnaire. Joey's first response caught in Elaine's chest, and she reread to make sure she'd seen it correctly. *I hired you as a coach because you saw strength and love and worth in me, and I want to learn to see myself that way too.*

The sincerity and simplicity could have come directly from her own heart. Joey had summed up in a single sentence the reason she was drawn to coaching. Any remaining doubts she harbored about Joey's actual interest in a non-romantic relationship dissipated as she read on.

Joey had only listed a few goals, but they were interesting. She wanted to get her degree, which wasn't a surprise given her insecurities about her education level. Under short-term goals she'd listed *be more confident, learn to utilize my strengths, and maybe go on a date.*

Elaine wasn't sure what to make of the last entry. A date was the most tangible of the goals, but Joey's uncertain "maybe" made her wonder if Joey's misgivings stemmed from her ambivalence about the goal or her discomfort about sharing it with Elaine after their earlier misunderstandings on the subject of dating. Either way, they'd have to address it eventually.

Moving on to the next section of the questionnaire, Elaine noted Joey's favorite pastimes, which weren't surprising. She knew Joey had close relationships with her father and Lisa, and her interest in sports made sense. She seemed athletic, though Elaine had nothing but her appearance to base that assessment on. Her interest in cooking and reading showcased a softer, subtler side that few people were probably aware of, but she'd known existed the first time she'd looked into those endlessly expressive brown eyes.

She turned to the next page to read Joey's response to *What five things in your past or present are you most proud of?*

Joey had numbered her responses.

1) I've had the same best friend since I was eight years old. That explained how Lisa was able to read her so well.

2) I haven't missed a day of work in over three years. While certainly an accomplishment, Elaine wondered when Joey found time for the things she loved. Joey didn't strike her as greedy or driven to succeed without balance. Did she love her job, or was there more to her dedication?

3) I've helped my dad financially since he got laid off. That explained the work ethic. Joey wasn't a workaholic. She supported the people she loved. That made more sense in light of her strong capacity to love and be loved.

4) I'm the person everyone calls in an emergency. Elaine grinned. It wasn't hard to believe. Even for all of Joey's bumbling and nervousness, she was clearly sensitive and dedicated to the people around her.

5) I helped my mom get the care she deserved in her final year

Oh, Joey. She laid down the papers and hugged her knees close to her chest. Joey had lost her mother, and if she'd loved her the way Elaine expected she would, the weight of her care and ultimately her loss would've consumed such a young, sensitive soul. Her mother's illness, her father's finances, and her role as caretaker would've put Joey in a position where most people would've crumbled, but Joey'd not only come through, she'd learned to value the sacrifices she made and see them as points of pride in her life.

Most of Joey's accomplishments carried heavy doses of sadness. Clearly the people she loved were her top priority and a big part of her motivations in life, and when they suffered, Joey suffered. It said a lot about her strength of character to view hardships as chances to overcome, to triumph. Many people would cave under less, yet she plowed forward, continuing to work, and try, and love with fortitude beyond her age. How many people who passed the boi behind the coffee counter ever glimpsed the remarkable woman Elaine was meeting through this questionnaire?

If Joey's accomplishments were so complicated, Elaine was afraid of what she had written as the things she'd had the hardest time overcoming. She was tempted to stop for tonight, but she needed to know what she didn't know about this woman who had entrusted her with her life's most meaningful memories. She had to have this information to do her job as a coach, but more than that she wanted, maybe even needed, to reach the bottom of Joey's pain, to see the worst and know that, in spite of it all, Joey was still the beautiful, whole, loving person she was getting to know.

She lifted the papers again and scanned down to the part where she'd left off. *What are the hardest things you've had to overcome/accept in your life?* Joey hadn't numbered these answers. She hadn't even spaced them out. They were run together in a quick sequence as if she had simply wanted to get them out and move on, like ripping off a Band-Aid. She'd written, *Losing my mom to a curable disease, having to drop out of college to help my family, and losing my first love to someone who could give her all the things I couldn't.*

She had expected the first two answers, though each one provided new details. Joey viewed her mom's death as a failure that could have or should have been prevented. She also confirmed Joey had left school because she had other obligations that she valued over her own dreams. What struck her the hardest, though, was the last piece of information. The woman lucky enough to have Joey's love had wanted or needed more. What had she found lacking in sweet, beautiful, honorable Joey? Had she convinced Joey she wasn't classy enough for her, not educated enough, not wealthy enough? Was that where Joey's insecurities about her worthiness as a partner came from? Had Joey listened to Elaine and heard the recriminations of this other woman?

She ached for the pain Joey had experienced, the pain she continued to experience. She tried to remain objective, neutral, professional. She couldn't carry the burdens of all her clients, no one could. She'd go crazy if she internalized every conflict she coached, but it was impossible not to care, especially in this unique case where she'd been an unknowing player in reinforcing Joey's inner critic. If only Joey had handled their introductions differently… She had to stop that. She couldn't see herself as a failed romance for Joey. She was her coach. She had to shut down any emotional response that carried her into any other space.

She quickly turned to the final question of the discovery form. *What would you like to do or accomplish during your lifetime (personally or professionally) so that you will consider your life to have been well-lived?*

Joey's words read with poignancy. *A well-lived life for me is one filled with love. I want to be a loving friend, daughter, wife, and maybe parent. I want to love and be loved in return.*

"Damn," she whispered. How in the world could she keep her emotional distance when Joey wrote things like that?

She carefully slid the stack of papers back into their envelope. She'd file them away with other clients' documents for reference purposes, but she wouldn't need to read them again. She'd remember every detail. If the way her heart continued to beat a little bit faster than usual was any indication, Joey's words would stay with her long after she should've compartmentalized them into a less personal part of her mind.

❖

December 3

Joey took her usual seat on the couch and obsessively ran her hands through her hair, hoping to flatten any stray strands rearranged by her stocking cap. She wished she could look in a mirror, but it was silly to obsess over her hair. Then again, not as silly as trying to come across as serious with her hair standing straight up. She shouldn't have worn the cap, but if she hadn't her ears would've frozen and the wind would've blown it out of place anyway.

Focus, Joey, your hair is the least of your worries. She exhaled slowly as she watched Elaine reenter the room with two steaming mugs of tea. She was as gorgeous as always in a worn pair of jeans and a fuzzy pullover sweater the same deep red as her lips.

"This should warm you up." Elaine smiled and set a mug in front of Joey before curling up in the chair opposite her. The warmth of Elaine's smile was all the comfort she needed, but she couldn't say that. She shouldn't even let herself think that, so she wrapped her hands around the mug, allowing the heat to burn some of the numbness from her fingertips.

"I can't believe you walked over here in this weather."

Joey shrugged. "I don't mind. I'm used to the cold. I actually prefer it in a lot of ways. Some of my best memories are in the cold and snow."

"Like what?" Elaine asked.

"Ice skating downtown, hockey on a backyard rink, sledding as a kid, then snowboarding in college. You grew up here. You know what I mean."

Elaine shook her head. "I remember snowball fights at school, but I never played hockey, I only skated a few times, and I don't know how to snowboard."

"You're kidding." She was amazed. "We couldn't afford to ski more than once or twice a season, but my parents used to take me skating every weekend. I thought everyone in Buffalo did the same thing."

"No." Elaine allowed a flash of sadness to cross her features before quickly pulling her expression back to neutral. "My mother was usually too busy to play."

"What about your dad?"

"He left when I was very young. I don't have any memories of him."

"I'm sorry," she whispered. "As bad as it hurt to lose my mom, I wouldn't trade knowing her for anything."

"She came up a couple of times in your discovery form," Elaine said calmly, her tone soothing the ache Joey always felt when the subject arose.

"She's been gone for over three years now, and I still pick up the phone to call her sometimes. She had liver disease. We didn't catch it soon enough. My dad was out of work. They didn't have insurance, and I'd just started college. She waited too long." She cited the facts. The words sounded hollow and empty, but if she let herself feel any of it, she'd be swallowed by the darkness that raced close on the heels of those memories.

"As soon as we found out, we got her help. I quit school, and Dad worked three jobs trying to bring in the money. Lisa helped too, but it was too late. We made her comfortable, though."

Elaine sat quietly, clearly in no rush to comment, but intently watching Joey, her blue eyes full of compassion.

Joey grew uneasy and searched for something meaningful to fill the silence. "After she died the bills were still there. I never went back to school."

"But you'd like to?"

"Yeah, it was important to my mom, and it was important to…" She sighed. She'd almost revealed more than she wanted to. "It's important to me too, but now it feels more like a dream."

"Dreams are important," Elaine said passionately. "They tie us to our authentic selves."

"Do you think every dream is meant to come true?"

"I believe every dream serves a purpose, and if it's your dream, your own heart's desire—not something someone else convinced you that you should want—then you need to chase it." She gestured with her elegant hands as she became more animated. "The dream may evolve or change as you grow, but to have a dream and not chase it would be terrible."

"Wow," Joey said. Elaine had come to life before her, the personal and professional blending into a passionate expression. "I'm impressed. Nobody I know talks like that."

Elaine's lips quirked upward in the tease of a smile. "It's something I feel strongly about."

"It's nice you're doing what matters to you." She grinned. "I wish I had that kind of certainty about my purpose."

"You don't strike me as someone who's unsure about what matters."

"No, I know what matters and what I want out of life. I'm just not sure how to get it," she said quickly, then added more timidly, "or if I'm even capable."

Elaine made a hand motion as if squeezing an invisible orange behind her ear. "That's the critical voice whispering in your ear."

"How do you know?"

"Because you're creative, resourceful, and whole, Joey. You're capable of doing anything you dedicate yourself to." Elaine's confidence made Joey believe she knew what she was talking about. "What do you want?"

"I want to be a teacher," she blurted.

Elaine smiled broadly.

"I want to get an education and a good job to support my family," she said more deliberately. "And I want to help other people get those things too. I want to help them access a better life."

"Sounds like you do have something you're passionate about."

Joey blushed at Elaine's look of joy. She hadn't told anyone she wanted to be a teacher in a long time, and it left her feeling exposed. "If it ever happens, it won't be for a long time."

"What's holding you back?"

"Oh, you know, winning the lottery." She tried to joke, but Elaine remained quiet and unmoved, waiting for an honest answer. Joey remembered her promise to commit herself to the coaching relationship so she could be worthy of the faith Elaine showed in her. She wouldn't willfully mislead Elaine, and she wouldn't sugarcoat the truth. She couldn't hold on to her pride or her distance. She wasn't on a date. Elaine was her coach, and she'd asked her a serious question.

Elaine's expression remained gentle and attentive while Joey sorted through her fears. "I'm afraid I can't work full-time and go to school. I'm afraid I won't be able to afford school without hurting my dad financially. I'm afraid because it's been five years since I've written a paper or taken a test, and I wasn't ever a straight-A student to start with. And I know that sounds like a lot of excuses, but I don't know how to stop being afraid."

Elaine nodded thoughtfully. "You've got a loud critical voice, and from what you've told me so far it likely developed as a survival skill over the last five years. You became overloaded and had to pour your strength into one area, so you shut down others in order to protect yourself, but that time has passed."

"So what happened before isn't important?" she asked, partly because she wasn't sure she believed that, and partly because she loved to hear Elaine talk. She was smart and passionate, and the things she said made sense to Joey on a gut level.

"The past is important to help you see the patterns you developed, but it's more important to focus on the now, and you're not in survival mode anymore. That's your critical voice holding you back. Your authentic self is pushing forward."

"How do I know what's the critical voice and what's a legitimate concern?"

Elaine rested her elbows on her knees. "The critical voice always has a negative feeling associated with it. It's mean, scary, and makes you feel bad. The authentic voice is neutral or positive. It makes you feel good or, at the very least, it allows you to examine it clearly."

"I guess I should try to examine those fears a little more closely, huh?"

Elaine grinned again, causing Joey's mood to lighten. "That sounds like a wonderful assignment for the next week."

She laughed, happy to see Elaine happy and thrilled that she'd come up with a good idea on her own. "So I gave myself homework?"

"You did. Think about what's holding you back. Try to weigh it against what you're missing by not chasing the dream. Break it. Examine what's truth and what's hot air. Meditate on your goals. Pay attention to where each feeling comes from."

Meditate? Joey tried not to giggle at the thought of herself cross-legged on the floor humming weird phrases. Maybe she could make a list of pros and cons.

"I'll try," she said, glancing at her watch. Their hour was up, and she respected Elaine's time. "Can we talk about this more next week?"

"Of course. We can talk about whatever you want, but if you have something else on your mind now, you don't have to go."

Joey stood quickly. She didn't need an invitation like that. She'd done a good job of keeping her mind on the coaching dynamics, but if she allowed herself to relax into just chatting with Elaine, she'd lose that battle. The boundaries she'd formerly found confining were now her lifeboat, and she clung to the formalities.

"No, I gotta go," she said, grabbing her coat. "I'll see you next Friday?"

"I'll look forward to it," Elaine said, rising to open the door for Joey.

"Me too," she said on her way out. Then halfway down the stairs she mumbled, "I'm already looking forward to it more than I should."

Chapter Eight

Elaine went to the kitchen. She needed something to do with her hands, so she turned on the stove. She wasn't much of a chef, but she could make a grilled cheese, and that was just the type of comfort food she needed now. She set a large cast-iron skillet on the gas burner and adjusted the blue flame, hypnotized by the way it flared out around the base of the pan. She took deep, even breaths, quieting her body and her mind.

Normally she felt calm after meeting with a client. She'd learned well how to induce peace. It was a skill she'd honed long before becoming a life coach. Her mother had worked long, hard hours as a waitress, often leaving her home with Amy at night, then later they switched roles and Amy left Elaine home alone with Brooke. The silence and uncertainty rattled around inside her until it would choke her, but Elaine refused to let it. She understood now that part of her ability to self-soothe was her natural introversion, but the other, harder part involved quieting her mind and the gremlins of doubt that hid there.

She buttered two pieces of bread, then added the cheese, dropped it into the skillet, and once again allowed herself to get lost in the hiss of the frying sandwich. Even before she'd known the terms for meditation, she'd learned to let thoughts flow unimpeded through her mind, examining them without bias or attachment, and let them go. That was how she'd kept the doubt from chipping away at her when her mother didn't come home immediately after her shift and how she'd managed not to get sucked into the emotional whirlwind of Amy's life. That was how she kept from going crazy when at fourteen she was left in charge of a colicky infant and a full load of her own schoolwork. She made peace with herself, her achievements and her failures, never obsessing over either. She'd developed some bad habits like compartmentalizing her own feelings, and she cordoned herself off from the people around her so she never had any trouble settling down.

So why did her hand tremble now when she lifted the spatula to turn over the grilled cheese? Joey had been the perfect client—open, willing, inquisitive, thoughtful, and respectful. She didn't seem to feel awkward about the new direction of their sessions. Elaine, for her part, had moved forward easily too. She hadn't hesitated in questioning Joey, and she hadn't been concerned with upholding protocol. Even with the disconcerting aspects of their former sessions, Joey was easy to talk to, easy to trust, and, most of all, easy to like. She wondered now how much she'd contributed. She merely gave Joey some vocabulary, but Joey had done the heavy connecting. She'd even come up with her own action plan. As a coach, she left the majority of the talking and reasoning to her clients.

They'd had a standard session. Nothing about their encounter should've shaken her, yet she fought a surge of something strange in her chest, a cross between joy and fear, anticipation and caution. She hadn't wanted Joey to go. She loved talking to all her clients and took immense pleasure from watching them progress, but with Joey those sensations were heightened. Joey had begun to think through her own patterns. She'd been on the edge of drawing major connections, and Elaine could almost see the sparks of potential trying to ignite. When Joey's eyes wandered when she was nervous or uncertain, then locked onto Elaine's when she found the courage to speak words she'd previously held to herself, Elaine had chills.

The smell of acrid smoke filled her tiny kitchen.

"Shit." She tossed the pan into the sink, then turned on the cold water, sending a plume of steam into the air. She threw open her one small window, trying to vent both the heat and smell into the frozen outdoors, but only managed to freeze herself out in a matter of minutes.

"That's what you get for daydreaming instead of cooking," she told herself. She was being absurd. There was nothing out of the ordinary in her session with Joey. They'd had an enlightening and fulfilling conversation, and now it was done. She couldn't spend the next week wondering where she and Joey would head next. She needed to focus on other things. She had clients to meet with between now and then, and needed to deal with the pesky little issue of her own life and relationships.

She'd been so caught up in coaching Joey and the drama surrounding their relationship she hadn't spoken to any of her family for over a week. She had to do better, but found the prospect of talking to Amy too daunting. She had enough going on in her mind. She couldn't add Amy's problems to the mix, nor could she add her own concerns to Amy's. Even if she were at liberty to talk about her experience with Joey, her sister would never understand. She needed to focus on something fresh, something enjoyable, a human connection she could enjoy without complications.

She quickly picked up the phone and dialed a number she'd posted on her refrigerator as soon as she'd moved in but had yet to use. When a little voice answered "hewwo" her turmoil faded. "Taylor, it's Aunt Lainie. Do you want to go out to dinner with me?"

❖

December 5

The melancholy hit Joey the moment she opened her front door. The house was cold and lonely with Lisa and her dad both at the football game without her. She'd missed the Bills game because she'd had to cover a shift at work. Franklin owed her big-time. She wouldn't get another day off until next Sunday, and the Bills were out of town then. She hated times when the drudgery of her job stretched on without giving her anything to look forward to. Her life was steady and secure but tedious, with few breaks for unabashed enjoyment. She tried not to hope for any major relief, merely taking her tasks a few days at a time, counting down to whatever little reprieves she made room for on her schedule. She ran through her mental calendar. When was the next time she'd get to do something simply for pleasure?

Monday and Tuesday she had to work split shifts. Wednesday and Thursday would be standard five a.m. until noon shifts, but she'd be so wiped out she'd probably go to bed right after dinner. Friday she'd work the early shift again, then go right from work to Elaine's. Elaine. She warmed at the prospect of seeing her and experiencing the peace she exuded. Anticipation of the way she'd feel when she walked into Elaine's tiny apartment Friday would carry her through the next week. In fact, the mere promise of her coaching session lifted her spirits.

Joey shed her coat and grabbed a few scraps of wood from the tinderbox. She knelt beside the large brick fireplace and struck a match. The kindling lit quickly, and she chose progressively thicker pieces of wood until the fire crackled and licked at the edges of the cast-iron insert. Warmth spread out through the room and into her body. The fireplace had drawn her to the house almost ten years ago and was still her favorite feature. She wished she could meet with Elaine here on Friday.

Where did that come from? It didn't matter where they met. What mattered was moving forward, both in their coaching relationship and in her own life. Speaking of progress, she still hadn't made any headway on this week's homework assignment. She sighed. She didn't want to spend her afternoon rehashing all her shortcoming and failures, but now was probably the best time she'd get. Still, the fire was nice. She could relax on the couch, read a book, or nap until Lisa came home. She'd worked all day at a dead-end job. Didn't she deserve a break?

"No," she said aloud. Elaine had asked her to do this, and she'd agreed to be worthy of her confidence. "I've put this off for years. Let's see what I'm so afraid of."

She grabbed a piece of paper and a pencil, then sat down on her living room floor. Okay, now what? She had plenty of reasons for not going back to school, and she knew them well, but she didn't know where to start.

You can't do it, her critical voice whispered. The tension pulled at Joey. Her shoulders tightened. "Why can't I?" She spoke out loud, the sound of her voice cutting through the silence around her.

You're too old, the voice hissed. *You'll look like a joke surrounded by eighteen-year-olds.* She wrote down "too old."

You weren't very sharp to begin with. You might not even get in. She added "not smart enough" to her list, then with a frown added "not accepted into program."

Even if you did get back in, how would you pay for it? Will you miss work to go to class? Give less to your dad? Work extra shifts that will take away from your study time? She set her jaw and wrote down "money," then, "time."

"Is that all?" she asked aloud. Somehow speaking made her feel stronger than staying in her head. It made the rebuttals feel real compared to the dark shadows and half-formed images of her fear.

Isn't that enough? She wasn't sure if her head or her heart was speaking now. Either way, the list was daunting. She read it several times, her grip on levelheadedness dissolving. It was so overwhelming, so negative, so uneven.

It's uneven because you filled in only one side. That wasn't the inner critic, because it felt good. She stared at the list and saw her answers didn't even fill up half the page. She hastily slashed a line under her last answer, effectively cutting the negative items off.

What were all the pluses of getting her degree? These answers came even more quickly and in a clearer voice. "No more dead-end job, insurance, purposeful work, self-respect, steady income, giving back to the community."

The lists had evened up quickly. She sat back and grinned. Every obstacle now had a counter-benefit.

But you don't get the benefits if you fail. The inner critic was back, landing a solid blow. Pursuing a dream didn't guarantee anything. She could fail, leaving her stuck where she was, and she'd have to live with knowing she wasn't good enough. She'd lose any hope or self-respect she'd been able to hold on to.

The front door opened. "The Bills lost," Lisa called while she kicked off her boots. "Shocker, right?"

"Yeah, didn't see that one coming," Joey mumbled.

"It's freezing cold."

"Another news flash."

Lisa put her frozen fingertips on the back of Joey's neck, and she jumped away from the human icicle. "Shit, what'd you do that for?"

"'Cause you're being a smart-ass."

"Sorry. I'm just cranky right now."

Lisa glanced over her shoulder. "Whatcha doing?"

"A pro-and-con list about going back to school."

Lisa scanned the list. "Looks pretty even."

"Yeah, but the pros aren't guaranteed. They only happen if I make it through, and the cons could set me back before I ever see any rewards."

"It could work the other way too. The cons aren't guaranteed either. You might not have any trouble and just get the rewards."

She frowned. "I hadn't thought of that."

"Of course you hadn't, Eeyore." Lisa laughed. "Is this little exercise for Coach Can't-Do-Wrong?"

"Sort of, and her name is Elaine. I'm supposed to examine what's holding me back from my dreams and figure out if each one's an authentic concern or my inner critic."

"And you do that by making a list?"

"Actually, I'm supposed to meditate, whatever that means."

Lisa snickered. "Maybe you could dance naked or walk on hot coals. Go ahead. I'll cook some tofu. Then I'll call the neighbors for a group hug."

"Shut up. We've had three sessions and she hasn't once sung 'Kumbaya.'"

"Then why make an all-practical list when she told you to meditate?"

She folded her arms across her chest. "I don't know how."

"How freakin' hard can it be?" Lisa snorted. "You cross your legs and say *om*."

"Surely there's more to it than that."

"Not in the movies."

"Seriously, that's all you've got to go on?"

"Naw, I went to MIT. All those intellectual types were always meditating in parks. They just sat on their brightly colored mats, humming to themselves with their eyes closed. Seriously, they didn't do anything."

"How will that help me?"

"I don't know, but Sting says it worked wonders for his sex life, so what do you have to lose?"

"Only my dignity." She groaned, but Lisa was right. Elaine had said to meditate. She was supposed to listen with her gut or her heart.

"Come on. We'll do it together. It'll be funny."

Joey grinned. "I don't think it's supposed to be funny, but what the hell do I know?" She sat up straight and crossed her legs while Lisa did the same and rested her hands palms up on each knee. Joey mirrored the move. "Okay, now what?"

"Close your eyes and breathe," Lisa whispered.

Joey did as instructed, inhaling deeply through her nose and exhaling out her slightly parted lips. "Now what?"

"Keep trying until it works."

"How do you know if it's working?"

Lisa pushed her shoulder. "We may never find out if you don't shut up."

She laughed and tried to refocus. She took another deep breath, then another. The muscles in her shoulders were less tense now, though she wasn't sure if that was because of the breathing or because of the laughing. Either way, she'd relaxed considerably since Lisa'd come home. She hadn't enjoyed being alone with a list of all the ways she could fail. But it wasn't just the possible pitfalls. She had positives to consider, too. Nothing was guaranteed. It was a crapshoot.

No, she didn't believe that. She didn't have Elaine's faith, but at the same time, she didn't believe life was random. She had some control. She didn't have the IQ of an astrophysicist, but she wasn't an idiot, either. She studied hard and loved to learn. She'd managed to get through her first couple of years of college with a respectable grade point average. And she might be a little rusty, but she hadn't gotten any dumber, and she'd certainly learned how to manage her time. If anything, she was more mature now. Her age wasn't a total detriment either. Sure, she'd feel silly sitting next to eighteen-year-olds, but no sillier than she felt scrubbing up their coffee spills.

More of Joey's stress dissipated, replaced by something lighter, nicer, more hopeful. She liked the feeling. Did that come with her authentic voice? She'd worked through the first two items on her list, age and intelligence. What about the more practical concern of actually getting back into college? *Just because you decide you're up to the challenge doesn't mean anyone at the college will agree with you.*

That was the inner critic. She recognized the way it echoed through her mind but refused to pass through. It *was* mean like Elaine said, but was it right? Could she get into Buff State? Would they check her high school grades, her SAT scores, or the grades she'd made there? She didn't know how admissions worked for returning students. The thoughts rattled around in her mind, but her heart was trying to get her attention too. It said her high school grades were good enough the first time around, as were her SATs, and she'd made a B average at the college. She'd left in good academic standing. There was absolutely no concrete reason why she couldn't get back in. Where had that fear even come from?

Three obstacles tackled. She enjoyed this meditation stuff. Was she actually meditating or just thinking, maybe daydreaming? Who cared? Her chest was light, her limbs strong, and her head clear. What should she tackle next? With so much positive energy flowing through her, she had a hard time remembering what had been overwhelming earlier. What had she written down?

She opened one eye to peek at her list and found Lisa staring at her cross-eyed with her tongue out and her nostrils flared. Joey laughed.

"Is it working?" Lisa asked.

"I think so."

"Really?" Lisa's eyes widened. "You're ready to go back to school?"

"I'm not quite there yet, but I think I could do it academically now."

"I never doubted you."

"No, but I did. I worried they wouldn't let me back in or I wouldn't be able to keep up."

"And now?"

"I did it once. Why couldn't I do it again?"

"I'll be damned." Lisa slapped her knee. "It *is* working. Teach me, teach me."

"What am I, Gandhi all of a sudden?"

Lisa stuck out her bottom lip. "Come on. I wanna learn. Do the next thing on your list."

"I'm not sure I can give a command performance," she said, but she did want to keep working through the things she'd written down. "I'll try."

She glanced at her list and saw her next challenge was time. "I'm going to close my eyes and breathe deeply, then I'll think about the time constraints I'll face if I go back to school."

"When you go back to school," Lisa said.

She rolled her eyes. She'd come a long way, but she hadn't made a final decision yet. When would she find the time? She had to work full-time to keep her meager benefits. *When can you go to class if you work forty hours a week?*

"What happened?" Lisa whispered. "You made a frowny face."

"Oh, I heard my critical voice."

"What did it say?"

"It said I don't have time for school since I need to keep up my hours at the coffeehouse."

"Tell it you can get off work by one o'clock every day."

Could she boss around her inner critic? *Why not? It bosses me around all the time.*

"What?" Lisa asked in an excited but hushed tone. "You smiled."

Joey giggled. "My authentic voice got sassy."

"I wanna hear her. It's a her, right?"

"I suppose." Joey shrugged. "I think it's me. Like the real me or something."

"Does she, I mean, you, have anything else to say to the inner bitch?"

Joey took another deep breath, her mind wandering back not to her fears but to the rebuttal welling up inside her. "I get two days off every week, and I'm the senior assistant. I can pick my days most of the time. I could rotate mornings and afternoons if needed."

"So it's settled?"

Joey paused, listening carefully. Was her inner critic laying low until she was alone again? What would it say tonight when Lisa went to bed and the house was quiet? She could sense something in the shadows of her mind, but she wasn't as afraid. She wanted to see it. Could she coax it out into the open? She sat still and listened. She could work mornings and go to class in the afternoon or evening. *When will you study? When will you mow the yard? When will you see your dad? When will you sleep?*

"Uh-oh." Lisa groaned. "Inner asshole is back."

"No. It's not just that."

As soon as the words had formed in her mind they moved on, pushed out by something stronger, something more real. She controlled her schedule and her priorities. She could arrange them as she wished. She had a week of vacation days, and she'd never used a sick day. She had plenty of time. She also got one weekend day off each week and shortened hours on Sundays. The authentic voice wasn't warm and fuzzy, but it let her examine it clearly and stood up to her scrutiny. It held steady at her core and showed itself fully, just like Elaine said.

"I'll find the time to study even if I have to use down time at work or take some of my paid leave. I can do this."

"Holy shit. You're the best meditator ever."

"I just needed to learn to listen for the differences between my inner critic and my authentic voice, but honestly, if I'd heard those terms from anyone other than Elaine, I would've written them off as extra crunchy." Joey laughed with amazement. "Something about the way she talked to me made me listen. Then when I really listened to me, poof. It wasn't hard to pick out the authentic stuff."

"Kumbaya, my Lord, kumbaya." Lisa began singing loudly. "Joey's chasing the dream, my Lord, kumbaya, going back to school, my Lord, kumbaya. Sing with me."

Joey didn't sing along, but she did laugh as she flopped back on the floor in relief. She was proud of herself. Elaine would be, too. Maybe she'd even go by the university tomorrow and pick up an application while she felt strong. That would shock Elaine if she'd already applied by the time they met on Friday.

Not that she was applying to please Elaine. She honestly hadn't thought of her reaction until now, but making her happy would be a nice side effect. Elaine had shown so much faith in her, and because of her guidance she shared some of that faith in herself. She looked forward to showing Elaine how much work she'd done and thanking her for providing the inspiration to move forward. If she also wanted to elicit one of those beautiful smiles she'd grown addicted to, there wasn't anything wrong with that, was there?

Chapter Nine

December 10

Elaine brushed a stray strand of hair from her face and fastened it loosely in a gold clip. She didn't linger in front of the mirror or allow herself to wonder what about her appearance inspired Joey's early devotions. She remained as neutral about her looks as she did about her clients, or at least she tried to stay neutral, but she didn't always succeed where Joey was concerned. Still, the more she fought her true feelings, the worse she felt, so she allowed herself the luxury of looking forward to seeing Joey.

She'd had a productive week with several successful coaching sessions, a new-client consultation, and even a civil Sunday dinner with her family. She'd also made plans with Brooke and Taylor for later that evening. It wasn't exactly a breakthrough, but it was progress. She was happy and wouldn't let her inner critic ruin her mood by pointing out the few things she could do better at. Working with Joey was in line with her purpose. She was passionate about coaching and didn't see anything wrong with enjoying her time with a client. Positive energy buzzed through her like the warmth of her tea, and joy fluttered about like the tiny, dancing snowflakes outside. She liked her work, she liked her new home, and she liked her afternoon schedule. That was enough for now.

She was so lost in her own reflections she didn't hear Joey approach until she knocked. Elaine had failed to shift into full coaching mode until that moment, but thankfully the transition was effortless. She didn't have far to go from meditating on her own purpose to facilitating those thoughts in others, though she had a momentary lapse of self-awareness when she saw Joey. She could've been in a catalog ad for Lands' End, with cargo khakis tucked into brown snow boots. Her navy-blue Columbia coat hung open, revealing a waffle-knit sweater that matched her espresso eyes. The remnants of snowflakes clung iridescently to her hair and eyelashes, reminiscent of dewdrops on a freshly awakened field.

"Hi." Joey grinned, eager, exuberant. "I filled out my application for Buff State."

"What?"

"I meditated, like you said, or I'm not sure if it was meditation, but I thought about it a lot, and I decided to go for it."

"Go for college?"

"Yeah." Joey blushed. "I mean, if you think I'm ready."

She fought the urge to throw her arms around Joey as a mix of pride and affection swept through her. "You're ready whenever you think you are, but come on in and tell me what you're feeling."

Joey shed her coat and sat down on the couch, still sitting forward but without giving the impression she might bolt from the room. "I feel good. A little brave, a little crazy."

"Bravery and valor was one of your top character strengths," she noted, pleased to see Joey put her strength into action. Aligning her actions with her purpose was a big step.

"Yeah, I actually thought about that when I got the application. I still haven't figured out how I'll come up with the money, but I worked through so many other issues I thought maybe I could just try to have some faith."

"What other issues did you work through?"

"You know, the critical-voice stuff, all the questions about 'Am I smart enough,' 'Am I too old,' 'Do I have the time?' When I pulled everything out and broke them down individually, it was a lot easier than letting all the insecurities shout at once."

It wasn't uncommon for a client to make a lot of the progress between sessions. Elaine had to ask the right questions and plant the right seeds. It was the client's job to foster that growth, and apparently that's what Joey had done. It wasn't unreasonable for a client to move quickly once she became aware of her purpose, but that wasn't to say action, even inspired action, was easy.

Before she could compliment Joey on everything she'd accomplished in such a short time, someone knocked on the door. "I'm sorry," she said, embarrassed. She never had visitors. "It's probably a UPS delivery."

"Go ahead and get it," Joey said.

Elaine reluctantly peeked through the peep hole and saw Brooke and Taylor waiting for her. She turned back to Joey. "I'm sorry, Joey. Will you excuse me a minute?"

"Sure. No problem."

Elaine wasn't so certain. She opened the door halfway and slipped into the hall. "Brooke, you're over an hour and a half early."

"Yeah, I know, I'm sorry, but another girl called off. I gotta work tonight. Can Taylor just go out to dinner with you instead?"

Elaine stared at her, disbelieving. Not only had she interrupted a session without calling first, she wanted to turn their dinner plans into an excuse to drop Taylor off for the night. "I'm with a client."

"Oops," Brooke said sheepishly. "Don't worry about Taylor, then. Just set him up with a video until you're done. He'll be quiet."

"I don't have a TV," she explained, "and even if I did, that would be completely unprofessional."

"Who's in there?" Taylor peeked around Elaine's leg and into her living room.

"Please stay here, honey," she said as Taylor tried to squeeze past her. "Brooke, I can't right now. Call your mother."

"I did. She's not home. Please, Aunt Lainie, I can't miss any more work. I wouldn't ask unless I really needed you."

Elaine wasn't sure she believed that, and she didn't appreciate being put in this position. She shouldn't have to choose between reconnecting with her niece and remaining faithful to the commitment she'd made to her clients. She deserved better, and so did Joey. She had to tell Brooke no, even if that meant further setting herself apart from her family, but Taylor had other plans. Clearly bored with the adult drama, he crouched down and crawled between her legs.

"Taylor, no," both of them called, but Taylor reminded her of Brooke at that age. She'd been deceptively fast, too. He dashed for Elaine's bedroom, but Joey's outstretched arm stopped him. In one fluid motion, she scooped him up and hoisted him to eye level. "Hello, young man. I believe you were ordered to halt."

"Who are you?" Taylor asked, totally unfazed.

"I'm Joey Lang."

"Joey is a boy's name."

Joey laughed. "Yes, but I like it much more than Joanna."

Taylor scrunched up his nose and giggled. "Me too."

The overabundance of cuteness made Elaine's frustration subside.

"So I'll pick him up at eleven?" Brooke asked, reminding Elaine why she'd been angry. This was her time with Joey, and Brooke was disrespecting that.

She snapped. "No. I'm in the middle of a very important meeting and—"

Joey laid a hand on her shoulder, causing her to turn and meet her deep, expressive eyes. Joey nodded to Taylor, who'd rested his head on her shoulder. "I appreciate that, but you've got a pretty important meeting right here, and he's listening to everything you two say."

Elaine sighed and leaned against the doorjamb. Joey was right. They shouldn't have this conversation in front of Taylor.

"I'm Joey Lang," she said to Brooke. "Do you mind if Taylor and I go out to the courtyard and build a snowman while the grown-ups finish their conversation?"

Elaine watched Brooke's expression change from surprise to gratitude to something stronger. "I'm Brooke, and that would be wonderful."

She extended her hand as she blatantly scanned Joey up and down. "You seem good with kids."

"Thanks," Joey said, clearly not as interested as Brooke was.

She passed Elaine with a sweet smile and headed downstairs chattering to Taylor about snowmen.

"Wow," Brooke said. "Who was that?"

"Brooke, I'm not at liberty to discuss my clients."

"Just a client?" Brooke asked, her tone more than suggestive.

"Not *just* a client." Elaine's temper flashed close to the surface. "She's a person, with feelings and goals and commitments, someone who deserves my undivided attention. It's completely inappropriate for you to interrupt our session and even more inappropriate for you to suggest what you're suggesting."

"Geez, sorry. I didn't know you were so touchy." Though Brooke apologized, her tone lacked sincerity. "If you don't want her, can you send her my way? I'm open-minded. I've never tried a woman before, but maybe I'd have better luck than with the guys."

Elaine's face flamed with anger at Brooke's failure to grasp the issue as well as a twinge of jealousy she chose not to examine.

"Just go, Brooke."

"Really?"

"There's no way to salvage this session now."

"Thank you, Aunt Lainie," Brooke gushed. "I won't dump him on you again."

"It's not Taylor I object to. It's the lack of warning."

"It won't happen again," Brooke reiterated, handing her Taylor's backpack. "Everything he needs is in there."

She left Elaine standing in the doorway holding a bag shaped like a penguin.

Elaine wandered back into the apartment to gather her thoughts. She'd lost her temper and Joey all at once. They'd been having such a lovely session before Brooke barged in. She'd wanted to keep moving forward, and if she was honest with herself she hated to lose out on Joey's company, too.

She heard a squeal of delight and looked out the window. Joey was rolling a huge snowball into the middle of courtyard while Taylor packed tiny handfuls of fresh powder on top. They made an adorable duo, and not even her wealth of frustration over the situation could dampen her longing to join them.

❖

Joey saw Elaine watching them from the doorway and waved. "Look who's here, Taylor."

He ran over and threw his heavily insulated arms around her legs. "I missed you, Anwainie."

The creases in Elaine's forehead vanished as her expression transitioned from guarded to sheepish. "I missed you, too," she said, clearly caught off guard by the easy abundance of emotion. Joey sensed Elaine hadn't spent a lot of time around children. She seemed unsure how to join in.

"Come on out and help us," she called, ready to lift an only slightly smaller snowball on top of the first.

"I haven't built a snowman in thirty years."

"Ah, well." She shrugged. "It's like riding a bike."

Elaine grinned and handed Joey her coat. "I haven't ridden a bike in twenty years."

"They say you never forget. Something about your inner child," she said. "But you probably know more about that than I do, Coach."

"I doubt that. You seem much more in touch with your inner child than I am. I'm sure you could teach me a few things."

"You could start by helping me lift Mr. Marshmallow's belly onto his bottom."

"Mr. Marshmallow?"

"Taylor named him already. Isn't it fitting?" she said with a wink to Taylor, who was watching them with rapt attention.

"Very."

They both bent over the large snowball, sliding their hands underneath to get as much leverage as possible on the packed snow. Their eyes met over the snowball, and Joey had to struggle to stay focused. "On the count of three, lift with your legs, not your back," she warned Elaine. "One. Two. Three."

Taylor squealed as they lifted the massive snowball, both of them stumbling a little under its weight and unwieldiness. With a few minor adjustments they stacked it on top of the other, then quickly added some extra snow to hold it in place. Elaine stood back, admiring their work, her cheeks pink from the cold and exertion. "On second thought, I'm not sure Mr. Marshmallow is a fitting name for someone of his heft."

Joey laughed. "Maybe you're right."

"He needs a head," Taylor said very matter-of-factly for a three-year-old.

"Should his head be bigger or smaller than his belly?" she asked, crouching down to Taylor's level.

Taylor considered the question seriously. "Smaller, but still big."

"Why still big?" Elaine asked.

"He needs a big brain to be smart."

"We can't argue with that, can we?" Joey smiled at Taylor, then up at Elaine. "How about I roll his head while you find something to use for his eyes and nose?"

She started packing snow together, glancing up occasionally to watch Elaine and Taylor wander around the small courtyard examining rocks and sticks. Elaine seemed nervous. She wrung her hands, her brow slightly furrowed in concentration as she nodded at something Taylor said. She liked to see Elaine with her guard down. She was always so composed, elegant, and unflappable that at times she seemed to transcend human error and awkwardness. Even after working with her for four sessions, Joey still had no trouble putting her on a pedestal, but watching her uncertainty with Taylor somehow made her more real. She clearly wasn't used to children, but she didn't shy away from Taylor.

Maybe that's what Joey liked best about this Elaine. Even though she was out of her element, she was tender and observant, and she listened to him with the same intense focus she used when coaching. Still, she hesitated when he reached for her to pick him up and looked perplexed when he rattled off a string of seemingly incoherent words. She enjoyed seeing Elaine forced outside of her poised, professional role. She adapted with grace and beauty. In fact, she was more stunning now than ever.

Elaine glanced up and caught her watching them. *Busted*, she thought, but if Elaine could read her mind she gave no indication. "Are you ready for a hand with Mr. Marshmallow's head?"

"Yeah, I'll need your height, too, since this snowman is going to be taller than I am," Joey admitted. She'd never worried about her height before. There was no use, but she would've liked to look into Elaine's pale blue gaze now when it was filled with mirth and laughter instead of the intense focus she was used to.

They got a good grip on the snowman's head, their gloved hands connecting beneath the snow. The lifting was easier this time but the balancing took more work. Both of them packed snow around the connecting points, their bodies colliding in several places as they raced to keep Mr. Marshmallow from losing his head. By the time they finished, they were laughing so hard they could barely stand up. Taylor ran over to join the excitement, giggling and spinning, happy to be part of the commotion.

Joey picked him up. "Did you find some eyes for Mr. Marshmallow?"

Taylor nodded.

"Where are they?"

He looked down at his empty hands. "Uh-oh."

"You dropped them?"

He nodded again, his bottom lip quivering.

"Not a problem, little man. I drop things all the time." She pulled him close for a quick squeeze. "I bet you can find them again, or maybe even some better ones."

He grinned so broadly his cheeks filled every inch of space between his hat and scarf. "I do it."

"I'll help," Elaine offered.

"No, I do it," Taylor said more forcefully as he wiggled free of Joey's grasp.

"Oh, okay." They watched him toddle across the snow in his little blue snowsuit.

"I'm sorry about your session," Elaine said quietly.

"I'm not. This is the most fun I've had in a long time. Taylor's great."

Elaine visibly relaxed. "Yes, he is. Thank you for understanding."

"He looks like you. He's got your eyes."

"He's got a shock of blond curls under that hat, too," she said, clearly amused. "It's kind of amazing, isn't it? He and I have so little in common. We're generations apart. I hadn't seen his mother for years and didn't meet Taylor until I moved back, yet I see myself reflected in his eyes."

"Is that why you moved home?" She didn't mean to pry, but she was genuinely interested.

"Something like that."

"Sounds complicated."

"When is it not?"

Joey shrugged. "Right now."

Elaine smiled. "You're right."

She thought she was used to Elaine's beauty, but when she smiled a certain way or stood in the right light or let down her defenses, Joey's breath caught again. This was one of those moments, Elaine's eyes bright, her long hair stirred by the breeze, her expression warm and open. Earlier, Joey had thought she seemed more human, but that glimpse of the real Elaine had actually made her more perfect.

"Anwainie, Jojo, I found them," Taylor shouted as he ran over.

"Good job, Taylor." Elaine lifted him up and Taylor giggled with pleasure as he stuck rocks on the snowman's face.

Elaine pulled a small, curved stick from her pocket. "How 'bout this for a mouth?"

Taylor clapped and added it to Mr. Marshmallow, giving him a little grin. He then turned to Joey with a look of anticipation.

"He's missing something, but what?" Joey stepped back and scratched her chin theatrically, pretending to do a critical evaluation. She circled the snowman, giving Elaine a little wink. "I've got it."

Joey pulled a scarf from her pocket and looped it around Mr. Marshmallow's neck. "What do you think?"

Taylor beamed. "I'm happy."

Elaine and Joey both laughed, and Elaine hugged Taylor tight. "I'm happy, too."

"Me three," Joey added. Leave it to a three-year-old to state something so clearly. She was happy, tremendously happy.

"And cold and hungry," Taylor added, snuggling into Elaine's neck.

"Oh, my goodness," Elaine exclaimed, "your little nose is frozen. Let's get you inside."

Joey followed them back into the building but stopped at the bottom of the stairs. She hadn't been invited up, and the time for their session had long passed. She'd had fun getting to know Taylor and seeing Elaine outside of coaching mode, but she was also edging dangerously close to slipping out of client mode. Going upstairs with them would be too personal. It would feel like a date, though not the most romantic one with a toddler in tow, but sharing family moments would make it hard to keep Elaine relegated to the professional realm. She'd done a good job of keeping her feelings in check, but if she let herself see how easy, how comfortable she could be with Elaine, she'd start to long for that on a regular basis. They'd established a good relationship, and she was seeing tangible benefits from their sessions. She was content with that set-up. She couldn't let herself want more. "I guess I'll see you next week?"

"Oh, Joey, you've got to be freezing, too," Elaine said. "Come in and warm up before you walk home."

"I don't want to interrupt your family time."

Elaine smiled sweetly. "You're not interrupting. Brooke interrupted your time, and you were nothing but wonderful and gracious. Now you're being invited. Accept it the same way."

Joey's resolve crumbled. She'd never had any willpower around this woman, and she wasn't about to develop any now.

❖

Elaine rested her shoulder against the doorjamb between the living room and kitchen. She'd gone to change into more comfortable clothes and came back to find Joey had perched Taylor on the kitchen counter. They were having an in-depth conversation about dinner. Taylor wore a set of little red pajamas with footies, his cheeks still pink, and his mop of gold curls fell across his forehead. He was cherubic, but Elaine's gaze kept wandering to Joey. She still wore her khakis and sweater, but she'd kicked off her wet boots and socks at the door. Her bare feet gave her the appearance of comfortable belonging. Elaine imagined waking up to a sight like this every morning and a sharp pang of longing sank deep into her chest. *Where did that come from?*

"Anwainie," Taylor exclaimed when he noticed her in the doorway. "I'm hungry."

"Oh?" She pulled herself back into the moment quickly. "What would you like, honey?"

"Hot dog," Taylor said resolutely.

"I'm sorry. I don't have any hot dogs."

"Okay, I have SpaghehttiOs."

"I don't have SpaghettiOs, either."

"Bologna?" he asked skeptically.

Joey's grin suggested she already knew the answer to the question.

Elaine shook her head. "We could go out for dinner."

"Do you have a car seat?" Joey asked quickly.

"No." She rubbed her forehead as she tried to come up with another option. What would she feed Taylor? What would they do all evening? Where would he sleep? Her frustration at Brooke returned.

Joey placed a hand lightly on her arm. "Do you mind if I look through your cabinets?"

"No, please do," she said, immediately settled by Joey's proximity.

"All right, buddy boy," Joey returned her attention to Taylor. "Let's see what chef Joey can whip up."

Joey opened up the cabinets and peeked around tins of tea and spices, grabbing a jar of peanut butter. "Do you have any bread?"

"Yes," Elaine said hopefully.

"Multigrain?"

"Yes."

"Scratch that." She grabbed a box of pasta shells, turning it over to read the details, then opened the fridge. She pushed around some fruit and grabbed a block of aged cheddar and some milk. "This might work. Taylor, do you like macaroni and cheese?"

He clapped his hands excitedly. "Yes, yes, yes!"

Elaine laughed. "It's his favorite, but he's probably used to the stuff from a box."

"Would you like some special Jojo macaroni?"

Taylor nodded.

"Okay, then I'll need some help from both of you."

She watched Joey become a flurry of action, moving confidently and purposefully around the galley kitchen. She occasionally asked for various pans or utensils, but mostly she engaged Taylor in measuring and pouring ingredients, leaving Elaine time to watch her. She was so different now, so sure of herself, with no hint of the bumbling or awkwardness that marked their early encounters. She laughed easily and smiled frequently, her expressions and body language open. Elaine had never had any trouble liking Joey, but now they'd reached a level of comfort beyond mutual respect, more akin to friendship. A nagging voice in the back of her mind said she wasn't supposed to be friends with her clients, but these were extenuating circumstances. She wouldn't make a habit of having clients cook barefoot in her kitchen, but there wasn't anything wrong with enjoying the twists life sent her way.

"Voilà," Joey said theatrically as she slid the pan of macaroni into the oven.

"Va-la." Taylor tried to imitate her.

"It'll take a while to cook, buddy," Joey said.

"Can I color? I have crayons."

"Ask Anwainie," Joey said, looking at Elaine as she practiced the name.

She rolled her eyes but couldn't hide her smile. "We can arrange that."

She rummaged through her desk and found an empty spiral

notebook while Taylor pulled a small box of Crayolas from his penguin backpack. He went to work, gripping a blue crayon in his tiny fist as he employed all the concentration a three-year-old could muster. Elaine kissed the top of his head and stood to find Joey watching her from the kitchen. Her chestnut hair was tousled, and one side of her mouth crooked up in a half smile. She was perfectly lovely, and Elaine saw a hint of the longing she'd felt earlier in Joey's warm brown eyes. She was drawn to that longing, whether she should be or not. She went into the kitchen and leaned against the counter facing Joey. They were too close, not physically, but emotionally, and they clearly both recognized it. She should tell Joey she was free to go, but it seemed unfair to dismiss her after everything she'd done simply because she was being too perfect.

Thankfully Joey gracefully transitioned to small talk with a touch of personable undertones. "Brooke is your sister?"

"No," Elaine said, grateful to discuss something tangible amid the unquantifiable aspects of her emotions. "She's my niece. Her mom is six years older than I am, and she had Brooke very young." She wasn't sure why she felt the need to clarify that point. Did she feel their age difference even if she hadn't consciously thought about it in some time?

"Were you close growing up?"

"With Brooke or her mother?"

"Either."

"Never with Amy. She always seemed so much older. By the time I was old enough to really interact with her, she was an unwed teenage mother. She didn't have the time or the energy to play big sister. I did watch Brooke a lot, though. We weren't peers, but Amy needed the help, and I liked that she trusted me with Brooke."

"No wonder Brooke trusts you with Taylor. She knows she can count on you to be steady for her son when she can't be."

She bit her lip, holding back a surge of emotion. "I hadn't thought about that."

"You don't think they consider you the steady one?"

"I didn't until now. I didn't think they thought much of me at all."

Joey seemed to sense her sadness and reflected it back in her expression. "It's complicated. You said so yourself."

"Right, it's always complicated." She smiled, comforted by the memory of Joey's earlier comment. "Except for right now."

Joey tried to return the smile. She didn't do a convincing job. "Is now really uncomplicated?"

Elaine sighed. The spell was broken. Her enjoyment of Joey's company and the soothing act of sharing herself was easy, natural, authentic, but certainly not uncomplicated. Then again, complexity wasn't always unwelcome. Given the choice between clear lines of separation and blurred boundaries of connection, she wouldn't trade complicated for distance and couldn't imagine regretting that decision later, no matter how it muddied future situations. "It is what it is."

Joey's smile was genuine now. "It is."

An hour later, dinner done and dishes washed, Joey said good-bye to Taylor, who presented her with a picture he'd colored, "just for Jojo."

Joey hugged him good-bye. "Thanks, buddy boy. Thanks for letting me play with you today."

"You come back tomorrow?"

"No, I'm sorry. I have to work tomorrow."

"I go to see you?"

"You can come see me anytime. I'll make you chocolate milk, and I'll make Anwainie some chai tea."

"Can we?" he asked excitedly.

"Probably not tomorrow, but someday soon," Elaine promised with a hint of his exuberance.

"Okay. Bye-bye, Jojo."

"'Bye, Taylor."

Taylor caught Joey's pant leg. "Hug bye-bye to Anwainie."

A faint blush crept into Joey's cheeks as she turned back to Elaine, the uncertainty renewed. She timidly wrapped her arms loosely around her shoulder. Elaine pulled her tighter for a second, eager to let her know it was okay while at the same time understanding they were dancing along a tightrope.

Joey stepped back. "Bye-bye, Anwainie."

"Bye-bye, Jojo." There was nothing more to say, or maybe too much that could be said. Either way, they had to tuck this evening into the space reserved for memories to cherish but not repeat.

Chapter Ten

December 14

"So did you tell your dad the big news?" Lisa asked Joey between bites of her pork chop.

Joey kicked her under the table, but her father's interest had already been piqued. "What big news?"

She glared at Lisa and took another bite, trying to figure out what to say now.

"What? I didn't know it was a surprise."

"What's a surprise?"

"Nothing, Dad," Joey said.

"Well, it's something, or you wouldn't be so grumpy."

"She's going back to school," Lisa blurted.

"No," she quickly said, "I applied to go back to school. Nothing's settled."

"But applying is a big deal, Jo," her father said seriously. "Don't sell yourself short."

"I'm not sure I'll get in." She repeated what her critical voice told her. The doubts had started to creep in almost the second she'd put her application in the mailbox on the way home from Elaine's last week. Everything had been clear on Friday. She'd felt strong, sure, and confident after her evening with Elaine and Taylor, like she could have the future she wanted, the future she was supposed to have, and she wanted to move toward it.

But the familiar gremlins had started to grumble again. Just because she'd felt close to Elaine didn't mean she'd ever be worthy of a woman like her, and even if she was, what did that have to do with getting her degree? She'd let a good night of blurred boundaries raise her hopes and had been trying to lower her expectations ever since.

"Why wouldn't they let you in?" her dad asked.

"Tell him about your professor."

"You're blowing that way out of proportion."

"It was an omen."

"What was?" he asked, clearly getting annoyed he had to keep digging for answers.

"I saw one of my old professors at the coffeehouse the other day. She remembered me."

Lisa pushed her. "Tell him what she said."

"She mentioned that since I never actually withdrew I might be able to get back into my program without having to go through all the admissions red tape for a new student."

"And…" Lisa wasn't going to let her cut any corners.

"And." Joey drew out the word to indicate her exasperation. "She'd vouch for me to the department chair if I wanted to apply for a waiver to take a couple classes next semester as a general student. Then I could apply for the major."

"That's not a coincidence," Lisa said, pointing at her with her fork for added emphasis. "That's an omen."

"Wait. Next semester? Like in January?"

"Yeah, January twenty-fourth, but I'd have to be accepted first, then figure out what classes to take. Maybe I should wait until summer or fall."

"Why?" he asked. "You're a smart kid. You've got the drive. You've had enough time off."

She didn't know what to tell him. She didn't even know all the reasons herself, and she wouldn't lay her main concrete worry on him. "It's all moving too fast."

He nodded thoughtfully. "It does seem fast, but you've thought about this for a long time without sending in the application. You must have a good reason for doing it now."

She blushed and stared at her plate.

"Jo?"

"I've been seeing this woman..." She stopped and started again. "I don't mean seeing her, but meeting with her."

He grinned at her. "I shoulda known a woman was involved. Women make you want more out of life. To be better."

"Well, yeah, but no. This woman is a professional."

He eyed her skeptically. "The same girl Lisa got you involved with?"

"Yeah, but that backfired in a big way. Anyway, we're not dating. I'm seeing her as a life coach."

"Okay." He nodded, then shook his head. "I'm sorry. I don't know what that means."

"It means I talk to her about my goals and she helps me work through stuff."

"Work through stuff? You mean like a shrink?"

"Not really," Joey said, then hung her head. She couldn't imagine what he thought of her. "She's not looking at what's wrong with me. She helps me see things differently. Like with applying to school, I'd got all hung up on all the reasons I couldn't, and she helped me work through that."

"And you pay her to talk to you about your problems?" There wasn't any judgment in his tone, only confusion. It couldn't be easy for a man who'd never complained about anything to understand his daughter paying a stranger to examine her personal failures.

"Yeah, Dad, I do. It's not what I set out to do. I mean, I didn't set out to do anything. Lisa did, but it's working out pretty well."

He was quiet for a minute, then pushed back from his plate. "I can't say I understand, but your going back to school is a big step. If your coach woman helped you do something you've been dreaming about, it's money well spent."

Relief washed through Joey. "Thanks, Dad. That means a lot to me."

"And you're sure you aren't holding out hope to date this woman?"

She blushed more profusely.

"Oh, for Godsakes, Jo." He laughed. "What else aren't you telling me?"

"No, nothing," she said. She didn't want to say that no matter how right their coaching sessions felt, she couldn't shake the sensation that they could be more. "She's wonderful, but she's my life coach. Those lines, well, you don't cross them."

Lisa cut in. "Joey could cross them. I think she *should* cross them, but you know her."

Her dad smiled. "Yeah, I do."

"I've got a lot to work out right now. School is a big enough challenge without adding other complications. I need Elaine to help me focus on being steady. I don't want to do anything to throw us off-kilter."

"I respect that," her dad said. "You've got a good head on your shoulders and a good heart, too. You'll do the right thing."

"Thank you." She was grateful for his unconditional support, not that she'd expected anything less. He'd always had faith in her. She wasn't sure she agreed with all his assessments of her, but she did want to do the right thing. She wanted to do right for him and for Elaine and for herself, but she didn't know what that was.

Later that evening as her dad was leaving, he threw his arm around Joey's shoulder and walked her out to the front porch. "I'm proud of you, Jo."

"Thanks, Dad, but I've still got a lot of stuff—"

"You're like your mother. You can't take a compliment."

"I don't think I've earned one yet."

"I'm your dad, and dads are allowed to be proud of their kids just because they're your kid. Someday you'll have kids of your own and you'll understand."

Joey's memory flashed to her and Elaine and Taylor building the snowman. Having a family of her own was a nice dream.

"But until then, you need to go easier on yourself," he said. "You're a good person, you take care of your family, you work hard, and it takes a lot of courage to admit you need some help, but you did that with this coach."

"You're not disappointed?"

"I'm surprised, confused, maybe, but not disappointed. Learning when and how to ask for help is an important lesson, and it's not an easy one. People who can't ask for help end up desperate and lonely, with nothing but silly pride."

She was shocked. Was this the man who never complained, never accepted a free ride? Did he speak from experience? She thought about her mom's death and how they both refused welfare or charity when the bills piled up. Now he'd lost his wife, his home, and his pension. He'd lived the only way he'd known how, a good life with a good woman, and he'd kept his integrity intact. Would he have done things differently? It was too late to wonder now. She hugged him tight.

"One more thing, Joey," he said, standing back.

She could tell by his expression she wouldn't like what he had to say.

"No more giving me money."

"Dad, I won't abandon you—"

He raised his hands, cutting her off. "You've paid more than your share of my debts."

"She was my mother. You're my dad. You took care of me. I want to take care of you. That's how it's supposed to be."

"You took care of her, and you've helped me, too, but we've paid off most of the bills. I'm working again, and it's not a lot of money, but it's enough. Let me take care of me, and you take care of you."

"Dad, I can do both."

He cupped her face in his hands and kissed her forehead. "I know you could, but all I want you to do now is graduate. That's what your mom wanted, too. After that we'll talk."

"Dad…" She couldn't think of anything to say.

He didn't wait for her to find the words but walked away into the frozen night. "Good night, Joey."

❖

December 17

"He just left," Joey said, her expression conveying a sense of disorientation.

"How do you feel about that?"

"I don't know. I mean, I'm not happy about him cutting me off."

Elaine fought a smile. When most people thought of their parents cutting them off, it meant the parents stopped giving their children money, not the other way around.

"I guess I should be happy, though. The money was the only real thing keeping me from school, and now I'll have more leeway financially."

Elaine had been ecstatic when Joey'd told her she'd not only sent in her application, but actually made provisions to take classes in a little more than a month. But Joey didn't have the spark Elaine had grown accustomed to seeing when she spoke of her dreams.

"It's weird. I've worked for so long to take care of my family, and now that's done."

"You mentioned on your discovery form that your family was your strongest motivator."

"Yeah," Joey said. "They're why I left school in the first place."

Elaine had worried their previous session would make it hard to focus on her coaching role, but her connection with Joey was strong, and Joey was clearly troubled, so Elaine fell back on what she knew. They'd addressed the situation through a series of questions for the last twenty minutes, and she finally started to see what upset Joey so much about her father's request to stop helping him financially.

"It sounds like you're feeling a little lost."

"I am. For such a long time I've been telling myself I made the right decision."

"And now you think you made the wrong decision?"

Joey tilted her head to the side. "No, I had to make it at the time, but I'm not sure what the right one is now. I've always had to choose between finishing school and taking care of my family. Now Dad's decided for me, and I'm not sure it's what I would've chosen."

That didn't sound right. Joey had sent in her application before her conversation with her father. "You would've put off college again?"

"I was trying to do both," Joey snapped with more ferocity than Elaine expected. It took all her training not to react to her harsh tone. She'd never heard a cross word from Joey, and for it to come now, on a question not all that different from the others, shocked her.

Joey must've realized how abrasive she sounded because she quickly covered her eyes with her hands. "I'm sorry, Elaine. God, I don't know what's wrong with me."

"Joey, you're fine. You're more than fine. You're wonderful. You're making such amazing progress so quickly. It's okay to feel disoriented. You're in a transition phase."

Joey shook her head. "I'd started to believe I could have it all."

She trod carefully, giving Joey extra time. More conflict lay below the surface of this conversation, she wanted to draw it out into the open, but she needed to respect Joey's authentic process. "It's not uncommon for people to experience crisis because they feel they've had to betray their values or choose one value over another."

"Somebody told me a long time ago I couldn't do both, and I believed her, but after all your talk about the critical voice I started to wonder if she was wrong. Like maybe I'd bought into a myth and didn't have to choose between my values, but she was right. Going back to school will take a big burden off me and put it back on my dad."

"Sounds like you've been through this before." Elaine needed to know more to see if a pattern emerged. She didn't put a lot of emphasis on a client's past, but Joey couldn't relegate the situation to her past if she insisted on carrying it into the future, and she couldn't coach Joey effectively if she didn't know the factors weighing on her decision. Any personal curiosity about the events that shaped Joey into such an amazing woman was purely secondary to her professional concern for Joey as a client.

"When my mom got sick and I had to decide whether to stay in school and get my degree or go to work to help pay the medical bills, my girlfriend wanted me to stay in school. She said if I dropped out I'd never go back. She said I'd end up like my parents, broke and lost, with no way out."

"This is the woman you mentioned on your discovery form." She swallowed the personal biases that rose within her. "Your first love?"

Joey's cheeks flushed. "Yeah. Serena. We'd been together since high school. I thought she was the one, and you know how I feel about people I love."

Elaine could only nod.

"Serena thought giving all my money to my parents meant giving up on our future together, and she didn't want to end up like them. She wanted safety and security that a college dropout barista couldn't give her, so she left me for someone who could," Joey said, then quickly added, "She wasn't a bad person. She was scared, and I disappointed her."

Elaine marveled at how quickly Joey protected everyone but herself. Even as she expressed the heartbreak and turmoil that had undercut her for over half a decade, she didn't want Elaine to think less of someone she'd loved.

"Anyway, I guess she was right."

"Really?" she asked, partially in coach mode and partially out of personal disbelief.

"She got out and I didn't. She graduated five years ago, and I'm still pouring coffee, still facing the same choice of helping my dad or helping myself. I don't have my own place or any money saved, and I'm still," Joey seemed to choke on the word, "alone."

Oh, Joey. She ached to hold her, to hug her, to stroke her cheek and whisper she wasn't alone. Instead, she remained planted in her chair and forced herself to focus on formulating the right questions.

"But you *are* going back to school, and you aren't going to work at the coffee shop forever, so she wasn't completely right."

Joey pursed her lips and looked at her shoes. "But she was still right that I couldn't do both at once."

"Was she?" Elaine asked. "You couldn't do both, or do you not need to do both anymore? Would your dad refuse your help if it was essential to sustain him?"

Joey sat back on the couch, the first time Elaine had seen her back come into contact with the cushions. "He'd accept the help if he really needed it. I don't know if I believed that a week ago, but I do now."

Joey's certainty surprised her.

"It'll make things harder on him, but it won't break him, at least not as badly as me giving up my dreams would. Do you think that's right?"

"I can't coach your dad, Joey, but he's a strong unique human being who's managed to raise a wonderfully compassionate daughter. He has a right to his values as much as you do."

"But what happens when his and mine conflict?"

"Are they conflicting or just finding new outlets?"

"I suppose they're shifting. I want to do the right thing for my family and for myself, and maybe those things don't always have to be different. It would be good for him emotionally to see me graduate."

"And would that be good for you emotionally?"

Joey grinned. "I've been stuck in this same space for a long time. I think I'm ready to move on."

"You think or you know?'

"Intellectually, I'm pretty sure, but what I know and what I feel don't always line up. So many things went wrong for so long that even when I start to get it right, I keep waiting for the bottom to drop out."

She was back in more familiar coaching territory. She knew the disconnect between the head and the heart well. "All right, then I've got some homework for you."

"Oh no." Joey feigned terror, her sense of humor shining through her turmoil.

"I want you to try on the decision to go back to school. Take the next week and wear it. Let yourself experience it without the doubts of whether you should. Tell yourself you're going back to school in six weeks. Then next week we can talk about how you felt." She didn't predict what was right for her clients, but she suspected Joey would do well with this exercise. "Can you do that?"

"I'm not committing to anything, so I don't have anything to lose."

"Right. It's like a test drive of a student identity. If at the end of the week you decide to return it, you can."

"Sounds good. I'm in."

She liked that Joey didn't try to fight her. She needed to give herself space to explore.

Joey glanced at her watch and stood. "I guess we're done for today."

Elaine hated to think of the clock cutting them off if they had more to say. She wanted their conversations to be authentic. "If you don't want to talk about anything else, we could wrap up, but there's no hurry."

"No," Joey said cheerfully as she put on her coat. "I'm good for now."

Elaine stifled her surge of disappointment. She wasn't eager to end their time together. "Okay, then I'll see you next Friday."

Joey stopped, her hand on the door. "Next Friday's Christmas Eve. I thought we'd take the weekend off. I don't want to keep you from your family."

"My family?" she asked, slow to process both the fact she would miss Joey and she was assumed to have other plans. She didn't.

"I figured you'd be with Taylor and Brooke, baking cookies and singing songs."

She smiled in spite of the fact she didn't see herself doing either. "Is that what you do on Christmas Eve?"

"We make hot toddies, play cards, and watch Christmas movies until it's time for midnight mass. It's not exactly a Thomas Kincaid painting, but it's tradition."

"It sounds nice."

"What does your family do?"

"I don't know. I've never been with them on Christmas Eve. I guess I'll find out." She forced a smile. *If I'm invited.*

If Joey picked up her uncertainty she had the good taste not to say so. "I hope you enjoy your first holiday back home, and if I don't see you again before then, Merry Christmas."

This time her smile was genuine. It was impossible for Joey's easy-going charm not to affect her. "Merry Christmas to you, too, Joey."

She waited until she heard Joey's footsteps fade into silence, then quietly closed the door. She flopped back on the couch where Joey had been sitting.

Christmas. She'd avoided the idea since Thanksgiving. Would she spend the day wishing she was at home alone or, even worse, would she spend the day wishing she was with Joey?

Chapter Eleven

December 22

Joey handed an eggnog to a brunette in a Buff State hoodie. "Happy holidays."

The girl smiled a little too brightly at Joey for her to write it off as holiday cheer. "Thanks. I'm glad finals are over, you know?"

"I bet. Now you can enjoy your holiday." And Joey could enjoy some peace and quiet. Most of the students had gone home, and the neighborhood was calmer without them, leaving her time to relax under the Christmas lights and garland she'd strung around the shop.

"Yeah, I'm headed back to Rochester to see the 'rents. I've put it off long enough. They know the semester ended four days ago. If I don't show up soon, they'll send a search party."

Joey tried to offer a sympathetic expression. "Bummer."

The girl laughed as she lingered. She had a silver stud in her nose and wore a ring on nearly every finger. "Do you go to Buff State?"

"I will next semester," Joey said confidently. She'd enjoyed her week of trying on her decision as Elaine suggested. She'd even picked up a course catalog to look at classes. Every time she started to wonder if she was doing the right thing, she simply shut her worry down, emotionally putting her concerns into a box to deal with next week.

"Cool. Maybe I'll see you around."

"Probably, but only if you survive Christmas with the 'rents."

"No joke."

"Good luck." This conversation had dragged on about two minutes longer than she would've liked.

"Thanks." The girl finally turned to leave, and Joey noticed Lisa smirking over the screen of her laptop.

"What?"

"What was the problem with that one?"

She shrugged. "Nothing. She was lovely."

"Lovely? Geez, are you eighty-five? That was a real-life lesbian begging you to ask her out."

"She was not," Joey said, but even she couldn't deny the signs. "Okay, maybe she was, and I was very polite."

"Yes, and you even used her to try out your new student lines, but on fourth and inches, you punted."

"I didn't punt. She just, I don't know…"

"She wasn't your type."

"You say that like having some standards is a bad thing. We all have types of women we go for more than others."

"Yes," Lisa said. "I go for women over eighteen who have a pulse."

"Then *you* should've asked her out."

"She wasn't flirting with me. No one ever flirts with me when you're around." Lisa pouted. "Next time you're going to punt, you could at least aim in my direction."

"How?"

Lisa came behind the counter and pretended to type on the register. "Here's your change. Thanks for flirting with me today, but I'm already hung up on Dr. Hot-Body. However, my smashingly beautiful best friend is single and sitting right behind that computer making boatloads of money."

"Fine, you go back and make your boatloads of money, and I'll practice my lines."

"Thanks." Lisa kissed her on the cheek and bounced back toward her computer.

"By the way, her name is Elaine," Joey called after her.

Lisa rolled her eyes and flopped down as the front door opened.

"Elaine," Joey said.

"Fine, I get it," Lisa said without looking up. "It's Elaine, for crying out loud. But Dr. Stud Muffin is more fun. This coaching business is killing your sense of humor."

Joey and Elaine both stopped and stared at Lisa until Elaine broke into a huge smile. "And you must be Lisa."

All the color drained from Lisa's face. "Shit. Talk about your speak-of-the-devil moments. Yeah, I'm Lisa Knapp, Joey's ex–best friend."

"I doubt that. Joey seems pretty forgiving." Elaine gracefully extended her hand to Lisa. "We spoke on the phone, but we've never been formally introduced. I usually go by Elaine, though I do quite like Dr. Stud Muffin."

Lisa's face turned redder than the holly berries strung around the coffee shop, but she managed to grin sheepishly. "It's nice to finally meet you."

"Likewise." Elaine turned to Joey, a mischievousness in her eyes Joey had never seen. "I didn't mean to bug you at work, but I'm glad I did if my coaching has killed your sense of humor. Maybe we could have an impromptu session to focus on your strength of humor and playfulness."

Lisa groaned and dropped heavily into her chair. "Have fun. I'm going to sit over here and be quietly contrite."

"It's easy to see why Joey loves you," Elaine said with genuine warmth, then headed toward the counter.

"Well, that was fun." Joey was giddy. She hadn't expected to see Elaine for more than a week, much less see such a playful side. "Can I get you a chai tea on the house?"

"I'd love one, but I can pay for it."

"Consider it a Christmas present," she said with a wink, then immediately regretted it. *Why did I wink? Could I be any nerdier?*

"Jojo!" A three-foot-tall bundle of fluff and wool burst through the door. Elaine caught Taylor before he crashed into the counter and pulled down his scarf, revealing bright blue eyes and pink cheeks.

"Hi, Taylor," Joey said, her happiness at seeing the child only slightly dampened by her disappointment at losing her personal time with Elaine.

"I can haves chocolate milk?"

"If it's okay with your Aunt Lainie."

Elaine turned and passed the question to Brooke, who had just pushed open the door.

"Taylor, what did I tell you about running ahead of me?"

"You said 'no, no.'" He answered in what must have been an impression of his mother's sternest voice. "I can haves Jojo chocolate milk, Mama?"

Brooke sighed. "I suppose it won't get you any more wound up than you already are."

"One chai tea, one chocolate milk," Joey recited. "And what can I get for you, Brooke? It's my treat."

Brooke's expression brightened. "You remembered my name."

"Of course I did. If you tell me your drink order, I'll remember that, too."

"I don't know," Brooke said, glancing at the menu, then back at Joey, clearly finding her more interesting. Her tone dropped an octave with a suggestive undercurrent. "I feel like trying something new today. Care to surprise me?"

Warning bells sounded in Joey's mind. She might need to punt and looked past Brooke to Lisa, who'd obviously read the situation the same way and was shaking her head.

She nodded and retreated to the back of the store. When she returned with the drinks, Taylor and Brooke had chosen a table near the window, but Elaine waited by the counter.

"Thank you, Joey." Elaine took two of the drinks. "I didn't mean to bombard you."

"I'm glad you did. It's nice to see Taylor again."

"He's asked about you every time I've seen him the last two weeks."

Her nervousness about Brooke faded. "I'll help you carry these over."

"Care to join us?" Brooke said as they approached the table.

"I don't want to interrupt your family time."

"It's no interruption. I'd like to get to know the woman my son is so in love with. Wouldn't you like Jojo to sit with us, Taylor?"

"Please," he said, his little lips already coated with a chocolate-milk mustache.

That's a dirty trick, she thought, *using your kid to get what you want*. Then she glanced at Elaine and realized she was equally willing to use Taylor as an excuse to get what she wanted. "I guess I can chat until another customer comes in."

"Is Santa going to come see you, Jojo?" Taylor asked eagerly.

"I hope so. Is he going to come see you?"

He held up three fingers. "In three more sleeps."

"Have you been a good boy?"

"Yes," he said, then glanced at his mom. "I tried."

"I'm sure you've been great. What did you ask for?"

"A hockey stick."

"Wow, me too," she said, causing Elaine and Brooke to laugh.

"Were you good?"

She grinned, looking over his head to Elaine. "I've been trying to be better lately."

"Joey has been very good," Elaine said. "Santa should be nice to her this year."

"You play hockey?" Taylor was oblivious to the depth of Elaine's comment or the thrill it gave Joey.

"I do play hockey. I just signed up for a pond-hockey tournament in Delaware Park on New Year's Day."

Taylor wiggled in his seat. "Can I go, Mama?"

"We'll see. Mama's never in good shape on New Year's Day, at least not if I had a good New Year's Eve." Brooke laughed. "Ya know what I mean?"

Elaine looked embarrassed, but Joey remained steady. "Nope. I don't drink. I always love waking up to a new year."

"You don't drink at all?"

"I did a champagne toast at a friend's wedding last year."

"Wow. I've never known someone my age who didn't hit the bars." Brooke's interest cooled a bit, but Elaine looked pleased.

"Joey's not an average twenty-something. She's an old soul," she said, then bit the corner of her bottom lip.

"What do you do to blow off steam?" Brooke asked, clearly not impressed by her old soul and searching for a better angle.

Joey shrugged. "I don't have a lot of steam. I like sports, watching and playing. I like to read, too, and when I have time I go see a movie or a play, but I work a lot. I don't have much spare time. And I'll have even less time in a few weeks when I go back to school."

She noticed Elaine hide a little quirk of a smile behind her mug of chai tea. It made her happy to make Elaine happy, and she liked to think they had an inside secret, like they were in on the same charade, but it didn't feel like a charade. The more she played the role of a student, the more it seemed real.

"You're going back to school?" Brooke asked. "Like in college?"

"That's the plan."

Brooke didn't seem impressed. "I guess you and Aunt Lainie probably have a lot in common, then."

Joey didn't see herself as having hardly anything in common with Elaine. She was several levels out of her league.

"She was always reading when I was little, always studying, trying to get out of here."

Elaine's eyes widened and a frown creased her beautiful features, but before she could speak Taylor cut in. "Anwainie get out of here?"

"No," Elaine said softly. "I'm not going anywhere."

"Jojo get out of here?"

"Nope, kiddo, I'm not going anywhere either." The door opened and a young couple bustled in, their arms loaded with packages. "Except back to work."

"You come play, Jojo?" Taylor asked.

"I wish I could, but maybe soon you can come play hockey with me?"

"Yay," he squealed.

Joey rose, patted him on the head and told Brooke it was good to see her again, then turned to Elaine. "See you next week?"

"Absolutely." Elaine gave one of her brilliant smiles, leaving her wishing they were meeting on Christmas Eve or any other day on the calendar. "Have a great holiday."

"You, too." Joey turned away quickly before she gave in to the urge to stay. She loved having Elaine as a coach, and clearly their sessions had helped beyond expectations. Her life held a new sense of purpose. If Elaine hadn't agreed to coach her, she wouldn't be returning to school, looking forward to her future, or have her new confidence and self-respect. But if Elaine continued to be her coach, she might never realize her bigger dream of being with the woman who truly captivated her.

❖

December 24

Elaine enjoyed the sounds of "O Holy Night" drifting from the apartment above, mixed with conversation and laughter. It made her feel close to something festive even if she wasn't part of it. Amy and Brooke apparently didn't celebrate Christmas Eve, though Brooke had invited Elaine over to watch Taylor open his presents in the morning, and Amy would host Christmas dinner later in the day.

She had considered inviting them to her apartment, but they weren't churchgoers and Taylor went to bed at eight, so it didn't make sense to try to do anything tonight. She wasn't used to big events on Christmas Eve anyway. In New York she'd usually spent the evening at dinner with a friend or maybe seeing a play. Occasionally she'd joined someone else's family for Christmas dinner. She probably wouldn't have treated the evening that differently from any other if not for Joey.

For some reason Joey's simple assumption that she'd have plans tonight drove home how much her life lacked special things. She loved her job and had peace and contentment in her day-to-day dealings, but when was the last time she'd looked forward to a major event such as a birthday or a holiday? Not since she'd moved back to Buffalo. Not that she'd done those things in the city, but at least she'd known more people. She had always had plenty of other single friends or colleagues around to share the holiday, but here in Buffalo her family had their own lives and their own ways of doing things. How strange that she'd left New York because her connections there were superficial only to return to Buffalo and not even have superficial relationships.

No, that wasn't true. She had meaningful relationships, but complications made them hard to simply enjoy. Wasn't there a happy medium? Maybe it was impossible to have a meaningful relationship that didn't leave her angst-ridden. Maybe she was incapable of maintaining a significant, personal connection.

She'd always had trouble opening up. Other people opened up to her. She was the steady one, the levelheaded one, blessed with an ability to carry their burdens, but without the ability to share her own. Then again, maybe she just used her intuition as an excuse not to reveal her own shortcomings. Maybe she couldn't maintain an equal relationship because she was deficient or somehow lacking. She'd never bonded with her own family, which was surely abnormal. What kind of person would rather spend her holidays alone than with her family?

No. Negativity was destructive. It allowed her critical voice to thrive. She wasn't immune to her own gremlins, but thankfully she was adept at walking away from them, literally.

She put on her thick wool pea coat, her best-insulated gloves, and a stocking cap and strolled out into the crisp, cold winter night. She let her internal compass guide her down Delaware Avenue. Almost a foot of snow lay on either side of her, but the sidewalks were clear, and she fell into an easy rhythm. She quieted her mind, blocked out the sounds of cars rushing along the expressway, and shut off the internal voices that suggested part of her was missing.

She became aware of the pulse each heartbeat sent through her. She paid attention as her lungs expanded, opening to the fresh air, then released the residual of negative energy on her exhale. Her mind flowed into her body as she returned to her truest form. She started from the center and moved outward slowly. She'd felt disconnected earlier. Her heart had been trying to lead her before her critical voice had cut in.

After she turned along the northern tip of Delaware Park, she took a path shaded by tall trees that cast a Rorschach pattern of shadow and moonlight at her feet. She wasn't lacking. She wasn't defective. She was whole but in transition. Her internal alarm had sent her signals to remind her of what she'd set out to do. What had she been searching for before she allowed herself to wander off track? Someone to spend Christmas Eve with? Someone to share herself with? Someone to build a lasting connection with?

Over the two decades since graduating from college, she'd slowly discovered her authentic voice. She'd done all the right things, but where were the results?

She strolled up the circular ramp to the pedestrian bridge over the Scajaquada Expressway, watching her feet land one in front of the other, spiraling deliberately upward, as though she'd found her own private labyrinth. "I'm going in circles," she said aloud.

I didn't connect with my family as a child, so I left, searching for something else. I wandered until I found myself and built the internal connection I needed before I could turn outward. Then I immersed myself in my purpose through my work, reaching out into the world, taking in little bits of other lives until I felt strong enough to return to where I'd started. Back at my point of origin, I'm regressing, forgetting the strengths I've already honed. Rather than spring forward again, I've hidden behind what I know, what's safe. I've pulled away from old challenges and anchored myself back in my work. I made a decision with my heart and then tried to implement it with my brain.

She reached the top of the bridge and looked out across her new, old city. She listened again, this time embracing the world around her, absorbing the lights of museums, the bustle of traffic, the peal of church bells in the distance. A soft breeze stirred her hair as snowflakes began to fall lightly, coating the landscape again, creating a fresh canvas. What could she make of it? What could it make of her?

A vibration from her coat pocket drew her attention, and she pulled out her phone. In the deep of night atop a parkway bridge, Elaine wondered if the universe had sent her a message as it plainly read, *Merry Christmas—Joey.*

CHAPTER TWELVE

December 31

It'd been snowing since yesterday, a steady, heavy deluge from what the weathermen liked to call a persistent snow band. Persistent didn't begin to cover it. They hadn't had a real break in over twenty-four hours, and the accumulation totals neared two feet, a lot even by Buffalo standards. Joey needed a shovel to get off her front porch.

"I can't believe you're going." Lisa stood in the doorway.

Joey shrugged. "I made a commitment."

"More like you haven't seen Elaine for a week and you're jonesing like a junkie in need of a fix."

"It's not about her. I'm feeling good about actually registering for classes. Every time I meet with her, I like myself a little more. Isn't that kind of progress worth a bit of effort?"

"If by 'a bit' you mean Herculean, then sure, I suppose so."

"I better get going. The trip'll take twice as long as usual."

"If you're lucky." Lisa still sounded skeptical. "What about the party? Want me to wait for you?"

Some of their neighbors had a yearly New Year's Eve party, and Lisa and Joey always went together. "I should be home by six, but if I'm not, go ahead. Don't monopolize all the cute girls, though."

"I'm sure whoever I pick will be more interested in you as soon as you get there."

"Then you better work fast." Joey liked to tease her. "I'll

probably feel good enough after my session to do something about it."

"That'll be the day," Lisa said, giving her a shove. "Be careful."

She walked down the middle of the wide Lincoln Parkway. There was little traffic out in the storm, and the fact that the street was one of the widest in Buffalo, along with its opulent homes and some of the oldest moneyed families in the city, assured it was plowed early and often in a storm. She had easy going all the way past the Albright-Knox Art Gallery and around the frozen serenity of Hoyt Lake, but as she turned off the parkway she couldn't find the path to the bridge over the expressway.

Stopping briefly, she thought about taking a detour along Elmwood. The busier street would be better plowed, but more dangerous with traffic on slick pavement. The detour would also lead her at least three blocks out of the way, and on a day like this, getting off track meant a lot more than spoiling a good walk. It symbolized diverting from her true course. She was done wandering, done taking the path of least resistance. She stepped forcefully onto the mound of snow at the road's edge, crushing the crust that formed from constant packing and frigid temperatures. Pushing off with her leg, she planted another booted foot firmly on top of the snowy embankment and tipped forward, hurling herself into uncharted territory.

Giddy at the implications of her choice she slogged uphill, knee deep in snow, toward the bridge. The shortest distance between two points was a straight line, so that's the route she intended to take. She plotted her course just to the rear of a big statue of David that kept watch over the travelers who sped past the art museum. She always passed behind him, mainly because that's where the path curved, but she liked the view from the rear better than the one from the front. At least from the back angle she recognized all the body parts. The cold seeped through her ski pants and thermal-lined boots by the time she reached the statue. As she looked up at David's chiseled granite ass, she couldn't help but chuckle despite her discomfort. "Sorry, old boy. I bet you're colder than I am."

She pushed forward, her path descending slightly. She'd expected easier traveling after the crest of the hill, but the snow had drifted on the downside, and she now sank to her mid-thighs. Each step took more effort to make less progress, and she doubted the resolve that had seemed so clear moments earlier. She could turn back. She'd already cleared a way in the opposite direction. The path in front of her was uncarved and unpredictable. Maybe she should cut her losses now and return to Elmwood. She wouldn't be giving up. She'd just go back before she could go forward. It would be a delay, but not necessarily a failure. She could probably make it to Elaine's only fifteen minutes late.

No. At the thought of Elaine, she pushed forward again. She wouldn't be late, and she wouldn't go backward. She'd promised Elaine she'd be up to the challenge. She'd made too much progress on this trip and on her larger journey to double back now. Sure, it would be easier to wait to start school. It'd be easier to go the long way to Elaine's. Hell, she could have stayed home. There was always an easier way, but she'd continue to face the same drudgery and disappointment. Nothing would improve. This might not be the smartest or safest choice, but she'd settled on a path, and it led to Elaine.

Her body warred with itself by the time she reached the spiral ramp of the pedestrian bridge. Her feet were frozen, numb with the exception of an occasional sharp bite from Jack Frost, but perspiration dotted the back of her neck and forehead. Thankfully the higher she climbed up the ramp, the shallower the snow became. Wind whipped through the railing, scraping the concrete bare of all but a few hard-packed inches of snow. Reaching the top, she glanced back in the direction she'd come. It wasn't far. On a clear day she could make it in three, maybe four minutes, and today it had likely taken nearly thirty, yet despite her distance or the time to get there, she did have a new perspective now.

A sense of accomplishment melted into the belief she could do more. Indeed, she might be able to do anything with the right motivation. She didn't linger. She wouldn't allow herself to acknowledge the burn of her muscles or be content with this measure of success. Her journey had new meaning, and she wanted her life to have the same sense of purpose. She didn't have time to rest. She wouldn't squander her momentum. She intended to ride it all the way to Elaine.

❖

"What do you mean she already left?" Elaine asked, unable to hide her shock. She'd called to talk to Joey about doing their session over the phone.

"Yeah, at least twenty minutes ago," Lisa said calmly. "She'll probably be there in ten or fifteen minutes."

"I haven't seen a bus go by in a long time."

"She's not on a bus. She's walking."

Her heart rate accelerated. "Walking? Lisa, have you seen it outside?"

"Yup."

"And you still thought it wise for her to walk all the way over here?"

"Nope."

"But?" This was maddening.

Lisa snorted. "But nothing."

Why was Lisa stonewalling her? Was she angry about their conversation at the coffeehouse? She thought Lisa had a good sense of humor. "Lisa, is there something you're not telling me?"

"Well, that's a loaded question if I've ever heard one." Lisa laughed outright, then said calmly, "No, Joey shouldn't be out in this weather. It's dangerous, but she isn't thinking about herself. She's thinking about getting to your session."

"Oh."

"Joey's on her way, and I couldn't stop her. Despite those big brown eyes and her need to please, she's not a puppy. Don't underestimate her."

"I don't," Elaine said, her breath shallow.

"Then go get ready to do whatever you two do. She left here determined to get to you, and that's what she'll do. If you respect her, you won't tell her she shouldn't have."

She breathed deeply, trying to steady the shiver that ran through her. Lisa's comment held too much power to acknowledge fully. Instead she simply said, "Thank you, Lisa."

She hung up the phone and jerked on her coat and boots. In the entryway of her apartment she grabbed a snow shovel and scraped her way out the door. She wouldn't let Joey do all the work. If she'd had any hope of getting her car out of the driveway she would have, but she settled for clearing as much of the path as she could. It wouldn't be easy. The snow was at least two feet deep, and Elaine hadn't shoveled in twenty years. The apartment staff always handled upkeep and maintenance tasks, but with the snow still coming down on a holiday, they wouldn't be by tonight.

She shoveled rhythmically, methodically as she dwelt on Lisa's comments yet tried to banish them completely. She fell into the repetitive work, not meditating but focusing on the concrete that appeared little by little. The muffled sound of a church bell reverberated along the wind, signaling four o'clock. Joey would be here soon; she was a greater force than the weather. Maybe she'd known even before she'd called Lisa. Joey wouldn't miss a session, and Elaine hadn't wanted her to. She'd looked forward to seeing her since Christmas Eve. She'd been preparing for this session all week, yet she wasn't in coaching mode.

She scanned the road Joey would take. Dusk and the dark clouds made the distance dim and hazy compared to the well-lit intersection her apartment building faced. She strained to see Joey approach, her hands trembling when she didn't find what she hoped to see. She'd never been this frazzled before a session. She had to center herself.

Why was she reacting to Joey's actions this way? She wasn't responsible for the risk Joey had willingly chosen. She wasn't responsible for the commitments Joey had gladly made or the determination with which she carried them out. Her body temperature rose with the labor of her shoveling, and she slowed. She had to stop being reactionary. Lisa was right. Joey wasn't a puppy. She wasn't fragile or foolish. She was a grown woman who'd invested a great deal of faith in Elaine as a coach.

What about Joey made her forget she was a coach? Granted, she'd only been coaching for a year and still had so much to learn, but no client had ever affected her on such a personal level. Had she underestimated Joey or simply her own resolve? Certainly she'd overestimated her ability to focus, because once again she'd fallen into her own turmoil rather than readying her mind for their session.

She stepped back, inhaling with all the deliberateness she could muster. She closed her eyes and willed her heart to beat more slowly. She forced her hands to steady and her internal voices to quiet. She had plenty of practice clearing her mind. It rarely required this much effort anymore, but she managed to adopt something resembling a neutral state. With one final breath she opened her eyes and unraveled again. Joey stood several yards away, her hands jammed casually in her coat pockets and a crooked half smile quirked across her lips.

"Hi," Joey said.

She smiled back, unguarded and unabashed. She couldn't help herself. "Hi, Joey."

"You're doing that wrong," Joey said, pointing to the shovel. "You're using your back instead of your knees."

"Am I?"

"And you shouldn't torque your upper body when you lift. Let me show you." Joey held out her hand for the shovel, and Elaine tossed it with as much grace and strength as she could muster, but it still fell a foot short, sinking into the top layer of powder. She threw like a girl, an unathletic one, but Joey didn't laugh. She simply stretched to get the shovel and set to work.

She bent her knees as she drove the shovel forcefully into the snow, straightened her knees so she stood upright, then turned her body a few degrees before starting another thrust to toss the snow off the shovel. She made several separate moves, but as she repeated the sequence more quickly, her body worked with a fluidity akin to a dancer's. No, not that delicate. Force and power flowed in her movement, as well as purpose. Elaine was captivated. Joey inched through steadily but slowly, efficiently scraping off three layers one at a time before hitting the sidewalk. Even with her strength and determination, the work would take an hour.

"Thanks for the lesson," she said. "Can you get through the snow? I'll finish later."

Joey regarded her with a curious expression, then looked at the snow between them. "Actually, I'd like to finish what I've started here."

Of course you would. "I'm not comfortable with you shoveling my walkway, Joey. We're supposed to have a session."

"Let's do both." Joey dug in for another load of snow. "We can have a session while I shovel."

"Our sessions are confidential."

Joey glanced around the deserted street. "Who's going to hear?"

"Why, Joey?" she asked seriously.

She stopped, crossed her arms, and rested them atop the shovel handle. "I want to deal with things the first time, clean the slate now so I don't end up slogging through the same stuff later."

"Okay." She nodded. Joey had been stuck in a holding pattern for years. She'd rehashed the same fears and insecurities incessantly since her mother died, and now she was finally putting them to rest. It made sense to take her new attitude into other areas, even the symbolic. It was actually impressive that she not only made connections on such a high level but that she articulated them so clearly. She'd learned to do for herself what Elaine had done with her over their last few sessions. She was ahead of schedule by every standard.

"Besides, I'm a kinesthetic learner," Joey said, her grin returning. "This will help me get through a conversation topic that'll probably make me jittery."

"Oh?"

"Pull up a chair, and let's get started, Coach."

Elaine grinned and settled in as comfortably as she could on the cold concrete steps of her apartment building while Joey began to shovel again.

"I'm ready when you are."

"I registered for classes. I start in three weeks."

"Wow." She wasn't surprised but she was thrilled. "That's fantastic, Joey. I'm proud of you."

"Thanks. I'm proud of me, too."

"So you liked trying on the role of student?"

"I did. It felt right, and it got easier every time I said I was going back to school. My authentic voice got stronger until it completely drowned out the critical one."

Elaine did a poor job of containing her giddiness, evidenced by both her expression and the excited tapping of her booted toes on the steps. "And how do you feel now?"

"Great." Joey sounded slightly amazed. "I know I'll have bad days. The gremlins will rear their ugly heads on my first day of class and when my first paper is due, but I can fight them now. Getting started is the hardest part. Once I commit to something, I follow through."

"That does seem to be a key component to your personality." She examined Joey more carefully. She hadn't faltered but still ratcheted through the same repetitive movements with grace and strength. "But why would this topic make you jittery? You seem more confident than ever."

"Yeah, well, about that." Joey stopped and shed her coat and hooded sweatshirt. Was her exertion alone or the change of topic causing her body temperature to rise? Either way, the move had the same effect on Elaine. She warmed at the sight of Joey's biceps flexing in the amber light that flooded the walkway. Joey had always worn long sleeves in front of her, and while she wasn't surprised that she was lean and fit, the toned muscles threw Elaine off-kilter.

"…so I thought we could talk about that today."

"I'm sorry," Elaine said, horrified. She'd been so busy staring at Joey's body she hadn't heard what she said. "When you took off your jacket I got worried about you catching a cold."

Elaine had seen Joey's sweet smile a hundred times, but now it seemed to carry something deeper, something stirring, a calm pleasure. "I just said since we've worked out my school goals, maybe we could apply that momentum to my other goal."

That made perfect sense. If she was a better coach, she would've already thought of that instead of letting a little skin distract her. What was Joey's other goal? She pretended not to remember immediately so she could take another deep breath. She had been preparing for this moment since she'd read Joey's discovery form, and those mental preparations had intensified when Brooke's eyes had wandered over Joey as they would a fine painting. But she hadn't expected to be looking at Joey the same way when the topic actually arose.

"So you want to talk about dating?" She was pleased that her voice sounded steady and neutral.

Joey, however, showed her discomfort as she worked more quickly, her eyes riveted on the end of her shovel. "I suppose we should. It's a goal, right?"

She chose her words carefully. "*Should* is one of those inner-critic words. Is this your goal or someone else's goal for you?"

"It's mine. I don't want to be alone, but relationships are daunting."

"Yeah, I know," she said, then realized she'd said it aloud. She quickly ducked behind her professionalism "It's a common coaching concern."

"I get hit on a lot," Joey said sheepishly, as if the fact embarrassed her. "But I don't know where to go from there. I suppose I should just ask for a phone number or something, but I don't know these women. We may have nothing in common. We might drive each other crazy, but how long will it take to find out, and how much awkwardness will I expose myself to while I'm playing guess-and-check? It doesn't seem like a good system to me."

She laughed. Joey was too perfect. She'd summed up many

of the thoughts Elaine had pondered for years. Why were they expected to put themselves at emotional risk for a stranger, knowing they'd get rejected more times than they got accepted? She'd yet to feel fully accepted. Not with her family, not with her social acquaintances, not with past lovers. They all accepted parts of her, some more than others, but with a girlfriend partial acceptance wasn't good enough. No wonder she'd shied away from working at personal relationships.

Pull it together. "Yet we keep putting ourselves out there, or at least we want to, so our hearts have to be telling us we need something."

"I guess so, but how am I supposed to look at a stranger and say, 'Sure, I'll offer you my heart for possible torture on the off chance you're the one.' Every time I think about it, I shut down."

"That's a lot to have on your mind when you consider asking a woman for coffee."

"No joke." Joey kept shoveling. She'd cut the distance between them by more than half.

"What do you hope to get when you ask a woman out?" Elaine fought to keep her interest professional and not mentally catalog Joey's answers for her own pleasure. "What causes the little spark that makes you want to know more about her?"

"That's the problem," Joey said. "I hate having to search for a spark. It's either there right away and I fall too quickly to keep my composure, or it's not and I'm left wondering if I'll ever feel anything worth putting myself out there for."

"You're an all-or-nothing kind of boi, aren't you?" she asked. Joey raised her eyes, humor and playfulness creasing her grin, and Elaine worried she'd sounded too flirty.

"You could say that, but what am I supposed to do when a woman comes on to me? I look at these girls at the coffee shop and think, 'She's cute enough. We may have a thing or two in common,' but I don't have any overwhelming urge to go any further."

She suffered a twinge of guilt for being happy that Joey didn't want to date every woman who noticed her. That was a long line, one she currently stood at the front of. "Are you listening to your heart or your head?"

"My head. Totally my head, but with women, my heart only gets me into trouble."

"How so?"

Joey stood upright, tossed off her stocking cap, and smoothed her hair with one gloved hand. She suddenly seemed impossibly close. Elaine could see the sheen of sweat and snow on her skin, the way her eyes caught the light and reflected it back, the curves and hollows of her throat. "I'm a hopeless romantic, and when I fall in love, I go in all the way."

Elaine's breath caught. She literally couldn't speak. Thankfully she often used silence to gather herself. Joey believed in an all-consuming passion, one that carried her away to the point she could barely function. She'd expressed similar sentiments before, and they'd always affected her on a deep level. She'd always found Joey sweet, sincere, and even adorable, but now, standing there, cut and firm, strong and sweaty, Joey was also devastatingly sexy. Try as she might, she couldn't find the cute, bumbling client in the face of the stunning woman who held her attention now.

"So how do I get around that?"

"I'm sorry?"

"How do I manage to find a woman who sparks those emotions but doesn't make me a bumbling puddle of nerves when I try to talk to her?"

"Practice?" Elaine asked, then immediately wanted to hide her face in her hands. *Role play.* Damn, this should've been easy. She should help Joey with a role play. She'd helped clients through goals like this plenty of times. She could help her if she'd just summon her strength. *I don't have it in me.*

"Like in the mirror?"

"Yes," she lied, her heart aching at her failure. She'd been distracted around Joey before, but she'd never let her personal feelings prevent her from doing her job. She was breaking their commitment and had to salvage the conversation. "Do you still feel unworthy of your dream girl?"

Joey stopped in mid-shovel, now no more than a few steps from her. "My dream girl?"

Elaine blushed profusely, remembering that Dream Girl was the term Joey had once used to describe her. "A hypothetical dream girl."

Joey returned to shoveling. "Hypothetical dream girls don't bother me so much, but the real ones send me into fits."

"And how often do the real ones come around?" That wasn't a coaching question but a personal one, though Joey didn't seem to know the difference.

"First I had Serena." Joey dug the shovel into the last mound of snow and lifted it. "There was a woman who used to work at the coffee shop, who I never asked out, then a grad student at Buff State I used to play hockey with. Never asked her out, either. Then one more."

Elaine watched the last bit of snow fall from Joey's shovel. "What happened?"

Joey shrugged. "Wasn't meant to be, I suppose, but she's an amazing life coach, so I'm not sorry I took the chance on her."

She scanned up the length of Joey's body and settled on her deep brown eyes. Was she still Joey's dream girl? She shivered away the surge of energy running through her.

"Oh, geez, Elaine," Joey said, reaching for her hand. "You're freezing."

"I'm okay." She was glad their gloves kept their skin from touching as she accepted Joey's hand and stood up.

"You're shivering," Joey said, her voice filled with concern. "I shouldn't have kept you out here. You'd better get inside and warm up."

She was already pretty warm, but content to let Joey think the cold had caused the chill she'd witnessed. "What about you?"

"Our hour's up," Joey said with a weary smile. "I'll head home so you can enjoy the rest of your New Year's Eve."

"Joey, no." Even in her lust-filled stupor, she knew that wasn't right. "You've been out in the cold for almost two hours, and you've overexerted yourself the whole time."

"I'm fine."

"But I'm not. If you left now, I'd spend my New Year's Eve feeling worried and guilty." *And if you stay with me, I'll spend my New Year's Eve feeling guilty and worried.*

"Okay. I'll come in, but I won't stay too long."

"Go." She held the door open and pointed to the stairs. As Joey moved past her, Elaine squeezed herself against the door to make sure none of her touched any part of Joey. She was being childish but didn't trust herself. She had no control over her thoughts, and she wasn't eager to see if the lack of restraint extended to her body. She started up the stairs behind Joey, careful to watch her feet instead of Joey's butt in those ski pants, and she was glad she did because she noticed the toe of Joey's boot catch on the lip of a couple of stairs on the way up. She was more exhausted than she'd let on.

When Joey got inside she sank to her knees to unclasp her heavy snow boots. Elaine studied Joey's trembling fingers as she fumbled with the buckles, then noticed she had to brace herself with both hands to get up off the floor. A muffled groan escaped Joey's lips as she stood. As a coach and as a woman, she knew it wasn't a good idea to have Joey in her apartment right now. She was incapable of thinking clearly. Even with self-admonishments rolling through her head, she still had to suppress the urge to reach up and tuck a stray strand of hair behind Joey's ear. But as a coach and as a human being, she couldn't justify sending a client, someone she cared about, out into the dark, snow-packed streets of Buffalo when she could barely stand.

"I can go," Joey whispered, clearly reading her hesitancy.

"No," she said, "you can't."

That was all she could say.

❖

Joey propped herself against the kitchen counter while Elaine put a kettle of water on for tea. "Can I get you something to eat?"

"No, thank you. I'm okay," Joey lied. She had no idea how

she'd make it home if she had to leave now, but she sensed something different between them. Elaine's guardedness made her nervous. Maybe Elaine had plans for the evening.

"Did you eat?"

"I had a peanut-butter-and-jelly sandwich," she said sheepishly, then added, "for lunch."

"Joey Lang." Elaine shook her head, but Joey didn't hear the reproach in the easy, intimate way her name rolled off Elaine's tongue. "I'm amazed you're still on your feet. Why weren't you going to tell me?"

"I've seen what you have to eat in this place." Joey liked to tease her.

Elaine burst out laughing. "I'll have you know I went shopping with Taylor last weekend. I have white bread, Froot Loops, SpaghettiOs, and chicken-and-stars soup."

"You're dying to have the SpaghettiOs, aren't you?"

"Not in the least."

"How about soup and grilled cheese, then I'll get on the road?"

Elaine stopped and leveled her intense blue eyes on her. "Do you have a good reason to hurry away from me and back out into that waist-deep snow?"

"No. Geez, no." She wanted to stay all night. She wanted to stay forever, but that wasn't the bargain. She couldn't let herself feel at home in Elaine's home. She couldn't feel like they belonged together. "I thought you probably had plans."

"I'm sorry to shatter any illusions you have of my social life, but…" Elaine held up a can of soup. "This is it for me tonight."

Joey laughed. "Well then, grab the butter, too, and I'll whip up a little dinner."

"No, Joey. You go sit down. I'll cook."

She didn't want to give in. Allowing Elaine to cook for her would be too much like a date, and she couldn't let her imagination wander down that path, not when she'd made so much progress. If she started seeing Elaine as something other than a coach, she'd fall apart. She couldn't revert to being a bumbling fool. She couldn't let Elaine be more than a coach. She had to keep it light. "I don't know if I trust a cook who has to shop with a three-year-old."

Elaine rolled her eyes playfully and pointed to the living room. "Go."

"Okay, I do need to call Lisa and tell her I'll be late getting home."

Elaine bit the corner of her lip like she wanted to say something, but she didn't, so Joey escaped to the living room and flipped open her phone.

"Hey, Lisa," Joey said when she answered. "I'm still at Elaine's."

"Cool, are you heading home now?"

"No, I'm going to stay and have some dinner."

"With Elaine?"

"Yeah."

"You're having dinner with her on New Year's Eve?"

Lisa made it sound exactly how Joey didn't need to consider it. "Not like that."

"What's it like, Jo?"

"I did some shoveling for her, and she doesn't want me to go back out in the snow until I warm up. She's a nurturer."

"And will she be charging you overages for the privilege of spending extra time in her presence?"

"That's not fair, Lisa."

"Maybe not." Lisa's voice softened. "Maybe I don't understand how your relationship works."

"Yeah, maybe I don't either."

"You've been doing so well lately, Jo."

"I'm still doing well. I'm going back to school. I'm happy. I'm more confident than I've been in years. You've seen the turnaround."

"Yeah, but I also see you playing Jojo to her nephew and risking your life to get to her and shoveling snow for her, and I'm sorry, but you've never stopped lighting up when she enters the room."

Joey shook her head. She couldn't hear this. Not now, not with

Elaine humming softly as she moved around the kitchen. If she let herself consider, even for a second, how perfect Elaine was, how stunning, how captivating… No, she had to stop right now. "It's not a good time for this conversation."

"I'm sorry. You know I love you and I don't want to be an ass, but I don't want you to backslide after everything you've accomplished in the last six weeks."

"I know." She felt the same way. Elaine came into the room carrying two bowls of soup. "Hey, I gotta go. Have fun tonight."

"Be careful."

"All right. I'll be careful coming home."

"That wasn't what I meant."

"I know," Joey said, then disconnected.

"Everything okay?" Elaine asked, setting the bowls on her desk.

"Yeah, just talking to Lisa."

"Have you two ever…I mean, were you two…?" Elaine shook her head. "I'm sorry. That's none of my business."

"No, it's fine. We weren't and we aren't. She practically lived with me in high school. It'd be like kissing your sister."

Elaine grimaced. "You obviously haven't met my sister."

"I've met you and your niece and your nephew. Was your gene pool somehow less kind to your sister?"

"No." Elaine tried to hide the shyness of her smile as she headed back toward the kitchen. "She looks like the rest of us, only a little older. She's actually very pretty, which is part of the problem. She learned early that 'pretty' got her what she wanted, at least on the surface."

"How so?" she asked when Elaine returned with their grilled cheeses and pulled up an extra chair to her desk.

"She found the attention she didn't get from our parents from a long line of boyfriends."

"And where did you find it?"

Elaine raised her eyebrows.

Joey froze, her spoon of chicken and stars a few inches from her lips. "Too personal?"

"No. It's just that no one ever asked me that," Elaine said. The crease in her brow appeared, signifying her deepest level of thought. "Maybe you should be the coach and I should be the client."

"You're a better coach than a client."

"Why?"

"Because you dodged my question."

"Nicely done, Joey. Okay, where did I find attention? I didn't. I learned not to need it."

"I'm sorry," she said, a rush of sadness mixing with her curiosity.

"Don't be. It saved me from the alternative."

"Which is?"

"Needing it and not getting it."

"Why do you think you wouldn't have gotten it?" she asked. How could a woman like Elaine not know she could be cherished?

"I saw too young how Amy's boys came and went. She thought everyone was 'the one' and then she got devastated all over again."

Joey frowned but didn't comment. She was getting too deep into Elaine the woman, and she wasn't sure either of them wanted that. Seeing her as perfect kept a kind of distance between them. If Elaine revealed herself as fragile and human, some of the walls they had established would crumble.

"What?" Elaine asked.

"Nothing."

"You have a terrible poker face, Joey. It was one of the first things I noticed about you."

She grinned. Walls or not, she couldn't deny this woman anything. "I just thought Amy couldn't have been completely devastated by her boyfriends if she managed to keep believing in love. That takes fortitude and belief in something bigger than herself."

Elaine bit the corner of her lip and interlaced her long slender fingers.

"What?" Joey asked, afraid she'd gone too far.

"Nothing."

"Your poker face isn't anything to be envied either, Elaine. You bite your lip every time you start to say something and change your mind."

"Do I?"

"You're doing it now."

"I've only ever considered how silly Amy and Brooke are to continue to give their hearts to men that disappoint them. I've never thought about what it takes for them to continue to believe it'll be worth the pain someday."

"And?"

"I guess they're the brave ones," Elaine said sadly, "but now I'm wondering what that makes me."

Joey sat back. She'd touched on something bigger than she'd expected, and that scared her. This wasn't life-coaching stuff or even casual-friend territory. Elaine was opening up to her, sharing herself in ways that revealed the depth she had only wondered at until now.

Elaine leveled her laser-beam blue eyes on her. "I'm forty-two years old and I've never had my heart broken."

This was where she should fall apart. She was too close to this beautiful, caring, thoughtful woman. She should be bumbling, terrified, and overwhelmed to the point of inaction. Instead, she covered Elaine's elegant hand with one of her own. "Have you ever been in love?"

"No," Elaine said without hesitation. "I've dated. I've had people I've cared about. I've loved so many people in a generic, regard-every-human-being-with-love sort of way, but I can't remember a single time I've ever let myself be *in love*."

"Because you don't think it can work?"

"Because I've never wanted to be devastated. Because I've never wanted to repeat Amy's mistakes. Because it's never worked out, so I haven't let myself believe it ever could."

"And now?" Her heart hammered an echo through her ears. She didn't know what she'd do if Elaine said she didn't believe in the all-consuming love she'd spent her whole life chasing.

"For the first time in my life, I'm jealous of my sister."

Joey flopped back in her chair, awash with relief that Elaine not only believed in love, she wanted to experience it. "It's not too late to turn that around."

"I don't know. I've never been able to let go and open myself up to a relationship."

"I've never had a successful relationship either. Does that mean I'm incapable?"

"No." Elaine snapped back into her life-coaching persona. "Of course not, Joey. You're—"

"Creative, resourceful, and whole," she said with a grin. "And so are you. Don't go back to coaching me right now. Let me hold the metaphorical mirror for you. You asked me once what I'd think of someone like me as a prospective partner. Turn the question back around on yourself."

Elaine smiled. "You're entirely too smooth, Joey."

"And you're dodging again," she said, trying to subdue her pleasure at having Elaine think she was smooth. She'd always been bumbling and inept around women of Elaine's caliber. Now she was not only conversing easily with Elaine, but also keeping up in the depth department. "What would you say to a kind and generous person, someone so loving to people she barely knew that she opened up her home and heart to them on a regular basis? Would you see anything that would make her incapable of falling in love?"

Elaine smiled so brightly Joey thought she might melt into her. A few months ago she would've sold her soul to have Elaine look at her like that. Now it terrified her. She worried she might kiss her. She could kiss her. The realization was sudden and complete. She wouldn't shy away or be rendered incapable of action. She wanted her so badly that if Elaine only slightly indicated that she returned those feelings, Joey would not only know what to do, she'd be able to do it.

"Well, I guess you've given me my homework for our next session," Elaine said, standing and breaking the mood. She reached for the empty soup bowl, then stopped and rested her hand on Joey's shoulder. "Honestly, thank you. You've given me a new perspective to consider for the new year."

"You're welcome." It was all she could manage to get out,

emotion still thick in her throat. Elaine had given her so much, so freely, without regard to the dubious way Joey had started their relationship. If she somehow gave back anything close to that, she was grateful for the opportunity.

"Why don't you go relax, and I'll make us some hot chocolate."

She rose to her feet, relieved for a more neutral topic. "I'll do the dishes."

"They can wait. Go relax."

She wanted to argue, but couldn't. The emotional strain of the previous conversation combined with her physical exhaustion overwhelmed her. She sagged into the corner of the couch. She was too at ease sharing a simple meal and a heartfelt conversation with Elaine. It was too natural to close her eyes and soak up the sound of her humming in the kitchen. Everything was just too close to perfect, and that should've terrified her. But instead of obsessing about how she shouldn't let herself get used to this particular brand of perfection, she let go and drifted off to sleep.

❖

Elaine didn't want hot chocolate; she needed the distraction it offered. Her conversation with Joey had overwhelmed her. Joey had deconstructed in a matter of minutes what she'd spent decades trying to come to terms with. She'd never let herself open up to someone who had the power to hurt her. That's why she didn't have a relationship with her sister, that's why she didn't have any close friends, and that's why she'd never been in love. How had Joey helped her see it so quickly when years of therapy and coaching had shown her only the fringes? She didn't make a habit of exposing herself to other people. Why had she revealed so much to Joey, and how had Joey reflected those things back so clearly that Elaine gained a new view of herself?

Was she still so rattled from her newfound attraction to Joey that she'd slipped into a less guarded state? Maybe she'd seen herself differently because she was off balance from the shock of seeing

Joey differently. But was her attraction to Joey something new? She flipped through her memories like photographs in a scrapbook, from being eager to see her each week, to feeling flattered by her compliments, all the way back to being captivated by her deep brown eyes in their first session.

If she was honest, she'd have to admit she'd always found something terribly attractive about Joey, but her sexiness tonight raised that attraction to a new level. Seeing her physicality blend with her newfound confidence and steady sweetness unleashed something raw and vital in Elaine. More than simple admiration or lust, this emotion mingled the two and amplified them. She couldn't remember the last time someone had affected her so totally. Maybe no one ever had. The sensation left her shaken and vulnerable, yet with Joey she was safe. If Joey had pushed even slightly, she would've surrendered completely, but Joey would suffer under the weight of her own will a hundred times over rather than impose even a shred of it on Elaine.

She usually retreated when she was lost. She turned inward or fell back on her work, and in this situation she had every right to consider her job. Her position as a coach was more than the perfect excuse, it was the logical, responsible thing to focus on. She had a habit of returning to the last place she'd felt secure, but instead of blocking Joey physically or emotionally, she'd drawn her close, invited her into her home and her emotions. What about Joey made her comfortable when she should've heeded the turmoil? Even now amid the noise and tumult rattling her mind, Elaine was drawn back to her.

She carried two steaming mugs into the living room and gazed at Joey sleeping in the corner of the couch. An ache settled deep in her chest. Torn between the urge to turn away and the compulsion to get closer, she moved nearer. She set down the mugs and sat on the edge of the coffee table. Joey looked almost angelic with her serene features, her lips slightly parted, and her chest lightly rising and falling. Elaine wanted to wrap around her, or be wrapped up in her, but she couldn't do either. She was dangerously close to crossing a line, both personal and professional, one she couldn't uncross.

She rose and quickly walked to the window. The snow had started again and was falling in sheets that sliced the air on brutal shards of wind. The weather was a fitting visual for her own internal state and a perfect foil for the peace that shrouded the sleeping boi behind her. She wouldn't send her into the cold. Joey had borne enough hardships. Elaine wouldn't pile her own on as well. She might not have been the life coach Joey deserved tonight, but she wouldn't compound the situation by also being selfish, and sending Joey away right now would be purely selfish. Then again, keeping her close had self-serving aspects, too. She looked from the storm outside to the portrait of serenity on her couch. If nothing else, she could take solace in providing Joey shelter from a storm despite the tempest she'd expose herself to by doing so.

She retrieved a blanket and pillow, then returned to her perch on the coffee table. Elaine allowed herself the luxury of watching Joey a minute more. She feared their time together was coming to a close, and she wanted to imprint this image on her mind. She traced a visual line up Joey's languid body, enjoying the splash of taut flesh where her shirt had bunched up, revealing her stomach and the now-relaxed muscles of her arms. The delicate hollow of her throat contrasted with the strength of her jawline. Elaine took in the soft curve of Joey's lips, the dark lashes against smooth skin, and the tuft of tousled hair splayed across her forehead. Then, surrendering to an impulse that cemented her fall from the role of Joey's coach, Elaine ran her trembling fingers through the stray strands of Joey's hair, tucking it into place before trailing the back of her fingers down the soft skin of Joey's cheek.

Joey's eyes fluttered open, a sleepy haze covering deep brown as she focused intensely on Elaine. She started to sit up, but Elaine rested a gentle hand on her shoulder. "Shh, relax. You're going to stay here tonight."

Maybe she sensed her resolve, or maybe she simply needed to accept it, but Joey didn't argue. She nodded and sank back on to the couch, alleviating the need for further discussion. Elaine handed her the blanket and pillow, dimmed the overhead light to almost dark, then quickly turned to leave before she had the chance to succumb to her desire to stay. She stopped only to unplug her laptop and whisk it into the bedroom.

She sat on the edge of her bed, the computer resting precariously on her knees, and opened a new e-mail, then typed a familiar address. With an amount of certainty equal to her decision to have Joey stay the night, she typed a message: *Marty, we have to talk ASAP. Elaine.*

After hitting Send and closing the computer, she lay back on the bed and resigned herself to a long, sleepless night.

Chapter Thirteen

January 1

Joey pushed off the hard pack of snow that ringed the pond, her skates gliding effortlessly across the freshly groomed surface. She had the ice to herself this early, the event staff too busy shoveling snow and arranging hay-bale barriers to pay her any attention. She watched with fascination as her blade scraped a clear line behind her, minuscule marks the only evidence she existed on this plane at all. Hundreds of others would soon cross the curls of her barely traceable trajectory, creating a massive abstract sketch and rendering her contribution indistinguishable.

What a silly thought to begin a hockey game with. The imminent clash of bodies didn't usually strike her as poetic. On the contrary, she liked how the press of competition cleared her head of anything other than the immediate. That's what she'd hoped for when she arrived at the pond early. She'd wanted to leave behind the overwhelming pensiveness that had plagued her since waking up at Elaine's.

There in the early light of a new day and a new year, she hadn't been disoriented to wake on Elaine's couch. She was comfortable, cozy, and well-rested. Her sleep had been deep and dreamless, but as awareness crept in, so did the gremlins. She didn't belong there. She was Elaine's client, not her friend, and certainly not her lover. She wasn't waking next to Elaine, but on the couch, a guest, and an unexpected one at that. She wouldn't be there at all if not for an act of nature, and now that the blizzard had passed, her welcome had also.

No. She sat up and rubbed the sleep from her eyes. She was welcome here. She'd offered to leave several times, and Elaine had wanted her to stay. She had been more than a coach last night. She'd shared parts of herself Joey sensed she didn't share lightly. They'd edged into something more than either of them had allowed before, which was actually scarier than anything the inner critic had to say. The beautiful, caring, and infinitely desirable woman asleep in the next room had invited her into a piece of her heart. How could she accept that invitation without wanting more?

She'd promised Elaine she'd stay dedicated to their coaching relationship and its power. She'd kept the appropriate professional distance and fostered only openness and authenticity between them, but how could she do that now? She couldn't remain distant and authentic when her authentic self thrived on their newfound closeness. She couldn't be honest with Elaine while pretending she wasn't falling for her all over again.

She had tiptoed into the bathroom and splashed some water on her face. She had to pull it together. This was Elaine; her one-time dream woman had become much more than a dream. A brilliant coach, a trusted confidante, and a personal inspiration, she was someone Joey valued on so many levels while still holding her on a pedestal, an almost celestial figure in her life. What would happen to their coaching relationship if Joey regressed to thinking of her as fantasy material? But was that what she was doing? She was no longer admiring her from afar or imagining all the wonderful things she could be. She actually knew her for the wonderful, inspiring, giving woman she was. And so much for watching from afar—Elaine was sleeping in the next room. Joey stood in her bathroom, surrounded by her blow dryer, her toothbrush, and her retainer.

Her retainer? She stared at the small piece of metal and plastic. *Elaine wears a retainer?* That wasn't the stuff of fantasies. That was real life, that was intimate, and so freaking cute. She had melted, the little imperfection somehow making Elaine more perfect.

"No, no, no," she had whispered as an unfamiliar sensation

built in her chest. It hadn't been unpleasant, but it was strong and disconcerting, and she had slammed the door on it before it could overwhelm her. She had to get out of there. It was hard enough to think of her as sexy and stunning and intuitive. She couldn't think of her as being in any way attainable.

She crept quietly to the living room and scribbled a note on a pad of paper, grabbed her boots, then slipped quietly out the door.

Making her escape before Elaine woke up had been cowardly, but what had scared her the most was how little she'd actually been scared. If she'd stayed and seen Elaine in the early morning light with her hair a mess and her sweet smile filled with the remnants of sleep, she wasn't sure she could have helped herself. This wasn't like the other times when she'd worried she'd dissolve into a bumbling, inarticulate mess. Now she worried she would've been strong and comfortable, and she couldn't trust her newfound, confident self to respect the boundaries Elaine had clearly set for them.

"You look guilty," Lisa called from the side of the ice where she laced up her skates.

Joey laughed. "How do you do that?"

Lisa pushed onto the ice. "You're easy to read."

"Elaine said that last night."

"What else did Elaine say?"

"She said—Hey, you called her Elaine. Why no funny nickname?"

"She's not funny when she keeps you for sleepovers and then dumps you out the next morning."

"It's not like that, Lisa."

"No? Why are you doing the solitary-pensive-skate thing figure skaters do in movies? You look downright maudlin."

"You're exaggerating."

"I'm not. Eeyore's back, and I don't know what good it was to make all that progress if she intended to leave you back where you started."

"I'm not back where I started. It's complicated, but it's not what you think. Last night Elaine was nothing but open and welcoming and wonderful in every way."

"Something's bothering you, and you aren't telling me what, so it's gotta be bad."

More people started to arrive, so even if she wanted to talk, now wasn't the time. "She didn't throw me out. I snuck out, okay? None of this is about her. It's me, and that's all that matters right now. We can talk about the rest when we get home."

"Hey, you two, knock it off with the heavy stuff and get warmed up," Carol, one of their teammates, called as she hit the ice. "No frowning, Joey. I need my coach to have a game face on. It's New Year's freaking Day. Let's play some hockey."

She was happy for the distraction, both for Lisa and for herself. She was the team leader, and she'd looked forward to this tournament for a long time. She pushed off hard and skated in full sprint to the other side of the ice, then kicked her skates sideways and skidded to a stop, throwing a satisfying wave of shaved ice in front of her.

"Show-off," Lisa yelled.

Joey laughed. She wasn't sure about much of anything at the moment, so it was ironic she felt most in control on a solid sheet of ice.

She flew through her warm-ups and into the opening match. Her team had the game well in hand, up two to nothing with less than a minute left to play in the first period. Joey had scored once and assisted Lisa for the other point, but now she'd shifted into defensive mode, her focus on the puck and its handlers on the other team. Her stick was light in her hand, and the wind whistled satisfyingly in her ear, drowning out any thoughts not immediately related to the game. Since there was no goalie in four-on-four hockey, she had to cover more ice to give her a location that allowed her to aggressively guard and deflect without actually goal-tending.

She skated backward past mid-ice, toward her own net, but as she entered the crease, she noticed Elaine sitting on a bale of hay to the side of the ice. Her breath grew shallow as warmth spread through her. Elaine looked gorgeous, as always, her blond waves of hair pulled back into a clip at the base of a stocking cap, her cheeks pink, and her eyes that striking shade of blue Joey found unnerving even from a distance. She watched the game intently, and Joey raised a hand of acknowledgment.

Elaine smiled and started to raise her hand to wave back, but Joey didn't see her finish the motion, as she caught a shoulder to her chest. While not a full body check, the hit was unexpected, and in her distracted state, she didn't have the spatial awareness to know which way to drive. Instead of using her body to block the onslaught from the other team, she hit the ice in a splay of arms and legs. She managed to shield most of her face with her arm, saving it from the initial impact, but the tip of her chin absorbed the brunt of her slide. She wrenched around to right herself in time to see the puck slide into the net.

"Nice one, Prince Charming," Lisa said, extending her hand to hoist her back onto her skates. "I'm sure Sexy O'Sweet-Thing over there was very impressed."

"Back to the nicknames? Does that mean you're not mad anymore?"

"Maybe." Lisa shrugged. "Or maybe I'd been working on that one for a while and I didn't want it to go to waste."

Joey laughed and skated to center ice for the face-off. She won, sliding the puck handily to Lisa, and sprinted for the other goal. She hadn't looked back at Elaine since her dive, but she wanted to redeem herself as much as possible before the end of the period. She dodged a defender and took a pass from Lisa up around the net, but the referee's whistle signaling the end of the first period and the beginning of a fifteen-minute break cut short her visions of grandeur.

Joey's shoulders slumped, but Lisa slapped her on the back. "Nice recovery, Gretzky."

"Hey, what happened out there, Coach?" asked Natalie, one of their teammates. "Did that chick level you?"

"No. I got distracted."

"You? Distracted?" Carol asked as she slid to a stop next to them. "Never."

"She's got a girl in the crowd," Lisa said.

"What? Who? Where?" Both girls hit her with a barrage of questions.

"Shh, she's not my girl," Joey said adamantly, though the idea thrilled her.

"She's the blonde sitting on the last hay bale near the other net."

"Stop," she whined when everyone looked at once. "She's gonna think we're talking about her."

"We *are* talking about her," Natalie said, pulling off her helmet to reveal the tight dark curls she kept cut close to her scalp. "I want to meet her, see if she blushes as easily as you do."

"She doesn't, and she's not my girl, and we're not in sixth grade, so please don't embarrass me."

"All right, Coach, settle down." Carol threw her arm around her shoulder. "We're just giving you shit. That's what friends do."

"You want to work on a game plan, Jo?" Lisa asked.

Joey's status as captain gave her the honorary position as coach, but she wasn't interested in the title. "Nah, we're fine. Let's just keep having fun."

"Then let's get off our skates for a few minutes," Natalie said.

"You go on," Joey said, glancing over her shoulder. "I'm fine."

Lisa shook her head. "If you go over there, you're a glutton for punishment."

She grinned and pushed off with a little kick of her skates. She tried to not blush anymore, but between the catcalls behind her and the mischievous twinkle in Elaine's eyes, that was a losing battle.

❖

Elaine fought the urge to remove her wool pea coat as she watched Joey approach and her body temperature rose. She was losing her grip on any remaining professionalism, but she'd known that when she decided to come down to Delaware Park. She simply couldn't face her empty apartment. Joey's absence this morning had shattered her usually peaceful solitude.

She had taken hours to fall asleep last night, and she'd officially seen the new year in by staring at her ceiling, but when she did finally sleep, it was deep and more restful than she would've thought possible. She awoke with a smile at the thought of sharing breakfast with Joey, only to find her gone. She'd folded the blankets neatly and left a short note atop the stack. *Thank you, Elaine, for everything. Joey.*

Elaine couldn't leave it alone, not after their conversation the night before and the way Joey had seen into her soul. She couldn't be content with a few short lines when she'd spent the night wrestling with her longing to hold her. Joey had done the right thing. She'd respected the distance they needed and had kept their time together from lingering into something neither of them would be able to ignore. Elaine had time and space to reassert herself in the professional capacity she usually clung to. Joey had given her a gift by being the one to leave gracefully, and she should've accepted it, but she didn't. She was drawn, like a pilgrim to Mecca, to the young woman who slid smoothly to a stop in front of her.

Joey tugged off her helmet and casually shook out her mop of dark hair. The move struck Elaine as something she might see in a movie when the heartthrob appeared on-screen. Did she consider Joey a heartthrob now? That was quite a transition from the bumbling, good-natured boi she'd seen on their first day together. Was the entire transformation in Joey, or had something shifted in her, too? Could the change be part of her new resolve not to go in circles?

"Hi," Joey said with a controlled grin, as if trying to contain her exuberance, but her face flushed and her eyes sparkled like the ice reflecting the sun.

"Hi," she replied, assuming her expression mirrored Joey's.

"Are you a hockey fan?" Joey asked as she stepped off the ice and sat on the hay next to her.

"Not generally, but you mentioned you'd be playing, so I thought I might as well see what all the fuss was about."

"And what do you think so far?"

She hadn't been thinking about hockey at all but about running her fingers tenderly along the scrape on Joey's chin. "It seems rough."

"Not really at this level," Joey said. "We play minimal contact."

"Doesn't seem like it to me," she said, giving in to the excuse to touch her index finger lightly to Joey's chin. *I've got the restraint of a toddler.*

"That was my fault." Joey laughed nervously. "I was, um, distracted."

"Oh? Did something catch your eye?"

She blushed and bumped her shoulder into Elaine's. "Not something, someone."

"Hmm." Elaine played coy, something she couldn't recall ever doing. "What a lucky someone that you'd sacrifice your beautiful face for her attention." Her remark was too flirty. She shouldn't have said it, but the words had spilled out. She'd been partially responsible for Joey's crash? While she felt guilty, she was also pleased she still had that effect on her sometimes. Joey had done such a good job of transitioning to her role as a client, lately she couldn't tell if Joey was still attracted to her. And since Joey's rise in confidence eliminated much of the nervousness around her, these occasional slips were the only indicator she wasn't facing this temptation alone. Then again, maybe if Joey didn't reaffirm their mutual attraction, she could better control herself. No, that wasn't fair. She'd crossed the line, she'd enforced these rules in the first place, and she was the one who had to uphold her ethics. None of that was Joey's responsibility.

"Will you stay for the second period?" Joey asked.

"I should go," she said.

"Should? I thought that was an inner-critic word?"

"Touché." She smiled. "I need to get ready for a session."

It wasn't a lie. She needed to talk to Marty, and she'd have to fortify and center herself for their conversation.

Joey sighed. "Can you at least stay until I redeem myself? I don't want your only impression of hockey to be me getting ice rash on my face."

She laughed. "How could I resist a request like that?"

"Hey, about last night. I was wondering…"

Elaine held her breath.

"Coach," Lisa called, causing both Elaine and Joey to start out of their oblivion.

"Yes?" they asked in unison.

"Hockey coach, not life coach."

"Oh, sorry." Elaine flushed.

"I hate to interrupt your coachiness, but the game's back on."

"I'll talk to you later?" Joey asked as she refastened the chin strap on her helmet.

"Of course. Go have fun."

Joey skated off, but Lisa remained, one eyebrow raised as she examined Elaine.

"I'm sorry," Elaine said. "I just wanted to say hello. I didn't intend to keep her."

"Maybe you should rethink that plan, 'cause she's a keeper." She skated off to join Joey.

Elaine silently considered Lisa's words. Did Lisa think she didn't appreciate Joey? If only she knew the opposite was true. Of course Joey was a keeper. Joey would make some woman very happy someday. She'd be an amazing partner to a woman her own age, a woman who shared her dreams and values. Someone capable of giving herself fully and to the same extent Joey did. Someone able to love her in the easy, uncomplicated way she deserved. Someone who was less complex with fewer obstacles to overcome. Someone other than Elaine.

The referee, or umpire, or whatever dropped the puck, and Lisa hit it to Joey, who skated off at a reckless speed. She slid the puck in front of her and around an opponent as though it was glued to her stick. Joey played hockey the same way she approached everything else, fully, exuberantly, passionately. Her move would've looked effortless if not for the exertion everyone else on the pond had to display in order to keep up. Even Joey's own teammates seemed at a loss for what to do with the burst of athleticism. Joey charged toward the net until she came within a foot of intersecting with the last defender, then abruptly stopped, pausing a half beat while the opposing player flew past her, then flicked her wrist, sending the puck easily into the unattended goal.

Elaine rose to her feet and cheered with a few other spectators, finally understanding what people saw in this game, but the excitement of the play didn't touch the thrill she got when Joey bypassed all her teammates to skate by her with unabashed exuberance across her beautiful features.

"Enjoy the rest of your day," Joey called as she breezed past.

She laughed. The rest of her day held nothing she'd enjoy as much as she treasured being a part of Joey's joy. No matter what else happened, she'd hold on to that moment in the days and weeks to come, and she hoped Joey would, too.

With that thought and the accompanying resolve, she started toward home.

She fought the urge to take her time, but she knew what she had to do. This morning was merely a reprieve from her responsibilities, not an abandonment. She'd crossed the line with Joey, and she'd already contacted Marty. She couldn't undo either of those things. Why not steal a few more minutes with Joey? She'd had fun flirting with her, and she needed some more fun in her life, but it couldn't come at the expense of her career, her values, or her sanity, so as soon as she got back to her apartment, she powered on her laptop and logged into Skype.

Marty was online waiting for her. They'd worked together for five years, and Marty knew her well enough to understand she wouldn't have demanded her attention unless she needed it.

"Happy New Year, darling," Marty said as soon as their video call connected. Her olive skin contrasted beautifully against her cream-colored turtleneck even on the dull computer screen. "I assume you've not had the best holiday?"

This wasn't going to be easy. She didn't even know how to answer that simple question. "It was wonderful, but for all the wrong reasons. No, the reasons weren't wrong, but the people were wrong. Maybe not wrong, but it's not right either. Oh, Marty, I've made a mess."

"Okay." Marty remained as calm and collected as she always did. "Let's start from the beginning."

"I'm attracted to one of my clients." The words poured out in a rush, and relief crashed into embarrassment behind them.

"Well, that is a starting point. Where shall we go from there?"

Elaine smiled in spite of her anguish. Marty wouldn't reprimand her. She was too good a coach. Nothing in her history suggested she'd get carried away in such an unprofessional fashion. Surely Marty had to be surprised, but she gave no visible indication. Her neutrality only made Elaine feel her own failure more acutely.

"I failed her in our session last night."

"So this began last night?"

She shook her head. "I became hyperaware of it last night, but it's probably been brewing in my blind spot for a while. I felt such a strong connection with her at our first meeting." She didn't want to get into too many details about Joey. It was essential to protect her confidentiality. "We got off to a complicated start, but we'd settled in beautifully, and she's made the most amazing progress."

"But you're no longer able to keep the appropriate distance between what you're feeling toward her personally and what you're doing as a coach?"

She'd certainly lost her emotional distance with Joey. There hadn't been a single disastrous moment, but several substantial breaches of her professional façade, all of them starting from the overwhelming attraction she'd felt the night before.

"Last night was the first time my attraction to her overrode my self-management skills. I didn't regard her neutrally, and I purposely avoided an exercise that could've helped her because it would've been too tempting for me personally."

"At least you recognized your limitations in the situation. You mentioned self-management, but don't forget self-care, too. I take it you're pretty upset?"

Self-care? How could she think of herself right now? Intellectually she understood that she needed to have her own needs met to be able to focus on her client, but her obligation was to Joey.

"Marty, I don't know what I am right now. I'm not the coach I wanted to be. I've failed a client, and that's enough for me to deal with. Whether or not I'm falling in love with her is a whole other issue."

"Interesting. A moment ago you mentioned only attraction to a client. Now you're falling in love with her?"

"I'm not sure difference matters much in this situation."

"True in the professional sense. Acting on either impulse would be enough to get you dispelled from the profession."

"I know, I know." She hid her face in her hands. How had she gotten so far out of control? A few weeks ago she worried she was incapable of forming an attachment of this magnitude with anyone, but she had her job to fall back on. Her role as a coach had been tied deeply to the identity she'd worked so hard for, and now it was being threatened by a dream she hadn't even fully formed until last night in Joey's presence. She'd had a shift in how she viewed herself, but at what cost?

"Just to be clear, you haven't already done anything to jeopardize your good standing in the coaching community?"

"No," she said. "I've brushed my hand against her twice, made a flirty comment or two, but I'm sure if you asked her, she'd say I was the consummate coach, which feels like even more of a betrayal, because she trusts me completely."

"You're very focused on your client, Elaine. Even in your own turmoil you're aware of her needs despite your fear you can't meet them. Have you considered how you've sacrificed yourself?"

"No," she said quickly. "I've been selfish enough in letting my own impulses take over. I need to focus on her now."

"Do you think you can help her when you haven't cared for yourself?"

She shook her head. "No. I know that intellectually, but then I see her, and everything I feel overruns everything I know. I can't help her. I can't help me. I have to stop."

"So you've come to a decision?"

"Yes. I've known since last night what I have to do." She

flashed back to the moment when she'd touched Joey's cheek. With a little brush of her fingers against Joey's beautifully smooth skin, she'd sealed their fate. "I have to terminate the relationship."

"And yet something's still upsetting you."

"I don't know why doing the right thing has to hurt so badly."

Marty's eyes brimmed with sympathy, reflecting a piece of Elaine's agony back at her, but there was nothing Elaine could say. She had to fill this silence.

"How do I tell her I can't find it in myself to see her anymore? She's done, everything I've asked of her. Even though this wasn't the relationship she wanted at first, she gave it all the trust and openness and dedication we always hope for. She's found her purpose, she's growing more confident, and her playful side is starting to emerge. If I cut her off, I just don't know what'll happen."

"You think ending the relationship will harm her?"

She pulled to mind the image of Joey on the ice earlier—her determination, her competence, her exuberance—and contrasted that image with Joey at their earliest meeting when she'd been nervous and apologetic. "I can't imagine her abandoning the goals she's already achieved, but she may never open her heart again."

"You don't think your stating your attraction to her would boost her confidence?"

"Should I phrase it that way? Wouldn't that open all kinds of unethical doors? Or maybe I'm a big coward for not wanting to admit what's happening here. God, I wish we had clearer rules for this."

"There aren't strict rules for coaching in challenging situations, but we have guiding principles of finding what's true and right for the individuals involved."

"Of course I want to honor what's true and right, but what is that? It's true I care deeply about her and she's opened herself to me. It's true I can't coach her effectively and that's going to upset her. All these truths, but none of them feel right."

Marty continued to nod sympathetically while she spilled her emotions and frustrations.

"First, do no harm, but what constitutes harm in this situation? Is there a way not to harm either of us? I think I've actually already harmed us both."

"Are you looking for a single answer here?"

She sighed. "I'm searching for something that may not exist. I can't imagine hurting her, yet I can't conceive of a way in which I don't hurt her. If I tell her I can't coach her because I'm attracted to her, but still can't date her, she's going to be hurt. If I use the clichéd 'it's not you, it's me,' she'll be hurt. And if I keep coaching her inappropriately, she'll end up getting hurt."

"If hurt is inevitable, may I ask what additional harm you see in telling the truth?"

Marty was right. Healing existed purely in truth, even as awkward as it would be to say. She'd broken her commitment as a coach in a myriad of ways. She couldn't compound the situation with a lie. One of Elaine's top strengths was honesty and authenticity, and Joey had worked so hard to connect with her true self, neither of them would find peace in deception. She owed Joey the same level of honesty and openness Joey had given her, and for the first time in her life she had to risk her own heart in order to spare the heart of someone she cared about more than herself.

Chapter Fourteen

January 5

Joey fought the urge to pound her head into the dining room table. Why couldn't she balance her checkbook? She'd added the numbers six times, and she was still off by a hundred and twenty dollars. She looked at her online banking statement. It was probably even something obvious, but what? She didn't have an eye for details, and all the lines had jumbled together in her exhaustion-induced haze. She hadn't slept well since New Year's Eve. Her body needed rest, but her mind refused to settle. Something was right below the surface of her consciousness that refused to grant her peace but wouldn't reveal itself completely either. It kept her awake at night and prevented her from focusing fully on anything else.

She punched the numbers into her calculator one more time, suspecting she was nearing the definition of insanity by doing the same thing again and hoping for new results.

"Damn it," she muttered when the figure resulted in the same difference.

Lisa glanced up from the Sabres game. "Want me to look at it?"

"Would you, please? I think I've got a blind spot."

Lisa took the checkbook and turned the laptop so she could see it better. She looked at one and then the other for all of thirty seconds before raising her eyebrows at Joey. "Yeah, I'd say you've got a blind spot. She's about five-seven, blond curls, striking blue eyes."

Joey's pulse accelerated. What was Lisa suggesting, and why was her chest constricting?

Lisa circled two lines in the checkbook. "Coacharella hasn't cashed the checks for your last two sessions. Sixty dollars a pop gives you one hundred and twenty dollars that apparently neither of you knows what to do with."

Why hadn't Elaine cashed those checks and, perhaps more important, why hadn't Joey noticed?

"Why didn't I see that?"

"I'm not a life coach, but I think you didn't want to see it."

"That's absurd. I've been trying to balance this for half an hour. Why would I purposely ignore two checks?"

"The same reason you've ignored the way you spent the night at Elaine's, the way you two were flirting this weekend, and the fact you're still in love with her."

She shook her head. "I promised I'd move on. I promised her I'd focus on the coaching."

"And you have. I'd say you're your old self, but you're like a whole new Joey. You're calmer and more relaxed, and you're starting school in a few weeks. The coaching has done its job."

"Right. Everything is going so well. I can't regress…" She felt a tug in her chest. The same feeling had kept her awake at night and nipped at her while she balanced her checkbook. Her heart was sending her a message, the same message it had been sending since that weekend. "I just, I um…"

"What?"

"I'm listening," she said aloud but to herself. She closed her eyes and inhaled, consciously letting the breath fill her lungs and raise her chest. She wasn't searching for something in her head. It was in her blind spot, her gut, her heart, and it had to do with Elaine. She needed to quiet her mind, mute the inner critic, and invite her feelings out into the open.

"What are we listening for?" Lisa whispered. "Love-at-first-sight-Elaine?"

"No, it wasn't love at first sight." The haze started to burn away, revealing the truth and allowing Joey to examine its outer edges.

"Fibber." Lisa laughed. "Don't try that revisionist-history crap with me. You got swoony the first time you saw her. You wanted to hug her and kiss her and have her babies."

"But I wasn't in love with her," she said with unfamiliar clarity. "I was in love with the idea of her."

"Whoa, heavy."

"I didn't even know her. I knew she was beautiful, but I didn't know what she did or how she was caring or smart or nice. Hell, I didn't even know her name. I saw a gorgeous woman, so I took all the things I love in a woman, mixed them with all my insecurities, and pasted them onto her."

Lisa stared at her as though she was either brilliant or crazy but couldn't decide which.

"I used her as an outlet for all the junk I have about women. No wonder I melted into a puddle of insecurities whenever I was around her. The more I got to know her, the more I saw her as a real, authentic person and not some caricature I'd drawn, the more comfortable I got."

"So you're saying you're not in love with her?"

"No." Joey shook her head slowly. "I said I *wasn't* in love with her. I was infatuated, I was a mess, maybe even obsessed, but I wasn't in love with her. She wasn't real then, and you can't be in love with something that doesn't exist. That's why I couldn't even talk to her."

"Wait. I thought she was out of your league and you couldn't talk to her because she made you all squimbly."

"Of course she did. I'd turned her into a ghost of girlfriends past. How do you talk to a figment of your imagination?"

"Who are you and what have you done with Eeyore?"

She smiled sadly. Even Lisa's humor couldn't cloud the reality of her situation. "I have to break it off with Elaine."

"What?" Lisa jumped out of her seat. "How did you go from all calm and self-awakening to crazy talk?"

"I'm still calm," she said truthfully. She wasn't happy, but a soothing certainty had replaced the unsettling sensations that had filled her moments earlier. “And I see myself more clearly now than I ever have. I’m not confused or infatuated or projecting. I’m not chasing a ghost or an idol. I see who I am, I see who she is, and I’m in love with her.”

“Holy shit.” Lisa dropped back into her chair. “I’m confused.”

“I’m not.”

“First you were in love with her, but then you weren’t, but now you *are* in love with her, so you’re going to break up with her? WTF?”

It did sound crazy. “I was infatuated with an idea, but I’ve outgrown that. Elaine helped me see my own patterns and in turn see who she is, and I’ve fallen in love with that real woman.”

“So why are you breaking up with her?”

“I’m breaking off the coaching relationship for several reasons, most important because I’ve failed to uphold my end of the deal. I’ve let my personal feelings supersede the coaching relationship. I’ve removed the power from the relationship and placed the emphasis on the coach herself.”

“Who talks like that?”

“People who quote from life-coaching contracts.”

“It kind of creeps me out.”

“I’ve met all the goals she can help me with. If I remained a client we’d work on dating issues, and it’s a lie to pretend I wanted to date anyone but her.”

“That’s better. I follow you now.”

“Let me go one step clearer, then. If I continue to pay her for coaching sessions focusing on my desire to date her, I become a john, and I take her profession, her essence, and prostitute it.”

Lisa winced. “Okay, yeah. You gotta get out.”

“I have to tell her Friday,” Joey said, her first wave of nervousness crashing in on her. “Easier said than done, right?”

“Are you going to ask her out?”

“I’ll be completely honest with her, but I don’t expect her to jump me. I think she’ll be disappointed in me. I made a promise I couldn’t keep. I’ve betrayed her trust.”

"I don't think that's how she'll see it," Lisa said. "I think she'll be relieved."

Her heart gave a little flutter. "Why?"

"Because she doesn't want to cash your checks for the same reasons you don't want to keep writing them."

"No, Lisa, I can't think about that. I can't let this become another elaborate come-on line. I can't let this be about her. It's about what I feel and what I have to do."

"Okay, dudette, I'm just saying—"

"Don't say it, please. I need to do what's right, not because of where it might lead, but because it's the right thing to do."

She couldn't afford the luxury of daydreams or nightmares about Elaine's response. That circle would spiral out of control until the inner critic took over. If she had any hope of remaining sane over the next few days, she had to stay out of her head and keep the lines of communication open to her heart. Then again, hope was the heart's domain. Perhaps there wasn't anything wrong with allowing a hint of desire to sustain her through Friday.

❖

January 7

Elaine fought to meditate, which was counterproductive. The harder she tried, the more frazzled she became. She couldn't find her center. Hell, she couldn't even find her breath. She'd never had a panic attack, and now when she absolutely needed to pull from her inner strength, she was about to hyperventilate. She knew what she had to do, but her body and her mind refused to allow her to do it. She'd never experienced such a terrible disconnect and felt she might be ripped apart from the inside. Internal discord was painful for anyone, especially for someone who'd spent her life striving to live in line with her purposeful, authentic self.

It also perplexed her. She'd understood being torn during her coaching conflict with Joey. Living outside her values, in this case her ethics, led to turmoil, but she'd decided to end the coaching relationship, to pull her actions back in line with her values, and in doing so she'd settled the conflict. She'd also decided to tell Joey the truth about why she had to end their relationship. She'd chosen honesty and authenticity, both of which were critical to her identity. She'd gone off her path, but in a few minutes she'd do what she needed to right her course. So why did she still feel awful?

Was she a coward or afraid of the damage the truth would inflict on her own ego? Was she really so vain she couldn't stand the thought of losing face as a coach? Did she simply dread letting Joey down? Certainly that concern had some truth. She didn't want to hurt Joey. She'd put herself through this ordeal in order to spare Joey more pain. If she just wanted to uphold her reputation, she could keep coaching her and fake neutrality. A less dedicated coach would simply enjoy the remainder of their time, then each of them would go her own way. A surge of nausea rolled through her, but why?

A gentle knock sounded against her door, causing her to jump. She didn't have to glance at her watch to know it was four o'clock. Joey was always on time.

With unsteady hands, she opened the door. She'd obsessed about this moment for a week and somehow was still caught off guard by the sight of Joey with her chestnut hair falling recklessly across her forehead but stopping short of covering those liquid chocolate eyes.

"Hi," Joey said with her signature grin.

"Hi." She returned the smile despite the tension, rendering the rest of her muscles useless. Joey had already shed her coat, and her cream-colored waffle-weave shirt fit snugly across her chest and torso, reminding Elaine of the muscled physique beneath it. Her immediate focus on Joey's body served as further evidence she was in no shape to continue coaching her. She had to end this quickly.

"Everything okay? Or should I wait out here for a while?"

She shook her head and stepped back. "No. I'm sorry. Come on in."

Joey breezed casually past her, close enough for Elaine to

smell her cologne or shampoo. It was subtle, fresh, and a little intoxicating. God, who was she becoming? "Can I get you a drink? Water? Tea?"

"Actually I'd like to get started," Joey said, sitting back on the couch. She was confident, comfortable, the image of a person sure about her place and her purpose. She was the perfect foil to Elaine's inner tumult.

"Of course," she said, taking her usual seat. *It's better to do this quickly.* Prolonging the situation would only make it harder. "I've actually thought a lot about our session this week. I think it's time we have a serious discussion about our future and—"

"I've thought about that, too, and I've made peace with a few aspects of myself that I need to share with you. Would you mind if I go first?"

Joey had never cut her off before. She rarely took charge of their conversations. Her good-natured personality usually made her open to being led by Elaine's questions. Something was off, and it wasn't just her own misgivings about the conversation she needed to have. Joey was too sure of herself. She wasn't simply having a good day or a positive attitude. Something had shifted. She didn't seem jubilant or even happy, but she carried a resolve that gave her a commanding presence. The change would've been alluring if she wasn't terrified of its implications.

"Elaine, the last six weeks have been amazing. I feel stronger than I ever have. I'm approaching life with purpose. I'm motivated and I'm working toward goals I'd given up on. I can't even begin to thank you for giving me this chance." Joey stopped. "This *second* chance. You saved me."

She flushed with pride and embarrassment. "Joey, you did all the work."

"But I wouldn't have without you," Joey said emphatically. "You made a commitment to me even after I deceived you. You were caring and genuine and generous, and you showed so much faith in me. I'll always be grateful that you're the coach you are."

She had to stop this. Joey's sincerity broke her heart. She

couldn't let her think she was perfect when in reality she was in the midst of an epic failure. "I'm far from perfect. I'm a flawed person and even less perfect as a coach."

"I'm not saying you're perfect, but you were perfect for me. You taught me to recognize my real self and put my values into action. That's why I'm going back to school, that's why I'm ready to start to date again, and that's why I can't see you as a coach anymore."

"Joey, I'm...what?" *She can't see me as a coach anymore?*

"On the day I committed myself to our coaching relationship, I promised to always be honest with you, but I haven't been faithful to that promise lately," Joey said. "Or maybe I've become more faithful. I don't know."

She waited, listening to the rush of her own pulse. What did Joey mean? Her confidence seemed to falter briefly as their eyes met and she grinned sheepishly and shrugged.

"I need to be honest with you, and you've given me the courage. You made me see I deserve better than what I've allowed myself to dream of. I've loved being your client, and I couldn't have done any of what I've done or what I'm about to do without you, but in order to honor the promise I made and my own authentic voice, I have to say I'm in love with you."

She made no attempt to hide her surprise. She was so far out of her coaching persona she couldn't even imagine neutrality. Joey loved her? Dizzy with emotion, she felt flooded with jubilation yet dreaded the knowledge that they were honor-bound to part ways. Her dream had come true. She wasn't alone. Joey shared her feelings, but the dream also held nightmarish qualities.

All her fears about her inability to have a meaningful personal relationship rushed in to remind her that she was primarily a coach. Even if she could set aside her fear of opening up, she could never undo her training as a coach. Opening herself to love was hard enough without complicating the matter with an ethics crisis. Even if they could get past their moral obligations, she couldn't unlearn her ways of relating to Joey as a client.

Still, of all the ways this conversation could go, they were both off to a good start. At least she knew she wasn't alone in her attachment to Joey and had the added solace that she hadn't spoken the words or broken the coaching contract. Joey had made the decision herself, based on her own needs. Elaine might carry her own doubts about her ability as a coach, but she wouldn't be responsible for burdening Joey with them.

Joey must have mistaken her silence for disappointment. "I know I promised you I'd put my personal attraction aside, and I did. This isn't a ploy, and our time together hasn't been an elaborate scheme. I've changed, and the way I see you has changed. I'm not telling you any of this to flatter you or because I expect you to return my feelings. I'm not even asking you out."

She's not asking me out? It stung a little that Joey could be so calm and logical when she had been a wreck all week and still couldn't find any words to convey how she felt.

"I know we can't be a couple, and I understand why, but I couldn't go on pretending I needed you to coach me when in reality I only wanted to be near you. You deserve better, and you've taught me that I do, too."

"I value your honesty, Joey, and believe me, I know how much courage it took to say what you just said…" She bit her lip. The coach in her said to let Joey go, to commend her on her progress and send her off on the terms she had chosen, yet another voice quietly pleaded with her to use Joey's courage as a mirror to her own. As she floundered in her indecision, she left Joey alone, twisting in her own emotions.

"I'm not sorry we had this time, and I'm not sorry for loving you, but I'm sorry I wasn't able to fully honor my commitment to you as a coach. I'm sorry we can't see each other anymore." Joey continued to fill the silence by baring her soul. "Even though I couldn't be the perfect client, you were the perfect coach for me."

Elaine's heart was being wrung out like a dish towel. She couldn't make eye contact with Joey, so she stared at her hands, slowly opening and closing them against each other, squeezing her knuckles white. Joey wasn't just expressing affection or respect or even love. She saw those emotions as a failure on her part. Elaine's authentic voice screamed at her not to let Joey take full responsibility for the downfall of their professional relationship. Then again, if she expressed her feelings, she could upset the peace Joey had made and throw them both back into turmoil. "Joey, I don't know what to say."

Joey shrugged and stood. "There's nothing more to say. I wish it could've ended differently, but I don't regret a minute we spent together."

Elaine rose and followed her to the door. Everything had happened too quickly. She needed time to think. She needed to sort through her options. She could grab Joey and hold her close, whisper soothing words in her ear, but what would that mean for Elaine as a coach, and how would her breaking down help Joey's resolve to move forward? No, she needed to focus on Joey, and Joey had chosen this path. She'd failed her before. She wouldn't compound the situation by failing her again. If only Joey didn't blame herself, she could convince herself everything was perfect.

As if reading her thoughts, Joey stopped and looked her in her eyes. "I know I've hit you with a lot, but I hope when the dust settles you know two things. One, even though I'm sorry for letting you down, I'm a better person for the experience, and two, if you ever want to talk about anything, I'd love to be there for you the way you've been for me."

Then she walked away. Elaine closed and locked her door, not to barricade anyone out but to prevent herself from chasing Joey. Though she couldn't run now anyway. Her legs were shaky and her feet heavy. Nothing made sense. She wasn't Joey's coach, or lover, or even her friend. They were nothing to each other, yet Joey meant everything to her. How had that beautiful, sweet, caring boi found the courage and strength to do what she'd just done? Joey gave the credit to Elaine and put all the responsibility on herself when Elaine saw it the other way around. She'd first failed as a coach and then as a human being. She hadn't been brave or honest, not with Joey and not with herself.

Joey would move forward and she'd succeed. She might have some short-term disappointment, but ultimately she'd have no regrets. The opposite was true for Elaine. She'd lied by omission. By allowing Joey sole ownership of their relationship and refusing to acknowledge her own feelings, she was complicit in a greater deception. She'd denied herself the peace and the healing Joey had offered. Even worse, by hiding behind her professionalism she'd failed on a much more personal level. She'd denied them the possibility of a future they'd both dreamed of.

CHAPTER FIFTEEN

January 9

"Fire," Lisa said, pointing to the grill with her beer bottle.
"Huh?"
"The burgers are on fire."
Joey glanced at the grill and finally noticed the flames surrounding her hamburgers, licking a foot high into the frigid night air and disintegrating the flurries that fell lightly overhead. Most of the country wouldn't consider fourteen degrees with light snow to be grill weather, but in Buffalo this was standard tailgate climate, not that the Bills had made the postseason.
"Shit, shit, shit." She doused the flames with her bottle of water while Lisa looked on, pink-cheeked and amused.
"You can't stop thinking about her, can you?'
"No." Joey's chest ached. Lisa didn't need to say Elaine's name. It hovered around her and hid beneath the surface of every conscious thought. In the forty-eight hours since their last session, she had spent forty hours reliving their conversation and eight hours dreaming fitfully about it. She'd rehashed every detail, examining every motive and its outcome from all angles. There was nothing left to consider or reconsider. Elaine had been a great coach, and while Joey had hoped for more, she understood they couldn't be friends and would never be lovers. Their time together had been amazing and purposeful, but it was over. Intellectually she'd let go;

even emotionally she wasn't a wreck. She hadn't cried or fallen into an impenetrable depression. She went to work, she played hockey, she bought her textbooks, and with the exception of flame-broiling the burgers, she managed to feed herself. She wasn't devastated, but she wasn't thriving.

"Something's off," Joey finally said.

"What?"

"I don't know." She watched her breath cloud, then disperse into the surrounding cold.

"Is this another one of your life-coachy, meditative, voodoo intuitions?" Lisa wiggled her gloved fingers at Joey as though casting a spell.

"Yeah." She no longer tried to explain herself to Lisa. She couldn't make her feel the connections, and she didn't have to. She was secure in her emotions, and Lisa respected her even if she did joke around. "I'm sure I did the right thing, but something's still nagging me about Elaine, and not just the stuff you'd expect like sadness or loneliness, though there's some of that, too."

"So what are you going to do?"

"I don't know. I've given everything I can to Elaine, first as an obsession, then as a coach, then as a love interest. I can't hold on to her any longer."

"The old 'if you love her set her free' business?"

"Clichéd as it may be, yes. She doesn't love me, not in the way I want her to, and if I really believe in having one true love, I have to believe she's not the one, or she'd return my feelings."

"I think you're wrong. She does return your feelings. I'm not blind. I've seen her look at you, and lately she can't stay away from you. She's at the coffeehouse, and the hockey game, and—"

She shook her head. "She stayed away from me when I told her how I felt, and she's stayed away for the past two days."

"You think she's content to let you walk away, no regrets?"

"Yes," Joey said quickly, but then thought about it. No regrets? Was that how Elaine had looked on Friday? She remembered the creases of emotion across her pretty features, the little V-shaped furrow of consternation between her brows, the way she'd bit her bottom lip when Joey said they both deserved better than what they'd settled for. "No, she was holding back."

Lisa glanced at her over the rims of her square-lens glasses. "Why? What did she say?"

"She didn't *say* anything. I blathered on while she stood there and bit her lip. She let me pour all my emotions out, but she held something back." Hope stirred in her chest. "I assumed she was shocked or disappointed, but I can see her so clearly now, and she wasn't disappointed. She was torn."

"Torn?"

"Yeah, she wasn't herself. Quiet yes, but not calm. She fidgeted. She didn't use any of her killer eye contact. Honestly, I think she was uncomfortable from the moment I got there. I don't think I was the only one who went to that session with something on my mind. She wasn't just upset about what I said, either. She had something bigger on her mind."

"She wanted you."

Joey didn't deny it. She couldn't be sure of what Elaine had been feeling, but if that was the answer, why wouldn't she say so?

"She wanted you, but she couldn't have you because you were a client. Man, the plot thickens." Lisa laughed. "What are you going to do?"

The hope crashed before it had a chance to form fully. It didn't matter how Elaine felt if she didn't feel it strongly enough to act on it.

"Nothing."

Lisa slapped her upside the back of her stocking-cap-covered head. "Of course not. It's fourth and inches again, and you're going to punt."

"This isn't a football game," she snapped. "It's my life, and Elaine's life."

"Which is why you've got to fight for her. You have to kick down her door, tell her you want her and you won't take no for an answer."

"No, I'm not sure what she's hiding from or why, but I'm not going to bully it out of her."

Lisa stared at her like she'd lost her mind, or maybe her spine. "You're going to let her go?"

"Why is it me letting her go?" she asked. "Why don't you see it as her letting me go? I'm the one who stood in front of her and bared my soul, twice. She knows me, what I have to offer as a partner, and how I feel about her. She sat stone-faced while I bled my emotions out for her. She either didn't return my feelings, or she felt the same way but she values something else more. I don't know if it's her pride or her job, but either way it's not very flattering for either of us."

"Are you saying you don't want her anymore?"

"I'm saying I don't want to do the chasing all the time. I don't want to be with someone who doesn't want to be with me or who values something more than me. She's taught me I have to stop cutting myself short. I offered her my best, and that wasn't enough. I want to be enough for somebody—more than enough. I want to be somebody's everything."

"Shit," Lisa said, rubbing her eyes. "When did you come to that epic realization?"

She chuckled humorlessly. "Just now."

"So how do you feel?"

"Like I got hit by a truck."

"So much for achieving your purpose making you happy."

"It might be my purpose, but it still sucks to realize she might love me a little bit, but not enough. In some ways that's worse. What's that say about me? And what does that say about her? Those questions could eat me up, and I can't let them. I'd go crazy. I don't want to be second best. I don't want a part of her. I deserve better."

"Damn right. So what are you going to do?"

She sighed. "Move on."

"Good for you," Lisa said with fake cheeriness only a best friend could've seen through.

"Yeah, good for me." She couldn't even pull off sarcasm through her sadness. "I'm a free woman."

"Don't sound so thrilled. You know all you have to do is put an open-for-business sign on your back, and women will line up to get a piece of you."

She grinned. "You're right. I need a fresh start. No more chasing women. I'm going to let them chase me for once."

"Really?"

"Sure. What's the point of getting life-coached if I go back to being Eeyore? The next girl who comes on to me wins the first date with the new-and-improved Joey. No more punting."

Lisa slapped her on the back. "That's my boi. Now let's go order a pizza, because the new-and-improved Joey may be a real Casanova, but she can't cook for shit."

She glanced at the charred rocks of burger smoking on the grill. "Pizza it is, and I'll make a mental note to look for a woman who can cook."

Lisa laughed and headed into the house, but Joey lagged behind. Taking a deep breath of icy air, she stared into the cloudy night sky. There were no stars to wish on, so she focused on a single falling snowflake and sent out a wish for Elaine's happiness. She focused all her positive energy onto the little flurry as it floated closer. She couldn't resist catching it in her gloved hand, but it melted the instant she made contact. She forced a smile. What a fitting reminder that she was done trying to hold on to something that wasn't hers. She found peace in letting go. Everything happened for a reason.

❖

January 14

"What the hell happened to you?" Amy asked when Elaine opened the door. "You look like shit."

"Thanks," she said wearily. She suspected she looked as bad as she felt, but she'd avoided the mirror so far today. She'd managed to stay present and focused on her clients throughout the week. Professional was her default position, and she'd clung to it with all her fortitude, but Friday was her usual day with Joey and her absence had left a cavernous emotional void. She'd managed to shower and eat, and while she was proud of her little victories, Amy hadn't seen her in anything other than business-casual clothes in nearly twenty years, so her sweatpants and fuzzy pink house slippers were probably a little jarring.

"Are you sick?"

"No." If only she had the flu. A virus would cure itself in a few days. She had no timetable for processing what plagued her now. Much more than her immune system was weakened. She was completely out of strength mentally, emotionally, and physically. Her heart and her head were so overloaded they seemed to have shut down on her. She'd given up on her turmoil. She had no right or wrong answer, only infinite questions, and she couldn't face them any longer.

Amy made herself comfortable on Elaine's couch. "You haven't stopped by in a while, and Brooke said you didn't want to go out to dinner with her and Taylor tonight."

"I'm sorry." She wasn't sure exactly what she had to apologize for, but she was sorry. Sorrier than she'd ever been. Regret weighed so heavily on her chest and limbs she refused to sit for fear the lethargy would consume her. "I'm not good company right now."

Amy looked up, her blue eyes bearing a family resemblance and their focus suggesting stubbornness was a genetic trait as well. "So you don't want to talk about this woman, or you don't want to talk about her to *me*?"

"How'd you know it was a woman?"

"I've been in love enough times to recognize the signs, and unless you've switched teams, there's a woman involved. The cute little client Brooke's been going on about?"

"How'd you—"

"I'm not as dense as you think."

"I don't think you're dense."

"Dense, or ditzy, or self-absorbed. On any given day I'm all of them, but I'm still your big sister."

She wasn't sure what this conversation was about, but she wasn't in the mood. She could only stare down at Amy, her expression likely as empty as her emotions.

"Don't look at me like that. I know I haven't been a good sister, but you didn't exactly follow the script, either."

"What script?"

"Oh, you know, the script we both hoped to read from, the one where sisters are close and braid each other's hair and talk for hours about love and life."

"I would've settled for fifteen minutes on something other than the weather, but we couldn't seem to manage that." She wasn't sure where her fit of honesty came from. Perhaps with her defenses down her internal filters had malfunctioned, too. "What did you want from me?"

"A second chance."

She hadn't actually been moving, but the comment stopped the internal loop she'd been mentally pacing for years. "A second chance for what?"

"To be the big sister," Amy said flatly, as though she'd said these lines to herself enough times to take the sting out of them. "I messed up when you were a kid. You must think I never realized I dumped all my problems on you, along with my toddler. I know I wasn't fair to you."

Elaine's legs gave way beneath her, causing her to sag into a chair opposite her sister, but some of her emotional strength returned. "Then why did you keep doing it?"

"I was such a mess, and so was Mom. You were the only steady person I knew. I'd made so many mistakes, and I just kept making them. I started to worry I couldn't be trusted, but I loved Brooke, and I loved you, and I thought maybe if I couldn't be good for either of you, at least you could be good for each other."

She visually traced the lines of her sister's face. She was a stranger. She'd always been a stranger, yet her patterns were familiar until now. Had this regret and reflectiveness been there for the last twenty years? How had she missed it? "Why didn't you tell me sooner?"

Amy stared at her interlocking fingers, and Elaine saw her own gestures mirrored in the move. "I didn't expect it to take this long.

I've been waiting for a time when I was the steady one and you were weak."

"You were waiting for me to fail?" Anger surged in her. The emotion was out of proportion to the situation, but it scraped against already raw nerves, and she relished the strength that came from having the capacity to feel something other than sadness. "You purposely waited until I was dejected to connect with me? You waited this long to prove yourself at my expense?"

"I've waited my whole life to be your big sister." Amy shot off the couch, anguish etching her features. "When I fell apart and you stayed so strong, I swore someday I'd do it the other way around. I'd show you how much I appreciated all the times you helped me. Every time I disintegrated, I'd keep from hating myself with the thought that someday when you had a broken heart I'd be there for you. I thought by going through it first and learning all my lessons the hard way I might spare you a little bit. That's how it's supposed to work with big sisters. You're supposed to cry on *my* shoulder, but you were too stubborn. You never needed me."

"I did need you. I never stopped needing you, but you never gave me any indication of any of this." Shock, anger, and hurt swirled together. She didn't know who Amy was now, not that she'd ever known. "I wasn't being stubborn. I was trying to find my way."

"Right. You had to do things your own way," Amy said. "You had to prove you could do it on your own, so you left."

"Stop right there. Brooke said the same thing, and it's not fair. I didn't abandon you. I went to college. That's what people do when they graduate, and it's not like you missed me. You only called me twice a year, when something went wrong. You never said you wanted me to come home, or even that you wanted a relationship."

"I was glad you left. I didn't want you to be weighed down by drama, but I didn't want you out of our lives. I did miss you, and I did want a relationship. Whenever my life fell apart, I'd call just to make sure even when everything else was crap, you were okay."

Amy shook her head, sadness clouding her expression. "If you'd just once asked for help or mentioned you'd had a bad day or a worry or a fear, I would've been there, but you never did. You're always so freaking together."

"I have fears, and I've had more than a few bad days. I'm having a pretty terrible one today."

"How could I know? For Godsakes, Lainie, you're so damn walled up in your philosophy and your self-esteem, and your I-don't-even-know-what-you-call-it, but you're this totally together life coach, and I'm your mess of a sister. I get as tired of the one-sidedness as you do. If I couldn't be good for you, I could at least get out of your way."

Elaine stared at her, seeing her for the first time in decades. The worry in her blue eyes, the creases of hurt across her forehead, the sleepless nights throbbing at her temples, the lines of laughter and frowns curving around her mouth—her beauty wasn't just superficial.

"You had more of an effect on me than you realized. I wasn't stubborn to spite you. I was stubborn to save me."

"What do you mean?"

"I never cried on your shoulder with a broken heart because you saved me from heartbreak altogether." Her lips twitched up in a crooked smile. "You were the Nancy Reagan of my love life. Instead of getting burnt, I learned to 'just say no' to love."

"That's not what I wanted." Amy's eyes welled with tears. "I wanted you to get your heart broken, but I wanted to teach you it's not the end of the world, that you were still you and love was still wonderful."

"No, it's not. It's awful." She started to cry.

She didn't know who collapsed into whom, but she was in Amy's arms, and they were both on the couch, tears streaming down their cheeks. "I keep trying to make it go away, to pull myself together, but I can't."

Amy shushed her. "You have to let it take over."

"I can't. It's complicated."

"It always is."

"She's my client. She's been hurt. I've never had a successful relationship. I don't know how to stop being her coach. She's Brooke's age…"

Amy laughed.

"It's not funny." She sobbed.

"I know, honey. You've picked a hell of a starter girlfriend, but anybody who makes my strong, self-assured sister turn into such a mess must be special."

"Joey's amazing." She sat up. "She's sweet, and she's got milk-chocolate brown eyes you could get lost in for hours. She's attentive and thoughtful. She risked her safety just to come talk to me, and she shoveled my walkway even though she was exhausted, and she's got biceps that make you want to feel her arms around you."

"Whew, I think I'd go gay for someone like her. If you don't want her maybe I'll try."

"I do want her." She started to cry again. "But I want her to be happy. I couldn't handle letting her down any more than I already have. She looks at me like I'm the most perfect thing she's ever seen, and I can't stand it because I'm not perfect for her. God, Amy, does it always feel like that?"

"No, not always, but it only takes once and you'll chase the feeling as long you live. You'll lie to yourself and make believe and try to force it when it's not there."

"Oh, God, what should I do?"

"Hold on to her. If you've really fallen in love, you need to do everything you can to keep her as long as you can."

"And what if I can't?" Terror cracked her voice. "What if I'm not built for this kind of emotion? What if I mess up, or mess her up, or—"

"You're already pretty messed up, and she probably is, too."

"How do you do it, Amy? How do you keep falling in love? Why haven't you closed up after as many times as you've been hurt?"

"Maybe I'm weak, or maybe it's wishful thinking, but chasing a dream forever beats not having any dreams at all."

Elaine gasped as the flashback lit up her memory. "To have a dream and not chase it would be terrible."

"Right."

"Joey was sitting right here when I told her that."

"What?"

"She asked me if every dream was meant to come true, and I told her every dream had a purpose and if it was her own dream and not something someone else had convinced her she should want, then she needed to chase it."

"What did she do?"

"She chased it. She was amazing. You should've seen her. She told me she loved me, and I left her hanging all alone."

"Why?" Amy shrieked. "She said she loved you, and you let her leave?"

"Even worse, I let her believe I was disappointed in her, that she'd failed me." Her hands trembled. "My top strength is authenticity and honesty."

"What?"

"My top strength is honesty, authenticity, and genuineness. Those are my guiding principles. I have to live my life in a genuine and authentic way."

"Well, that's nice," Amy said, clearly having lost the direction this conversation had taken.

"I taught Joey to live in line with her values, and then I refused to do the same. No wonder I'm miserable. I value honesty and being true to myself, and I acted like a hypocrite, hiding behind my job and her age and my past."

"Then go be honest with her. Tell her you have to have her."

"I can't. I can't put my own will on her, and I can't pretend to be anything I'm not."

"But you *are* in love with her."

"And I'm terrified of her, and I'm worried about me and not sure what's right in this situation. If I tell her the truth, I have to tell the whole truth. I can't play coy, and I don't think that's how dating usually goes."

"Well, you don't generally tell someone you love them

and you're scared of them and you don't think you can make a relationship work."

She snorted. "I suppose that's not a very romantic start, but it's the only way for me. She's already opened up. I know her fears, her insecurities, and exactly how she feels about me. I can't live with that imbalance."

"Lainie, I wouldn't recommend that route, but what the hell do I know? She fell in love with you despite all the crap you two have against you. What can it hurt to lay it out there?"

The tears threatened to overtake her again. "It could hurt us both a lot."

"Would it hurt more than living without your honesty and authenticity and whatnot?"

She shook her head. There was nothing left to discuss. She had to find the courage to act.

CHAPTER SIXTEEN

January 17

"I hoped you'd be working today." It was the same Buff State coed who'd stopped in before Christmas.

"Hey, I'm glad to see you survived two weeks with your parents."

The girl laughed easily. Joey liked that. She also liked how she didn't wear any makeup. She had a nice smile, too; not as nice as Elaine's, but nothing good would come from comparing the two. Elaine didn't want her, whatever the reason, and this girl did. That was the only real difference that mattered.

"I didn't get your name before. I'm Joey."

"Hi, Joey. I'm Indigo."

"Good to formally meet you, Indigo. What can I get for you today?"

"I'd like a tall, skim, decaf mocha," she said, then nervously added, "and I'd like to know if maybe you'd want to go out sometime. I mean, nothing formal, but maybe we could grab a cup of coffee or something."

Joey grinned with the exuberance of letting herself enjoy the moment. A woman had asked her out, and Indigo's nervousness was endearing. She wasn't gorgeous, and it wasn't love or even lust at first sight, but she was good for Joey's self-esteem.

"I mean, only if you want to."

She glanced around, playfully, catching Lisa's eye for a second.

She was done punting. "Well, we happen to have some coffee right here."

The shop was dead today. The business lunch hour had passed slowly, and most of the students weren't back on campus from their winter break. With the exception of one lonely emo-kid scratching out poetry on a little notebook in the corner and Lisa tapping on her computer, Joey hadn't seen anyone in half an hour. Franklin could handle any customers that trickled in.

"Really?"

"Yeah, why not? I can take a break, at least for a little while."

Indigo brightened, causing Joey's confidence to surge. "Awesome."

Lisa smirked, but Joey didn't pay attention to her. She'd been asked out on a date. She made someone nervous. Someone was excited about her. Of course, she would've liked those feelings to have been mutual, but if unevenness was unavoidable, she preferred this side of the equation.

She quickly made Indigo's mocha, grabbed a bottle of water for herself, and joined her at a table. She sat facing the counter so she could keep an eye on Franklin in case he got busy, and also because it put Lisa out of her line of sight. She didn't need a chaperone.

"What's your major?" Indigo asked.

"History education."

"Cool."

"Yeah, what's yours?"

"English."

"So, do you want to teach?"

"No, I don't really like kids."

"Oh." Joey's interest waned.

"I like to read," Indigo said, "and I like to write."

"I like to read. What do you write?"

"Poetry."

"Oh, that's great," she lied. "I don't read a lot of poetry, but I respect poets." *You respect poets? Oh, my God, that sounded stupid.*

"What do you read?"

"A lot of biographies, history, the classics, even a little romance, everything."

Indigo grinned. "Everything but poetry."

"Sorry. Maybe I should give it another try. You never know, right?"

"It's okay. It's not for everybody. What about TV? What do you watch?"

"Sports mostly. Any sport. Football, hockey, tennis, baseball. I couldn't pick a favorite. What about you?" Her interest rose on the hope that sports could save them, but Indigo's interest seemed to evaporate in inverse proportion.

"I'm more of a reality TV person. I know it's trashy, but I can't turn away from the train wreck."

"I've never seen any reality TV. I pretty much turned off MTV when they stopped playing music videos."

"You like music?" Indigo asked, seeming near frantic to find something to connect on.

"Yeah. My mom was a classic pianist, but she loved singer-songwriters, too. My dad is more of a classic rock influence. I can appreciate anything with a strong melody or powerful lyrics. I'm into Serena Ryder and Jennifer Knapp right now, but I've got Springsteen and Mellencamp in my blood, so the heavier rock stuff also resonates."

"I've never heard of any of those people. I listen to a lot of hip-hop with a little pop, but mostly I like to drown out my thoughts with a big bass beat."

"Huh." Joey shrugged. This was a total disaster. At least Indigo had dimples and was eager to connect. That had to count for something. "I suppose opposites can attract."

"Thanks for saying that," Indigo said, relief filling her voice. "It's hard, you know?"

"Yeah, I do." She covered her hand in a motion of solidarity. Finding a connection was hard, and maybe all they had in common was their willingness to risk something that wasn't easy. She wasn't sure relating should be so hard, but it was, and maybe that was okay, too.

❖

Elaine stripped off her deep green turtleneck and tossed it into a pile on the bed, along with the seven other tops she'd already discarded. This was ridiculous. She'd never acted like such a schoolgirl, even when she'd been a schoolgirl a very long time ago. She was self-aware enough to realize her indecision about her attire served as an outlet for larger concerns about what she planned to do this afternoon, but if she was going to crash and burn, she wanted to look good while doing it.

Maybe she should wear a skirt. A skirt could be sexy or sweet. Then again, she'd never thought of herself as sexy, and she certainly hadn't been sweet lately, but maybe if she projected the image she wanted, she could align her internal identity with it.

"Oh, for crying out loud, it's two p.m. in Buffalo in the middle of January. Wear jeans, Elaine. There's nothing sexy about frostbite.

"And now you're talking out loud to yourself. Lovely."

She didn't know how to be sexy or alluring, and she wasn't even sure she should try. She had to be honest about her fears and admit her shortcomings, but what would that even look like, a burlap sack? No, she needed to feel good about herself. She needed to be comfortable but confident. She reached for a plain white button-down shirt and left two buttons undone, enough to show her collarbones, but traded her plain white underwear for something a little silkier, then blushed.

"Those aren't for Joey to see tonight, or maybe ever. Those are for my own personal state of mind."

Then she quickly covered them with a pair of her tightest jeans in a compromise between utility and appeal, exactly how she hoped her discussion with Joey would present her. Plus the jeans helped hold things in their original place, as opposed to where forty years of gravity wanted them to go. She wasn't twenty-eight, and she couldn't do anything about that, but she didn't have to advertise her age.

Not that it wouldn't become clear if she ever did come fully up against Joey's flat planes and dimpled muscles, and…oh, God, did she really need to think about what they'd look like together naked? She had enough on her mind. She couldn't worry about how their age difference would manifest itself in bed. That prospect was so far off she'd have other days to obsess about it, but only if she made it through today's conversation.

Would Joey even want her after what she told her today? She had fallen in love with the perfect life coach, a composed, elegant, reserved woman. Would she want a complicated nervous wreck who poured a load of insecurity at her feet? She couldn't think like that either. She had to be honest, but she didn't have to flagellate herself. She had to do what was right, regardless of what Joey would decide. She topped off the ensemble with a pair of black snow boots and a black belt. She left her hair down, hoping it would soften her appearance and shed some of the professionalism she never could shake from her persona. She refused to stand in front of the mirror finding fault in every detail, but she did glance at her reflection on her way out the door.

Stopping short, she bit her lip and unfastened one more button, then hurried out. She could lie to herself all she wanted to about trying to induce confidence, but who was she kidding? That little bit of extra skin wasn't a mental exercise; it was for Joey.

Striding across frozen sidewalks, she was glad she'd chosen appropriate footwear instead of something more elegant. She didn't need to worry about literally falling on her ass. That concern was real enough in the figurative sense. She tried to focus on the physical act of putting one foot in front of the other as quickly as possible, but when she rounded the corner to the coffee shop, her determined pace faltered. Through the large front window she could clearly see Joey sitting at a table, her hand over that of another girl, and she was a girl, not a woman. She was young, maybe no more than twenty, and the contrast made Joey look older and stronger than she had ever seen her.

They both laughed, and Elaine's chest constricted. Were they friends? She couldn't see Joey's face, but their postures said they were doing the awkward dance that came with getting to know each other, and the brush of their hands spoke of the possibility of intimacy, however subtle. Had she waited too long?

The coffeehouse door opened, and Lisa stepped out onto the sidewalk, then waited until it had closed fully behind her before she spoke. "What are you doing here?"

Elaine wasn't sure how to answer, so she simply shrugged.

"Wrong answer," Lisa said flatly. "If you're looking for a cup of coffee or want to check up on her, you need to go."

"Lisa, I don't know what to say. If she's moved on, I want her to be happy."

"Well, that's a very PC answer, but I'm neither a coach nor a client, so I'm going to level with you. That's a train wreck in there." She gestured over her shoulder to where Joey and the girl sat. "She's flailing, and it's damned painful to listen to the awkwardness, but she's trying, and that's more than she's done in years. She's got hope, and if you're just here to remind her of what she can't have, you need to leave."

Her frustration welled up again. "That's not fair. I've never meant to hurt Joey. If anything, I've protected her too much. You told me she wasn't a puppy, and you were right. She's a beautiful, sincere, capable woman who doesn't need either of us to tell her when or who or how to love. I didn't see that at first, but I do now."

Lisa smiled broadly, then swung the door open wide and nodded for her to enter.

❖

Joey turned around when she heard someone enter the coffeehouse. Even on break she was always prepared for the next rush of customers, but she wasn't prepared for the rush of emotion that surged through her at the sight of Elaine. All the fragile traction she'd achieved over the last few days blew away like straw in a storm. Her stability, her fortitude, her confidence vanished, leaving her hurt and longing exposed, yet like a firefly she was drawn to the pain over the numbness she'd been dwelling in. Those eyes, those legs, those lips, everything about Elaine snapped one of the threads anchoring her resolve. Elaine smiled with a shyness in her expression she had never seen before, and Joey returned it fully, the burn of blush spreading across her cheeks.

Indigo clearly read the change in Joey's body language. "I should let you get back to work."

Joey looked from Elaine, the woman who could have her heart but didn't want it, back to Indigo, who wanted her affections but didn't inspire them. It was a terrible choice, but one she'd already made. She was done chasing women who didn't want to be caught. "No, it's fine. We can keep talking if you want."

She could see Elaine only out of the corner of her eye, but she noticed her shoulders sag as she continued past them to the counter. She tried to refocus on the conversation they'd been having, but she hung on Elaine's voice as she ordered her chai tea, then listened for her footsteps to fall lightly past on her way out the door, but they didn't. The scrape of a chair across the tile floor said Elaine had taken a seat on the other side of the coffeehouse.

"You're a million miles away," Indigo said.

No, I'm just across the room. "I'm sorry. I'm not good at this."

"Actually you're very good. You're sweet. We just don't have much in common." Indigo squeezed Joey's hand, then stood. "But if you have a sister who's into trashy reality shows, please send her my way."

She grinned. "Actually, the dashingly handsome woman behind the laptop over there is the closest thing I have to a sister. I can guarantee she's been eavesdropping on us, and that's a sort of reality show, right?"

Indigo glanced at Lisa hiding behind her laptop, then grinned and grabbed an ink pen. She scribbled down a phone number on a napkin. "Tell her to watch this week's *Dancing with the Stars* and give me a call."

With that she was gone from the coffeehouse and from Joey's mind. She'd vanished from her focus when Elaine walked in the door, but Joey continued to stare at the wall. She wanted to see Elaine. She missed her terribly, both as a life coach and as the object of hope, but if she went to her now, Elaine wouldn't be either of those things. She had to learn to relate to her in a new way, but what was she to her now? She was so absorbed in her own musings she didn't hear Elaine approach.

"Joey, if you need your space, I want you to have it, but you said if I ever needed to talk to you, I could. And I do. I mean, I'd like to talk to you. At some point."

The uncertainty in Elaine's tone commanded her full attention, if for no other reason than the way it tore at her heart. She stood to meet those devastating blue eyes. "I'll always be here for you. You can talk to me about anything."

Elaine glanced over her shoulder, and Joey followed her line of sight to Lisa, who quickly ducked behind her computer.

"Hang on a second," she said, grabbing the napkin with Indigo's phone number. She balled up the napkin and threw it at Lisa, dropping it on top of her keyboard. When Lisa looked up with a sheepish grin, Joey smiled. "There, I punted to you."

Then she turned to Franklin at the counter. "I'm taking my break. If I'm not back in fifteen minutes, call one of the other clerks and tell them something came up and I need them to cover the last part of my shift."

"Not a problem, boss."

She turned back to Elaine, whose smile transitioned from shyness to a mix of admiration, joy, and perhaps a little fear. Joey fell into that smile the way she had a hundred times before. She had intellectually resolved to move on, but her heart refused to acknowledge her decision. "Come on. Let's go for a walk."

They left, wordlessly strolling slowly along snow-packed sidewalks. She had the strongest urge to hold Elaine's hand, but she suppressed it. Elaine gave her no indication of what she wanted to discuss. As they got farther from the coffeehouse, the silence stretched to the point of discomfort, but she wouldn't break it. Her curiosity mixed with an unsubstantiated dread. Clearly this wasn't a casual meeting, and the suspense nearly suffocated her, but she waited. Elaine shouldn't and wouldn't be rushed into anything. They strolled past the Albright-Knox Art Gallery toward Hoyt Lake, turning onto a park path around the water's edge. Thin lines of snow traced the tree branches overhead, and a fresh dusting crunched beneath their feet.

Elaine sighed several times before finally saying, "Do you mind if we sit?"

"Of course not." Joey steered them toward a park bench at the edge of the lake and brushed the snow from the wooden slats. They both stared at the blue-gray sheet of ice encasing the water.

"Joey," Elaine said, then stopped and took a deep breath, exhaling slowly. "I'm afraid I've been a terrible hypocrite."

"What?" That was the last thing she'd expected Elaine to say.

"I told you to chase your dreams, and I told you to live in line with your purpose, but I haven't done either of those things. I've let fear rule me and I've hidden behind my job, letting my own dreams falter and fade."

She searched Elaine's eyes, trying to find what she hoped to see there, but found only anguish. She was familiar with that feeling and wanted desperately to soothe Elaine. "I don't understand."

"I know you don't because you're wonderful and you dealt with everything you needed to, everything I asked of you. How did you do it?"

"Do what?"

"How did you manage to get over your fears and the past and my job and tell me you loved me even though you knew it probably wouldn't work?"

"It was the right thing to do, and I knew I'd be a wreck until… Wait a second. Did you just suggest you're…Elaine?" Joey wouldn't use the L-word. She didn't want to put any words in Elaine's mouth, but especially not that one.

Tears filled Elaine's eyes. "I am and I do. I'm falling in love with you."

Joey's heart beat like a bass drum against her rib cage, but somehow there was a disconnect between the words and their delivery, as if Elaine continued to withhold something crucial. "Why do I get the feeling there's a 'but' in that sentence?"

Elaine smiled though her tears began to fall. "I wish this could be like in the movies. I wish we could both say 'I love you' and the music would swell and the scene would fade out on our embrace so we could live happily ever after. You deserve that, but I'm not the kind of person who can give it to you."

"But you're falling in love with me?" She wasn't trying to ignore the other stuff, but she had to grasp the big issue first.

"Yes. I'm a mess. I've been a mess for weeks. I should've told you. I wanted to tell you. I was even prepared to, but you were so sure of yourself, and you seemed to have made peace, and I was anything but peaceful. I had nothing to offer you but fear and insecurity."

"About what?" It was hard to hear anything with tears streaming down Elaine's beautiful face. The urge to hold her, to comfort her, to love her was enough to break her, but she had to get to the bottom of that pain or she'd unravel.

"About what?" Elaine sniffled and wiped her eyes with her sleeve. "I'm forty-two years old. I've never been in love. I'm your life coach, for Godsakes, Joey. I'm not attractive relationship material."

"Are you still my life coach?" she asked in mock horror. "I thought I fired you."

"You fired me?" Elaine looked startled, then burst out laughing.

Her easy, melodic laugh thrilled Joey. "Okay, fine. I broke up with you."

"That's so much better." Elaine sighed. "We've broken up before our first date."

They hadn't had a first date. After all the time they'd spent together, all the obstacles they'd already overcome, and admitting they were falling in love, they'd yet to go on a date. This wasn't how it was supposed to happen. This was supposed to be a happy moment, and yet here they were both overwhelmed with drama, Elaine crying and Joey in a shocked stupor. How had they come to this? Better yet, how could they fix it? Couldn't they go back to the beginning or build a new one that gave them the chance they deserved?

"Joey?" Elaine asked, the insecurities creeping back into her voice.

"Yes?"

"What are you thinking?"

"Would you like to go ice skating with me?"

"Right now?"

"I've waited an awfully long time for a date with you. I'd rather not wait any longer, but I will if you've got other plans—"

"No." Elaine paused, her lips curved slightly upward as she mulled over the offer. Joey could feel the uncertainty radiating from her, but she refused to dwell on possibilities of what might go wrong. They both knew the risks, and they'd gotten a taste of what life was like apart from each other. Shouldn't they at least give their potential a chance? She could overlook anything for a few hours of possibility. Apparently Elaine was willing to delay the inevitable, too, because she finally said, "There's nothing else I'd rather do this afternoon."

Chapter Seventeen

Elaine hadn't ice-skated since high school, but she couldn't muster much nervousness with Joey beside her. Her exuberance was contagious, and Elaine was grateful she had neither made light of her concerns nor given in to her gremlins. They crossed Elmwood Avenue to the Buffalo State campus. Her lighter side rebounded in the face of Joey's playfulness, and she hoped that could sustain them. She wanted to enjoy herself and Joey, even if only for now, especially if only for now.

Joey handed an ID to a young man behind the counter at the entrance to the college ice arena. "We need two skate rentals."

"Hockey or figure skates?"

"Hockey size seven for me."

"What's the difference between hockey skates and figure skates?" she asked.

"Toe pick," Joey and the young man said in unison.

She wasn't sure what that meant, but decided to follow Joey's lead. "I'll have hockey skates in a size seven as well."

The employee went to a back room to fetch the skates, and Joey grinned at Elaine. "Who would've thought we wore the same size shoes."

"Do you want to borrow some of mine sometimes?"

"Maybe. Do you have any cute black strappy heels?"

"When was the last time you wore cute black strappy heels?"

Joey cocked her head to the side in her endearing way as she pondered the question. "When I was eight. I had a piano recital. My mom and I wore matching outfits."

"I bet that was precious."

Joey blushed. "It was awkward. The next year I wore a suit coat like my dad."

"I bet that was precious, too."

The employee returned with their skates and Joey's ID, but when he laid the card on the counter Elaine snatched it up, realizing it wasn't a license, but a student ID. *I'm a forty-two year old woman on a date with a college coed.* "When did you get this?"

"Last week," Joey said shyly, staring at her shoes.

She turned back to the picture. Joey's expression in the photo was one of sheer pride, and she wished she could have a copy, but she wasn't comfortable blurting that out yet. Instead she handed it back to Joey. "It's a flattering photo."

"Thanks."

They sat on wooden bleachers to put on their skates.

Joey laced up quickly and confidently, but Elaine fumbled nervously. Ice-skating? What had she been thinking? Her last date had been at a wine bar a block off Broadway, and she'd barely survived. How on earth would she manage not to kill herself while trying to stay graceful on a thin blade and a sheet of ice? As if their age difference wasn't stark enough, now she risked breaking a hip.

Joey knelt beside her and took the skate laces from her hands, tying them swiftly and tight. "Don't worry. I'll catch you if you fall."

"How'd you know what I was thinking?"

"When you're worried, you get this adorable little crease between your eyebrows, and in this case I figured you were worried about falling on the ice or falling for me. Either way, my response is the same."

How did Joey manage to be so perfect when she was so shaky? Joey's heart had been broken. She understood the pain Elaine could only guess at, yet she remained so wonderfully hopeful.

"Come on." Joey took her hand and led her onto the rink. "Don't give the gremlins time to start chattering."

She didn't lose her balance the minute her skates touched the ice, which was better than she'd feared. After making a few tentative shuffles she got bolder, pushing off more forcefully. She didn't fall. With each stride she grew more confident, not that she displayed any Olympic-caliber skill, but she hadn't hurt herself yet.

"You're doing great." Joey skated backward a foot in front of her to watch her form. A rink attendant sat on a bench at the edge of the ice, but other than that they had the place to themselves. Two o'clock on a Monday clearly wasn't peak ice-skating time, and she liked it that way. She'd spent so many hours alone with Joey, but this felt like a first for them. The boundaries hadn't disappeared, but they'd been set aside for the time being.

Eager to get out of her head and into a conversation with Joey, she asked, "Do you still play piano?"

"My dad has Mom's piano at his house, and I tinker on it, but I'm not the musician she was. Thankfully, she never expected me to be."

"How did they take it when you came out?"

"They didn't throw me a parade or anything, but I had it better than most. My mom worried I'd have a hard road ahead of me. My dad was genuinely perplexed, but they both said they loved me, and that's what mattered. What about you?"

"My family didn't care."

"It didn't bother them or they didn't care?"

Joey was much more perceptive than she'd originally noticed. "They didn't care. My mother's health had deteriorated. My sister was a single mom of a five-year-old, and I hadn't visited them in years. I just slipped it casually into a phone call with Amy."

"You slipped it in casually?"

"I said something like, 'I'm seeing a woman now. We've been dating a few months, but mostly I'm focused on school. By the way, did Brooke like the teddy bear I sent for her birthday?'"

"Wow. Didn't leave much room for a conversation, did you?"

"I guess I didn't. It's funny. At the time I thought I'd opened a big discussion. Now I see I made a declaration."

Joey turned around so they were both skating the same direction, slow, easy laps around the edge of the rink. "I take it you've always preferred to let other people do the talking?"

"I don't know how much of that's natural introversion and how much is learned, but I do live in my head a lot."

"Ya think?" Joey teased her. "I'm at a disadvantage here. You've got a full discovery form on me, and I know virtually nothing about you."

"Huh." She kept skating.

"Come on. Don't huh me." Joey laughed. "I'm not asking you to list ten goals for this relationship."

The mix of allusion to her role as a coach and reminder of how far she'd strayed from their original purpose shattered her concentration. One of her skates went out from under her, but before she had a chance to flail, much less fall, Joey's arm wrapped around her waist, gently stabilizing her.

"I've got you," she said calmly, her proximity and her low tone causing goose bumps to rise along Elaine's neck. *God, she's sexy.*

"Thank you."

"My pleasure," Joey said with a wink, "but don't think you'll get out of my questions so easily."

Joey was right. It wasn't fair for her to do all the revealing, all the opening up. She didn't purposely withhold parts of herself. She'd just developed those habits from years of staying safe. "I don't mean to dodge. What do you want to know?"

"Start with all those awkward, first-date questions. What kind of music do you like?"

"That is a good, small-talk topic. I like singer-songwriters, folk, a little bit of soul."

Joey nodded. "I'm right there with you. What about TV?"

"I don't own one."

"Right. I never saw one in your place, but I thought it could be in the bedroom."

She grinned. "Have you been speculating about the TV or the bedroom?"

"No, I haven't, I've never even thought about…I mean obviously

I know you have a bedroom, but not during our sessions…anyway, you don't have a TV. That's cool."

She laughed. She liked to know she wasn't the only one unnerved by her attraction. Joey had become so confident over the past weeks, it was refreshing Elaine could still affect her. "It's okay, but are you a TV junkie?"

"Not hardly. I'm a sports junkie. If the TV is on, I'm watching a ball or a puck."

"That makes sense. You're very athletic."

Joey's blush made Elaine ache to touch her. "I'm not really, but what I lack in grace, I make up in gusto. I suppose that's true of life in general."

"That's interesting you think you lack grace and feel the need to compensate."

Joey stopped. "I find it interesting you just used your coaching voice on me."

"Did I?" The insecurities rumbled to the surface again. She'd used her life-coaching persona because that was how she was used to relating to Joey. It was easy and comfortable and fitting. "It's a hard habit to break. Let's try again. I think you're very graceful, both physically and with life in general."

"Thanks, I wasn't fishing for compliments, but that's a nice one coming from one of the most graceful women I know."

How did Joey manage to gently call her out, get her to open up authentically, then leave her high on a rush of gratitude?

"Back to sports. You're a Bills fan, right?"

"I don't really follow sports."

"Okay, I know what you *said*, but you have to understand I *heard*, 'Yes, of course I'm a Bills fan.'"

She laughed. "Okay, good to know."

"Where'd you go to school?"

"Columbia for my undergrad and then, a few years later, NYU for my master's."

"Impressive schools."

The clearly visible flash of panic in Joey's beautiful eyes

reminded her that education was still a complex subject, but she stifled the urge to soothe or protect Joey. She wasn't her coach now, and the impulse to revert into that mindset would only hurt them both. Still, she had a hard time finding an appropriate answer. "I was very studious."

"That's not surprising. I would've been shocked if you'd said you weren't."

"You don't see me as a party girl?"

Joey shook her head, causing a stray strand of hair to fall across her forehead. Elaine fought the compulsion to run her hand through it. "Nope, you don't strike me as the kind of girl who's ever done a keg stand."

"And have you?"

"Maybe." Joey's grin turned sly. "A long time ago."

"A long time ago? What, when you were ten?"

Joey's laughter echoed into the rafters of the arena, warming Elaine despite the surrounding ice. "Sometimes it feels like that long ago."

"You had to grow up quickly."

"That's something we have in common." Joey said.

She hadn't made that connection until now. Neither one of them had had the luxury of aging into responsibility and steadiness. At times Joey's interpersonal experiences made her seem older, though Elaine had carried burdens beyond her years in other areas. Maybe their similar emotional age outweighed their chronological age difference. If it was really just a number and true compatibility lay in their capacity to relate on deep levels, maybe they were a better match than she had allowed herself to believe. Or perhaps being close to Joey rendered her incapable of focusing on anything.

❖

After nearly an hour of skating, talking, laughing, and enjoying each other's company, they took a break in the bleachers so the Zamboni could refresh the ice.

Joey couldn't stop stealing glances at Elaine. At times it was so easy to be with her, their connection completely natural, but other moments she'd get a jolt of awareness that she was actually on a date with the woman she'd dreamed about. She found it hard to believe this stunning, caring, intelligent woman wanted to be with her. She was radiant as she lounged casually on the bleachers with her feet kicked out in front of her and her elbows resting on the bench above where they were seated.

The position elongated her torso, drawing Joey's attention to the subtle rise and fall of her chest with each breath. She had to readjust her line of sight several times, but her eyes kept straying to the tantalizing bit of skin between the open buttons of her white oxford. She didn't intentionally stare at Elaine's chest, but she did appreciate the hint of sexuality she'd never let herself indulge in within the confines of the coaching relationship. Not that Joey wanted to objectify Elaine's body just because she wasn't paying her, but she did give herself a little more leeway.

Joey blushed at her line of thought and forcibly turned her attention to Elaine's eyes, which were no less sexy than the part she'd been admiring. If anything, she found the intense blue gaze more alluring.

"So what did you think of ice skating?"

"I enjoyed myself. I'm pretty sure I'll feel the effects in my leg muscles for days, but it was worth it."

"You did really well. I kind of expected to have to hold your hand the whole time."

Elaine's smile widened. "Oh, so that's what you were going for."

Her cheeks warmed. "You can't fault a boi for trying."

She wanted to take Elaine's hand now, but what if she pulled away? She got the sense Elaine still felt uncertain about a lot of things, and she didn't want to scare her by going too fast, but she also didn't want to miss an opportunity. There wasn't a playbook for first dates, especially first dates with as much baggage as they'd brought along. She decided to give Elaine some space.

"We don't have to stay if you're tired. I could walk you home," Joey offered, praying Elaine wouldn't accept, then more hopefully added, "Or we could go get some hot chocolate or something, maybe dinner?"

Elaine mulled that over. She stared at the Zamboni and the smooth surface it laid over their tracks on the ice. She hoped that if she was a metaphorical person, Elaine saw the smooth ice as indicative of a fresh start rather than a message to wipe clean the progress they'd made.

"I'd like to have dinner with you, but…"

Joey's breath became labored under the weight of the suspense. *Please, please, please, say yes*. "But?"

"No SpaghettiOs, okay?"

Laughter rode the waves of relief that spilled out of her. "Deal. In fact, why don't we go back to my place?"

Elaine raised her eyebrows.

"No." Her blush heated to the point she wondered if her face would ever cool. "I didn't mean we, I thought at my house, I meant… I'd like to cook dinner for you."

"I'd love to see what you can really do in a kitchen." Elaine's smile was sweet with equal parts amusement and adoration. "And I'd like to see your house, too."

"Really?"

"That's one area where you know more about me than I do you. You've been in my apartment. You even slept there, but I've never seen your home."

"I hadn't thought about that." They unlaced their skates.

"You've also met my family. Taylor even likes you more than he likes me."

"I doubt that, but he's a pretty great kid. And those eyes, he's got your eyes. Do they run in your family?"

"Yeah, the baby blues come from my mother. She was very Nordic. What about you? Do you favor your mom or your dad?"

"I'm a lot more like my dad overall. I've got his mannerisms and his interests and his personality, but I look like my mom. She was small with darker hair. I've also got her eyes, which is only fair because she used those brown eyes on me my whole childhood. She hardly ever yelled, but if her eyes started to water, I knew I'd disappointed her or hurt her feelings, and you'd never seen a kid clean a room faster than I did when I got one of her guilt trips."

"Then you do have her eyes," Elaine said softly. "Yours are the most expressive ones I've ever seen. I noticed them about you first thing. I should've known I was in trouble right then."

"Really?"

"Absolutely," Elaine said. "I've spent a lot of time wondering what would've happened if my top strength had been bravery and valor. If I'd had a touch of your courage, maybe I would've said yes the first time you asked me out."

She stopped tying her boots. She couldn't believe what she'd just heard. Elaine had been attracted to her all along? "Why didn't you say something sooner?"

Elaine considered the question as she bit her lip, causing Joey to wonder what she was holding back. "It's not easy for me, Joey. I know it wasn't for you either. Especially after today I understand how much you put yourself on the line, but it took me longer to get to the place where you started. You've always understood our purpose better than I have. I wish I could follow your lead, but bravery and valor are in your top strengths. Mine are caution, prudence, and discretion."

That sounded daunting, but at least she acknowledged she wanted to believe in their potential. Elaine's cautious side wasn't an earth-shattering revelation. In fact, maybe her prudence had ended up saving them. Joey was a different person now than she'd been when they met. The inner critics occasionally whispered about how much Elaine outclassed her, but now they didn't cripple her, and she had Elaine the life coach to thank for that.

"I'm sorry if I killed the mood."

"No, not at all. I was actually thinking that everything has its purpose. You told me that at our first meeting, and it's true. Our purpose is just evolving."

Elaine's smile returned to full force. "Did you memorize everything I ever said?"

"Maybe." She stood, offering her hand. "Or maybe I just held on to the stuff I hoped to turn around on you someday."

"And what was that?"

"You'll have to stick around longer if you want to find out."

Elaine accepted her hand, giving Joey a thrill completely disproportionate to the amount of skin she was touching. Her elegant fingers closed around Joey's, captivating her with the same softness and grace that marked every other interaction they'd shared. The simple touch made her ache for more. She wanted her arms around Elaine's waist, her lips against the soft skin of her neck, her body pressed into the hollows and curves mirroring her own.

Then Elaine bounded down the stairs and out the door ahead of her. She stifled a groan at the disconnect. She couldn't let a little tease of possibility throw her back into the chase. Elaine needed time to adjust, and she refused to pressure her, so she followed at a respectable distance. It might not be the level of closeness she'd hoped for, but at least from this angle she could enjoy the view.

❖

Elaine wanted to take Joey's hand as they walked back across campus. She longed for it in a way she'd heard described in love songs but never experienced. She craved her touch with a frightening intensity. She could reach for Joey as easily as Joey could reach for her, but years of practice rendered her incapable of putting desire into action. She couldn't break down twenty-five years of defenses in one day, but how long would it take to unlearn those bad habits? How long could she ask Joey to be patient? How long could she stand waiting when the want burned so strongly inside her?

They crossed Elmwood and strolled down past the art gallery and on to Lincoln Parkway. The farther they went, the deeper she retreated into her own head. What had she been thinking? She'd had such a wonderful time playing with Joey she had let herself forget they faced a world full of obstacles. Emotionally, Joey was perfect in every way Elaine was flawed, but her openness, her faith, her trust added to the overwhelming responsibility weighing on her shoulders. Joey loved her, and she was falling more in love with Joey every second, but she worried what devastation she'd bring if she couldn't quiet the gremlins. She wanted a real relationship, but she wouldn't be able to live with herself if she disappointed Joey. Her inadequacies kept her from relaxing fully, no matter how much she wanted to.

"It's only dinner, you know? We don't have to pick out wedding rings or baby names," Joey said, a half smile tugging at her lips.

Elaine stopped and stared at her. "Joey, do you have psychic abilities?"

Joey threw back her head and laughed, her dark hair shaking out in waves that begged to be touched. "I was mostly talking to myself, but I'm glad it resonated with you. Were you trying to decide on a name for a boy or a girl?"

She shook her head, and they started walking again. "I think we've moved out of the awkward-first-date questions."

"What, you don't think asking someone on a first date what they want to name your unborn children is awkward?"

"Good point. I haven't decided on kids' names yet, though."

"Quite all right. That's more of a second-date conversation, after the U-Haul."

"See, I'm out of practice. I don't know the Robert's Rules for lesbian dating."

"It's okay to be nervous. I've got the jitters, too." Joey's words were laced with an earnest sweetness. "It's not like I'm any more current in the dating department than you are."

"I don't know, I haven't had a first date in over a year, and I haven't had a second date in…I can't even remember how long it's been since I had a second date."

"Well, I suppose I'm slightly better off than you are. I had a first date this afternoon, though nothing I'd like for us to emulate."

Elaine did an admirable job of ignoring the pang of jealousy that lanced through her chest. "Is that what I interrupted back at the coffeehouse?"

"You put us both out of our misery."

She released the breath caught in her throat. "I'm sorry your first time back out there wasn't more reaffirming."

"Are you?"

"No, I'm not. I'm glad it was terrible. I don't know if I could've stood it if you'd wanted to see her again. I don't even know why I said that."

"You didn't." Joey grinned. "My life coach did."

"I'm glad *you* can separate the two."

"I can't, but it seems to make you feel better when I try," Joey said with her characteristic shrug. "You know you're still a life coach, right?"

She nodded, tension encasing her back and tightening her throat.

"You can't escape your job, and I don't want you to. It's a huge part of you, and if not for that part of you, we wouldn't be here now. I'd still be a bumbling mess of nerves. I would've fallen completely to pieces after my crash-and-burn attempt at dating this morning. The old Joey would've seen that as reaffirmation of all my inadequacies and hidden for months. I sure wouldn't have been able to go on another date, especially one that actually mattered, a few hours later."

"I'm afraid you've fallen for Elaine the life coach, and you'll be disappointed by Elaine the woman."

"Try me."

"What?"

"I know you think you'll let me down, and there's nothing I can say to make you believe I see so much more in you than your job, but give me a chance to show you."

She didn't know what to say. The sincerity of Joey's plea ripped at her heart. She wanted to kiss Joey and run away simultaneously, but instead of engaging either of those authentic emotions, she chose the safe path and changed the subject. "Now I know we've moved into second-date material."

Joey looked like she wanted to say something, as if she were considering calling her out, but instead she kept walking. "Maybe we can label this our second date. I think we know each other well enough to be on the accelerated program. First date ice skating, second date dinner."

"Two dates in one day, can you handle that?"

Joey teased her. "Technically, I've had three dates today."

She bumped her shoulder into Joey playfully. "If you can pretend I'm a Bills fan, I'm going to pretend the other date never happened, okay?"

"Deal."

Maybe they could make a pact to ignore all the things they didn't want to face. Maybe they could pretend to be ageless, jobless women with no romantic pasts.

"This is my street," Joey said, turning down Granger Place. "Ours is right there."

The moss-colored Victorian with maroon-and-cream gingerbread trim was squeezed into a row of similar style homes, but it carried a charm all its own. An impeccably shoveled walkway led to an inviting front porch and a maroon door with a leaded-glass window. There was a second-story balcony, and light spilled from every window into the growing dusk. Joey bounded up the stairs and threw open the door, revealing hardwood floors and an intricately detailed stairway. The large living room had a sizable fireplace that effused warmth even though it wasn't lit. "It's beautiful, Joey."

"Thanks. Lisa owns it, but we've done all the restoration together. I refinished the floor and built the mantel over the fireplace. She did all the decorating, though."

"Is she home?"

"Doesn't look like it." She wandered into the dining room and picked up a note on the table. Elaine read over her shoulder. "Dear Eeyore, the receiving team would like to thank you for punting. I caught the ball and ran right to dinner and a movie. Don't wait up. First down, Lisa. P.S. Can't wait to review your highlight reel tomorrow."

"Are those a bunch of sports references I don't get?"

Joey turned around, drawing attention to the proximity of their bodies. "I, um, I could explain if you wanted, but basically we have the house to ourselves tonight."

Elaine watched the pupils of Joey's already dark eyes dilate as the scent of her cologne filled her senses. She was close, too close. Joey's lips parted but no words came. *She's going to kiss me. Please kiss me. God, I'm going to kiss her. If I kiss her now, I may never stop.* The words rolled through her mind and reverberated to the tips of her toes, but the soundtrack of her desire wasn't the only voice in her head. The chorus of inner critics began chanting, too. *She's practically a child. You failed her as a coach. You'll fail her as a lover. You'll get hurt. She'll get hurt. You're both going to get hurt.*

She couldn't take any more, so she wrenched free of her trance and took a step back. "Great. So what does the master chef have planned for dinner?"

Joey smiled through a heavy sigh and headed toward the kitchen with forced cheerfulness. "Let's just say I hope you're not one of those girls who starves herself on weird diets, because in the Lang household we eat both meat and carbs."

Elaine squeezed her hands into fists and released them several times, trying to make the blood circulate back to her tingling extremities. What was wrong with her? She had an infinitely desirable woman alone and practically pressed up against her. They were two consenting adults who connected physically, intellectually, and emotionally. She'd never experienced anything like this encompassing attraction, and on top of it she was falling in love with someone who returned her love with equal if not greater ferocity. This was as perfect as it was ever going to get, and still she couldn't let go.

Maybe her subconscious was telling her something. She stilled her mind and listened. She couldn't distinguish her inner critic from her authentic voice, or maybe they were both saying the same thing for once. Either way, the voice had a clear message.

She was a coward.

❖

Joey carried two plates of steak Alfredo penne into the dining room, and Elaine followed with a basket of garlic bread. "This smells fantastic. I can't believe you just whipped it up out of nothing."

"It didn't come out of nothing. I mixed cream and parmesan and garlic, a bit of veggies, and a lot of beef."

"I know. I watched you, but this looks like something from a restaurant."

"Well, it's not SpaghettiOs, but I hope it's worthy of your praise."

Elaine shook her head. "Funny boi."

She grinned but felt the tension under the jokes. They ping-ponged between beautifully unguarded moments of pure enjoyment to flashes of hyperawareness of who they were and how badly this could go wrong. The seesawing of her emotions was taking its toll, and she compensated by working to keep the tone light. "Would you like a glass of wine?"

"I'd love one."

"Red to go with the beef, or white to match the pasta?"

"Which do you recommend?"

"I don't know. Lisa is the wine connoisseur of the house. I don't drink."

"You mentioned that to Brooke. Is there something I should be aware of?"

"My mom died of liver failure, and my dad spent the next year drinking himself into a whiskey coma to numb the pain and had a hard time reining it back in. Both sides of my gene pool have sufficiently warned me to stay away from alcohol, but unless your DNA sent you similar messages, please don't pass on the wine."

Elaine mulled over her decision while Joey waited. She wasn't nearly as comfortable with silence as Elaine. Did she worry about Joey's reaction? Did she see her as fragile? Joey didn't need protection, pity, or caution. She wanted to be Elaine's equal. She wanted to give her space and time and freedom, but they needed to be in this together, and Elaine was handling her with kid gloves. She couldn't stand for Elaine to see her as the old Joey.

"I'll try the white."

"Great." She beamed and bounded back into the kitchen.

She poured a glass of wine and returned to the table a touch more confident. Elaine had already eaten several bites of her pasta. "Sorry, I couldn't wait. It's amazing."

She let her pride run unencumbered. "Thank you."

"Where did you learn to cook?"

"Both my parents, really. Mom made miracles with just a few ingredients. Dad never met a piece of meat he couldn't grill. I guess I combined their styles."

"My mother was actually a pretty good cook, too, and so is Amy. Don't get me wrong. I'm passable, but nothing like this. I'm not above cereal for dinner a couple times a week."

The idea of Elaine snuggled up on her couch with a bowl of Cheerios was actually pretty wonderful. Those personal touches made her love Elaine the real woman even more than Elaine the impeccable life coach.

"What?" Elaine asked.

"Huh?"

"You just gave a little twitch of a grin, like you had a nice thought you wanted to keep to yourself."

"Who's psychic now? I think it's sweet you eat cereal for dinner."

"Sweet? A cook like you doesn't find that horrifying?"

"I know you think I'm just into the image you project, but believe it or not, I love the fact you eat cereal for dinner, the way you bite your lip when you're holding something in, how you don't pretend to understand my sports references, that you couldn't wait to start eating, and that this list of things I love about you makes you a nervous wreck."

Elaine's lips parted on a silent breath. "I'm sorry, Joey. You're so amazing. You're perfect, really, and I'd give anything for a fraction of your openness. It's not that I don't feel those things or don't want to express them, but I don't know if I'm capable."

Not capable. The words echoed through the emptiness in Joey's chest where her heart had been beating. Here was the "it's not you, it's me" speech. She'd known this was a possibility, but she hadn't really believed it would happen. She was a hopeless romantic. Despite all her past heartbreak and all the progress she'd made with Elaine's coaching, she was still an "all you need is love" kind of boi, and when Elaine admitted she loved her, she thought the rest would eventually fall into place. What an idiot.

"Joey, please don't look like that. You're wonderful, and if I could ever let go and love anyone recklessly it'd be you. You're everything I could ever dream of."

"But I'm still not enough."

"I find it interesting that I've listed my own crucial fault, yet you've still placed that burden on yourself. What would you have said to me if the reverse were true?"

"Please don't," Joey whispered.

"Don't what?"

"Please don't coach me right now." She pushed her hands roughly through her hair. "If we're not right for each other I can handle that. Somehow I'll get through. But if you go back behind your professional façade and leave me with my heart beating outside my chest, I don't know if I'll ever find my dignity again."

"You're right." Elaine bit her lips as a tear spilled down her cheek. "This is ripping me apart, too. If I could be someone else for you, I would."

"I don't want you to be someone else. I've only ever wanted you."

"I'm sorry."

"Stop apologizing." She rose and walked over to Elaine. She couldn't take any more distance between them. She pulled Elaine into her arms. This wasn't the way she'd hoped to be close to her, but Elaine was in anguish, and Joey loved her. As much as she wanted to curl up in her own hurt, her desire to soothe was stronger. "It'll be okay."

"I never wanted to hurt you."

"I know you didn't, but I've never had any regrets with you, and I don't want you to have any about me. I don't want to be a lapse in judgment for you. I don't want you to think of today as a failure." Her voice cracked. "I don't want to be tied to your sadness."

Elaine rested her head on Joey's shoulder. "What's the matter with me?"

"Nothing." She pulled Elaine close, running her hands up her back, soaking up every sensation. This memory would be all she had to sustain her in the long nights of heartbreak ahead. She needed to imprint the perfection of Elaine's body on her heart and mind. She had to fortify herself with everything right about holding Elaine in order to find the strength to let her go. "To me, you're perfect."

She took a deep breath, then stepped back.

Elaine stared at her with red-rimmed eyes. "You're perfect, Joey."

"We're just not perfect for each other, and that'll have to be okay."

"I have to go," Elaine said.

An icy resolve spread through her. If she couldn't be the one to keep Elaine happy, she could at least minimize her pain by giving her up gracefully. "Can I take you home?"

"No, the walk will be good for me."

Joey nodded, grateful she wouldn't have to keep up her bravado much longer. She followed Elaine as far as the front porch.

Elaine turned tearfully to her, letting the unspoken settle between them, then looked away. "You really don't have any regrets?"

She paused, suspended between what she knew she should do and what she wanted to do. This might be her last chance, and she truly wanted to make sure she left her conscience as clean as possible. She didn't have anything left to lose. "Just one."

"What's that?"

She cupped Elaine's face gently in her hands, threading her fingers through the soft hair at the base of her neck. "I regret not doing this sooner." She closed the breath of distance between them, bringing her lips lightly across Elaine's.

She expected Elaine to stiffen or pull away. She prepared herself for that final rejection. She hadn't kissed her in hopes of changing her mind. She'd kissed her because it was her last chance to do so, one final fix for a need that would never subside. Still, the softest caress of Elaine's lips told her this thirst was unquenchable. She could deepen the kiss, draw it out all night, or repeat it a thousand times, and still want more.

❖

Elaine melted into Joey's kiss. No logic, only need. Maybe somewhere in her intellect she was aware of the havoc this kiss could bring, but her intellect lost its power the instant Joey's lips touched hers. For once she acted on pure instinct. Her heart, her gut, her authentic self took charge and emboldened her as she snaked an arm around Joey's waist, drawing their bodies against each other. Parting her lips, she sought Joey more completely. For a woman who'd been walking away seconds earlier, she certainly couldn't get close enough now. No question, no fear, no concern for the past or the future, only the most profound understanding of how right this was.

Then, as unexpectedly as she'd started the kiss, Joey ended it. Wrenching herself free, she stared at Elaine. Her deep brown eyes swirled with lust and agony. "I can't do this."

Elaine staggered slightly backward, breathless and raw from the void Joey's body had left against her own. She wasn't sure whose agony she felt more acutely. Perhaps the two couldn't be separated.

"I can't take this back-and-forth. I can't hold you and then let you go." Joey threw back her head, as if searching the heavens for some divine intervention. "I can't stand to keep kissing you, then watch you leave."

She was wrong. If she left right now, Joey would survive. She'd hurt, but she'd heal. Elaine couldn't say the same for herself. Her choice was no longer between safety and consequence. It wasn't even between the familiar and the unknown. She knew now where she was meant to be, and to deny that for any reason would be to reject her essence. She couldn't leave Joey any more than she could command her heart to stop beating.

"I don't know what you want, and I'm not sure *you* even know what you want or don't want," Joey said.

That might have been true a minute earlier, but now she knew what she didn't want. She didn't want to be responsible, or safe, or strong. More important, she finally knew what she did want. Joey. She needed Joey, needed her in a powerful, uncontrollable way that would've terrified her if she were capable of fear, but the only thing she could process was her irrepressible desire.

"I can't kiss you like that and then stop," Joey whispered.

"Don't," she answered. "Don't ever stop kissing me like that."

This time when they collided, Elaine took control, pressing her lips, her chest, her legs to Joey's. The kiss was furious, without any of their previous emotional or physical distance. She clung to Joey, their mouths parted in bruising exploration. She'd spent decades fighting, dodging, and protecting herself from even the hint of something all-consuming, but now, in the face of true passion, desire, and love, she couldn't summon a single doubt. Where was her resolve to walk away, to save them from themselves? Had it really evaporated when Joey's lips touched hers? She ran her hands up Joey's arms and over her shoulders, sinking her fingers into Joey's thick, dark hair. She wanted to pull her in completely. She couldn't get enough of something she'd been abandoning just seconds ago.

Oh my God, I almost turned away from this. Her legs weakened beneath her, but Joey's arms around her waist held her securely. How had she been so blind? She'd examined their relationship a hundred times, driving herself crazy with doubt and indecision as she weighed the pros and cons from every intellectual, professional, and rational standpoint, when all she had to do to find the clarity she craved was listen to her gut, her heart, her body.

She'd known this was right all along on her most fundamental level, yet she would've likely kept denying it if Joey hadn't kissed her. She shivered at the thought of how close she'd come to leaving perfection.

Joey halted the kiss but didn't break the contact between them. "Are you cold?"

"No," she whispered, resting her forehead on Joey's. "I'm scared."

"Scared?" Joey started backward, giving her the distance to search Elaine's eyes. "Of me? Of this?"

"Absolutely not. I'm scared of me. It's terrifying to think I almost let you go. And now these emotions are so overwhelming."

"Okay," Joey said. "Maybe we need to slow down and think this through."

"No," she said forcefully. "I don't need to think. I just need you."

Joey's smile was effervescent. "You've got me."

"I need more of you." Her body surged to life again. Now that it had been heard, it wouldn't go back to being ignored. She practically threw herself at Joey, pressing her against the front door as their mouths connected again. She moaned as Joey's tongue swept across hers. She couldn't and wouldn't be fulfilled on the front porch, so without breaking contact she reached past her and opened the door, causing both of them to stumble into the entryway.

Joey must've gotten the message, because she didn't waste time, walking backward up the stairs. The path wasn't easy with their mouths locked together and their hands grasping each other's clothes. They successfully kicked off their shoes as they went, but after only a few steps they stumbled, sinking down onto the stairs. She didn't care. She couldn't wait any longer.

Clutching the hem of Joey's shirt, she pulled it over her head, revealing a thin white T-shirt. She could clearly make out the outline of Joey's small, firm breasts and the rippled planes of her stomach. Hungry for bare skin, she slid her hands under Joey's shirt and started to work it up over her head, but Joey's foot slipped over the edge of the step and sent them both down a level with a thud.

Joey laughed and wrapped an arm around Elaine's waist, pulling her up. "Come on. Let's do this right."

They giggled as Joey half pulled, half carried her up the remaining stairs and through her bedroom door. Joey turned and looked at her, her laughter dying out as her eyes grew serious and intense. "I need you to know I don't take this lightly. I want you so badly I can hardly stand, but I also respect you, and I care about you and…" She shrugged and grinned with a mix of sweet and sexy that drove Elaine wild. "I love you."

She cupped Joey's face in her hands. "And I love you." Then instead of closing the remaining distance between them, she placed her hands flat against Joey's chest and pushed her back onto the bed. She stood with her eyes fixed on Joey's as she unbuttoned the last three buttons of her shirt, then let it fall to the floor. A surge of power and passion mingled in her as Joey's dark eyes dilated with lust. She lifted her hand to unclasp her bra, but Joey sat up and scooted to the edge of the bed, placing her hands on Elaine's hips and drawing her into the space between her knees. She placed light kisses down Elaine's abs and stomach, the heat in her touch rebuffing any criticism Elaine had for her own body. Joey slowly worked back up to Elaine's bra and ran her lips over its lace cups. The warmth of her breath teased Elaine's skin, and she sank her hands into Joey's hair to hold her close. Joey unclasped the bra, then gently lowered the straps from Elaine's shoulders before letting it fall to the floor. Joey leaned back as if to get a better view, but Elaine couldn't handle the separation and guided her back against her again. She wanted this experience to last forever, but she couldn't wait that long.

She needed more of Joey against more of herself. She swiftly removed Joey's T-shirt so she could fully see the body she'd been imagining for weeks. Joey was compact and toned, her breasts firm and her body even more alluring than expected. She wanted to touch every part of her, but the sound of her zipper being lowered broke her concentration. Joey popped open the button on Elaine's jeans, then kissed the newly revealed skin before sliding the denim over her hips and down her legs. She was infinitely glad she'd gone with the sexy underwear as Joey drew her fingertips lightly over the lace before peeling it away. She watched Joey's reaction to the final revelation of her body. Awe and wonder burned heavy with passion in her eyes, stirring something powerful in Elaine.

She nudged Joey back onto the bed, then climbed on top, straddling her hips. Connecting their lips in a kiss that took their passion from sensual to smoldering, she indulged her senses further by tracing her fingers along the lines of Joey's body. She caressed Joey's rib cage, the sides of her breasts, the curve of her hips. Reaching between them she flicked open the button of Joey's jeans and slowly lowered the zipper. Continuing to let her fingers explore the subtle ridges along Joey's muscled torso, Elaine moved lower, kissing along Joey's neck, shoulder, and collarbone. She thrilled at the low grumble that escaped Joey's lips when she passed lightly over her breasts, breathing, teasing, caressing.

Joey laced her fingers through Elaine's hair, not pushing or even guiding her head, but gently urging her closer. She complied, taking her more fully into her mouth, but only briefly before she moved lower, placing hot, wet kisses down Joey's stomach. Joey arched up, allowing her to slide her jeans over her hips and down her legs so she could continue her trail of kisses unimpeded. She kissed slowly down one leg and up the other, pausing to tease Joey's inner thighs.

Joey reached for her, catching her shoulders and pulling her up so their eyes were level. She kissed Elaine quickly, then tried to roll her over. She was strong and fast, but Elaine had a better position and held firm. "What's wrong?"

"I want to make love to you," Joey whispered.

"I need to make love to you." She spoke the simple truth guiding her since their first kiss. She couldn't be a passive observer. She needed to embrace Joey and everything that came with her. "I need you."

Elaine worked her hands between the press of their bodies, into the tangle of their legs, seeking out warmth and wetness, then slid quickly inside. Joey bucked up beneath her but didn't close her eyes. She watched her own reflection in the liquid dark of Joey's pupils. She could see herself in Joey and feel Joey all around her. They were indistinguishable now—friends, lovers, coach, and women inseparable. She rode the rhythm of their bodies, rocking gently into Joey, pressing fully along the length of her, eyes locked until Joey's breath became erratic and she cast her head to the side, a low groan building into a steady shout, as she tightened and pulsed against her.

Withdrawing slowly, she moved to the side and rested her head on Joey's chest. She listened to the rapid heartbeat and marveled at how it matched her own. She'd spent so many years avoiding this feeling only to find it was what she'd been made for. She hugged Joey tight and kissed her bare shoulder, then whispered, "I'll never let you go again."

❖

Joey was in a haze of lust, love, exhaustion, and disbelief. An hour earlier she'd given up all hope of a future with Elaine, and now she lay naked in her arms. Everything had happened so fast she hadn't had time to overthink it. Their bodies had made demands they couldn't ignore, and she had been swept up in the passion. She'd hoped for a good-bye kiss, a memory to cherish in the face of loss, but it had changed everything. She wished she could take credit, but even she understood that as soon as their lips touched, Elaine took over. She was dealing with a different woman completely, only not completely. It had most definitely been Elaine's intense blue eyes she'd stared into as they made love, but this Elaine hadn't been reserved or cautious. She'd held nothing back. She was completely in her body and, damn, what a body. She luxuriated in the feel of Elaine pressed against her back. The heat of her body, the curve of her hip, the swell of her breasts, the flutter of her breath on bare skin, every part of Elaine stirred her.

Her eyes flashed open, and her breath caught painfully in her chest. *Oh my God, I'm in bed with the most amazing woman ever to walk on earth.*

"What's the matter?" Elaine asked

Joey rolled over to face Elaine, exhaling softly at the love she saw reflected in her blue eyes. "I can't believe you're here."

Elaine smiled radiantly as she ran her long, graceful fingers through Joey's hair. Her touch was exquisite, and Joey's pulse accelerated again. Her adoration and attraction for Elaine now mixed with an unfamiliar hunger clawing its way to the surface. She was afraid of the magnitude of her need, terrified she'd frighten Elaine and worried she wouldn't be able to restrain herself once she started. She deserved better than a bumbling mess of nerves and excitement. Someone much more adept than Joey should make love to her.

Joey trembled as the old insecurities ran though her. What was Elaine doing in bed with her? A beautiful, smart, sexy, and innately talented lover like her could have her pick of women. She loved Elaine with every ounce of herself, but all the love and desire in the world couldn't turn her into some sexy super-lover.

"What's on your mind?" Elaine asked.

"I told you. I can't believe you're here."

"I thought that was just an expression." Elaine laughed lightly. "What's to believe, Joey? I'm here. For the first time in my life, I am really, truly here."

Elaine took her hand and placed it against the curve of her hip. Joey's fingers tightened automatically, a physiological response sent straight from her sex drive. She lost her grip on the logical.

Elaine propped herself up on her elbow and traced a line down the center of Joey's chest with the tips of her fingers. "You want me here, don't you?"

She swallowed audibly. "Yes, I want you very much."

"What do you want to do to me?"

"I want to make love to you until you can't move," she said in a voice so low and gravelly she barely recognized it as her own. "But I'm just—"

"No buts," Elaine whispered. "Kiss me."

She complied, her doubts melting as she surrendered to her body. It wasn't important why Elaine had chosen her. She'd chosen her. She was sexy and desirable and worthy in her eyes. The surge of pride and confidence gave her courage to slide her hand farther down Elaine's side, grasp her thigh, and pull it toward her. She hooked Elaine's leg over her hip, giving her access to everything she craved, but she didn't take it yet. Even in her newfound boldness and desire, she was aware this wasn't something to rush.

She kissed Elaine deeply, reveling in the beautiful mouth she'd admired for so long. There was so much of Elaine she longed to kiss and touch and explore. She moved her hand over the length of Elaine's side, every place she touched more arousing than the last. Elaine wriggled her elbow out from under her, allowing her head to loll back on to the bed, and Joey seized the moment to kiss and lick her way along the delicate curve of her neck.

"God, you smell good," she muttered against Elaine's skin, flush with the subtle scent of sweat and jasmine. She ran her tongue down the hollow at the base of Elaine's throat, rewarded by a soft whimper. Elaine skated her hand over Joey's chest, her fingernails pressing lightly into the sensitive flesh. Emboldened by the hint of

Elaine's need, she dipped her head lower, gliding her mouth lightly over her breasts, teasing her way from one to the other until she registered the weight of Elaine cradling the back of her head and pushing her closer. With increased pressure, she nipped and sucked as she went, and Elaine snaked her fingers into her hair and tightened her grasp. She eased on, exhilarated by Elaine's responsiveness. She skimmed a flat palm down Elaine's abs and across her stomach, stopping to watch its path. Elaine was stunningly beautiful. Joey wanted to kiss every inch of her until she knew every detail of the amazing body before her.

"Please." Elaine breathed the word, her voice raspy with a palpable desire.

She was drawn back into the moment, her senses alive and attuned to the cues Elaine's body was sending. She saw the arch of Elaine's hips as she lifted them to urge her touch lower, heard the ragged intake of air as she slipped between her legs, felt the pulse and rush of heat when they connected. Everything she gave was returned exponentially. When she sought, Elaine met her. When she pushed, Elaine pulled her in. When she rocked forward, Elaine matched her rhythm. She'd dreamed of what it would be like to love Elaine, to hold her, to touch her, but her imagination couldn't have conjured anything this exquisite.

Her doubts were nonexistent now as Elaine clung to her, holding tight with arms and legs, her breathing increasingly erratic. Elaine needed her, and she filled that need. Her confidence surged with each moan that escaped her lover's lips, and they were lovers now, with nothing but love between them. She wanted to hold this moment forever, but she didn't have to cram forever into one night. They would have more opportunities. Elaine's need burned hot, a twin flame to her own, destined to consume them both.

Connecting their mouths again, she increased the pressure at every point where their bodies connected, half-riding, half-absorbing the tremors that crashed through Elaine. She held on, marveling at the way Elaine shuddered in her arms and urging her to continue embracing every sensation until she collapsed, limp and panting in her arms.

Joey couldn't restrain her smile. It burst through her even as she placed soft kisses along Elaine's cheek.

"I love you." She said the only truth she could absorb.

"I love you, too." Elaine's voice was still thick with the remnants of her desire.

"I believe it now."

"Hmm," Elaine said, "I find it interesting that you—"

"No." Joey kissed her quickly, stopping that line of thought. "No more coaching."

"Joey." Elaine sighed. "Are you going to get skittish every time I make an observation about you?"

"Maybe," she said. "I don't want you to remember you were my life coach first because I'm afraid if you return to that role all your professional distance will roar back."

"Never." She trailed her fingers lightly down Joey's chest. "I can't be distant from you, not ever again. I was a fool to hide behind my career as long as I did."

"Really?"

"Yes, I used my job as an excuse not to do all the things my job is supposed to help people do. I let it overrule my authentic self, and my real self is madly in love with you."

"Wow." She might never fully lose her wonder at hearing that Elaine loved her.

"But if I'm embracing my real self, it's worth mentioning that another part of my real self is a life coach. I love asking questions, I love making observations, and I love searching out what makes people who they are. I can't turn that off, and I don't want to, but I'm not coaching you. I'll never tire of getting to know you."

Her chest swelled with pride. "Well, when you put it like that, observe away. I think I'll be able to keep my insecurities in check."

Elaine rolled Joey flat on her back and climbed on top, straddling her hips, her expression filled with mock seriousness. "I find it interesting you'd harbor any hint of insecurity while I'm getting ready to have my way with you again."

She grinned, unable to remember what insecurities they were referring to. "Did you just use your coaching voice to turn me on?"

"Maybe," Elaine said coyly as she slid her palms up Joey's chest. "Don't you find me irresistible when I do that?"

"Maybe." She bucked her hips, pitching Elaine forward and catching her in her arms. "Perhaps you should do some hands-on research to see how irresistible we can be together."

"No, there's nothing left for me to find out in that area," Elaine said with a kiss. "My heart knew the answer to that question all along."

About the Author

Rachel Spangler never set out to be an award-winning author. She was just so poor and so easily bored during her college years that she had to come up with creative ways to entertain herself, and her first novel, *Learning Curve*, was born out of one such attempt. She was sincerely surprised when it was accepted for publication and even more shocked when it won the Golden Crown Literary Award for Debut Author. She also won a Goldie for her second novel, *Trails Merge*. Since writing is more fun than a real job, and so much cheaper than therapy, Rachel continued to type away, leading to the publication of *The Long Way Home* and *LoveLife*. She plans to continue writing as long as anyone, anywhere will keep reading, and most likely even if they won't. Her fifth novel, *Spanish Heart*, is forthcoming from Bold Strokes Books (October 2012)

Rachel and her partner, Susan, are raising their young son in small-town western New York, where during the winter they all make the most of the lake effect snow on local ski slopes, and in summer they love to travel and watch their beloved St. Louis Cardinals.

Regardless of the season, Rachel always makes time for a good romance, whether she's reading it, writing it, or living it.

Rachel can be found online at www.RachelSpangler.com as well as on Facebook.

Books Available From Bold Strokes Books

Burgundy Betrayal by Sheri Lewis Wohl. Park Ranger Kara Lynch has no idea she's a witch until dead bodies begin to pile up in her park, forcing her to turn to beautiful and sexy shape-shifter Camille Black Wolf for help in stopping a rogue werewolf. (978-1-60282-654-0)

LoveLife by Rachel Spangler. When Joey Lang unintentionally becomes a client of life coach Elaine Raitt, the relationship becomes complicated as they develop feelings that make them question their purpose in love and life. (978-1-60282-655-7)

The Fling by Rebekah Weatherspoon. When the ultimate fantasy of a one-night stand with her trainer, Oksana Gorinkov, suddenly turns into more, reality show producer Annie Collins opens her life to a new type of love she's never imagined. (978-1-60282-656-4)

Ill Will by J.M. Redmann. New Orleans PI Micky Knight must untangle a twisted web of healthcare fraud that leads to murder—and puts those closest to her most at risk. (978-1-60282-657-1)

Buccaneer Island by J.P. Beausejour. In the rough world of Caribbean piracy, a man is what he makes of himself—or what a stronger man makes of him. (978-1-60282-658-8)

Twelve O'Clock Tales by Felice Picano. The fourth collection of short fiction by legendary novelist and memoirist Felice Picano. Thirteen dark tales that will thrill and disturb, discomfort and titillate, enthrall and leave you wondering. (978-1-60282-659-5)

Words to Die By by William Holden. Sixteen answers to the question: What causes a mind to curdle? (978-1-60282-653-3)

Tyger, Tyger, Burning Bright by Justine Saracen. Love does not conquer all, but when all of Europe is on fire, it's better than going to hell alone. (978-1-60282-652-6)

Night Hunt by L.L. Raand. When dormant powers ignite, the wolf Were pack is thrown into violent upheaval, and Sylvan's pregnant mate is at the center of the turmoil. A Midnight Hunters novel. (978-1-60282-647-2)

Demons are Forever by Kim Baldwin and Xenia Alexiou. Elite Operative Landis "Chase" Coolidge enlists the help of high-class call girl Heather Snyder to track down a kidnapped colleague embroiled in a global black market organ-harvesting ring. (978-1-60282-648-9)

Runaway by Anne Laughlin. When Jan Roberts is hired to find a teenager who has run away to live with a group of antigovernment survivalists, she's forced to return to the life she escaped when she was a teenager herself. (978-1-60282-649-6)

Street Dreams by Tama Wise. Tyson Rua has more than his fair share of problems growing up in New Zealand—he's gay, he's falling in love, and he's run afoul of the local hip-hop crew leader just as he's trying to make it as a graffiti artist. (978-1-60282-650-2)

Women of the Dark Streets: Lesbian Paranormal by Radclyffe and Stacia Seaman, eds. Erotic tales of the supernatural—a world of vampires, werewolves, witches, ghosts, and demons—by the authors of Bold Strokes Books. (978-1-60282-651-9)

Derrick Steele: Private Dick—The Case of the Hollywood Hustlers by Zavo. Derrick Steele, a hard-drinking, lusty private detective, is being framed for the murder of a hustler in downtown Los Angeles. When his brother's friend Daniel McAllister joins the investigation, their growing attraction might prove to be more explosive than the case. (978-1-60282-596-3)

Nice Butt: Gay Anal Eroticism edited by Shane Allison. From toys to teasing, spanking to sporting, some of the best gay erotic scribes celebrate the hottest and most creative in new erotica. (978-1-60282-635-9)

Initiation by Desire by MJ Williamz. Jaded Sue and innocent Tulley find forbidden love and passion within the inhibiting confines of a sorority house filled with nosy sisters. (978-1-60282-590-1)

Toughskins by William Masswa. John and Bret are two twenty-something athletes who find that love can begin in the most unlikely of places, including a "mom-and-pop shop" wrestling league. (978-1-60282-591-8)

me@you.com by KE Payne. Is it possible to fall in love with someone you've never met? Imogen Summers thinks so because it's happened to her. (978-1-60282-592-5)

Bloody Claws by Winter Pennington. In the midst of aiding the police, Preternatural Private Investigator Kassandra Lyall finally finds herself at serious odds with Sheila Morris, the local werewolf pack's Alpha female, when Sheila abuses someone Kassandra has sworn to protect. (978-1-60282-588-8)

Awake Unto Me by Kathleen Knowles. In turn of the century San Francisco, two young women fight for love in a world where women are often invisible and passion is the privilege of the powerful. (978-1-60282-589-5)

Rescue Me by Julie Cannon. Tyler Logan reluctantly agrees to pose as the girlfriend of her in-the-closet gay BFF at his company's annual retreat, but she didn't count on falling for Kristin, the boss's wife. (978-1-60282-582-6)

Snowbound by Cari Hunter. *"The policewoman got shot and she's bleeding everywhere. Get someone here in one hour or I'm going to put her out of her misery."* It's an ultimatum that will forever change the lives of police officer Sam Lucas and Dr. Kate Myles. (978-1-60282-581-9)

High Impact by Kim Baldwin. Thrill seeker Emery Lawson and Adventure Outfitter Pasha Dunn learn you can never truly appreciate what's important and what you're capable of until faced with a sudden and stark reminder of your own mortality. (978-1-60282-580-2)